Runaround Sue

A Sweet Quirky Romantic Entanglement

Jennifer Lynn Cary

Tandem Services Press

What Readers Are Saying

The Crockett Chronicles trilogy

"I love historical novels and this one did not disappoint. I was caught up from the first sentence and completely in love with the Crocketts by the end. Can't wait to follow along their next journey. Well done!" –Virginia Denise

"I love this book! The story is soooooo engaging! I can hardly put it down!"—DeNage

Tales of the Hob Nob Annex Café

"This is a well written book that hooks you on the first page. It's a very enjoyable read that makes you forget about all your troubles and step back in time. I loved this book and look forward to what this author writes next." –Ann Ferri

"I loved reading this book! It had me intrigued from the first page, and as the stories began, I could hardly wait to turn the page to see what happened next! Love the mix of true facts mixed with some good, clean, fun fiction! Easy, quick read. I highly recommend this book!" –CatSmit

The Relentless Series

"I lost my heart in this book, caught up in the lives of each character. I remember these times, which made it more real to me. I had tears of joy, tears of sorrow, grief, and smiles in the unexpected. Great story and hard to put down. Keep reading.... You won't regret it."—Novabelle

"I enjoyed another book by Jennifer Cary! As with all her books the story held your attention from the beginning to the end and I look forward to reading all her future books!"—Mary Rima

"I live in Indiana so I know of the places this book talks about. I so absolutely LOVED this story. It's the first one in this series I've read. I'm glad because I feel it should be the first book as it tells of the 2 families & how they connect. It so touched my heart that at times I cried. I couldn't put it down after starting it so anxious to know how things would turn out with all the difficulties Val & Jimmy had. I'm sure the other books in this series are equally as great."—Pat

The Traveling Prayer Shawl

"When her sister's inheritance depends on it, Cami must do the thing she resolved she'd never do, the thing which will break her heart as well as add one more tough task to her already overstuffed calendar. She must fulfill her grandmother's last request - and what's more, there's a deadline that puts in jeopardy her major project at work. As she begins working on the request, she finds even more complications. The inheritance may raise a conflict of interests. How Cami negotiates these and other potential pitfalls made for an interesting and warmhearted story.

Recommended to those who enjoy Christian Women's Fiction and readers who enjoy Debbie Macomber's stories."—Dana McNeely

"I loved this book so much I hated for it to end!"—Cindy

The Weather Girls trilogy

"I just finished all three of the Weather Girls books on my Kindle Fire! I found that once I started, I couldn't stop - and went from one to two to three - in a matter of 4 days! I work so had to leave my evenings to reading - but oh I hated to quit and go to bed! And then I'd run the story through in my mind again!" —Novabelle

"What a fun series! I'm loving spending time in the past with this family and learning more about the girls and their unique personalities." —Erin S

The Forgotten Gratitude Journal

"This incredible book is written in split time. I don't want to give any more away about the story. It's so enjoyable and I couldn't put it down, needing to know what happened to Molly and RJ!"—Annmarie K

"Jennifer Lynn Cary has written a beautiful split time story about love, love lost and love found again! Throw a mystery villain in the mix and you have a romance with suspense and drama! Such a good read for any romance lover!"—Anita Stafford

Cheryl's Going Home

"This book will touch your heart and soul. Cheryl and Aaron's heart-warming story is full of emotions, and you can feel every one of them. This book will make you laugh, cry and feel every emotion in between. I loved it and highly recommend this book and the entire series." —Ann Ferri

"The book is Christian fiction, but it is not heavy handed and fits the characters and the early 1970ties. The book is Cheryl's story, but also her estranged husband, Aaron's story as well. Their two stories, expertly woven together, share the experience of the rebuilding of their relationship from each of their POVs. It's a lovely journey evoking the time and place with musical and celebrity references from the era."—MLRumph

Judy in Disguise

"Wow. I usually don't read strictly romance but this book captured my attention from the back cover and did not disappoint." —Cheri Swalwell

"I love how this author can transport readers back to the 1970's and brings the past to life." —Connie Hill

Sylvia's Mother

"Sylvia's Mother of The Weather Girls Wedding Shoppe and Venue series will take you on a journey like no other and transporting you in the 1970s and showing you the lessons of God's Redemption, overcoming major obstacles, and showing what it means to be a Child of God." —lesliejune

"I was captivated by the storyline from the very first page." —familym-grkendra

In memory of Mary England.

I love you and miss you.

Therefore if any man be in Christ,

he is a new creature:

old things are passed away;

behold, all things are become new.

2 Corinthians 5:17

Published by Tandem Services Press

Post Office Box 220

Yucaipa, California

www.TandemServicesInk.com

Ebook ISBN 978-1-954986-79-4

Paperback ISBN 978-1-954986-78-7

Cover design by Alt 19 Creative

Contents

The Cardinal in the Sycamore

Once upon a time, a legend grew from the native people living in Central Indiana.

If a couple really loved each other and they kissed beneath a certain sycamore tree *and* a cardinal landed on the branch above them, they would have a long life together.

In the late nineteenth century, a gas boom hit the sleepy farming town of Kokomo.

A family named Ferguson made their wealth with the event and built an impressive mansion on the grounds of the old sycamore tree. When they did, word of the legend came to them, and they passed it down their generations.

Finally, in 1970 the last member of the family sold Ferguson House to Sunny Day Whitcomb who, along with her sisters Stormy Day Crawford and Windy Day Norman, opened the *Weather Girls Wedding Shoppe and Venue* in the old mansion.

Now when couples come, they have their photos taken beneath the shade of the old sycamore and hope for a cardinal sighting to add spice to their kiss.

Welcome to the stories of the *Weather Girls Wedding Shoppe and Venue* series.

Chapter 1

Tuesday, June 20, 1972 Kokomo, Indiana

"I am not being difficult, Tracy, nor am I a misanthrope." Sue Mitchell ran her hand over her forehead, swiping her bangs from where they'd slipped out of the bobby pins she used to pin them back. There wasn't time for this phone discussion during working hours.

That is, if any work still needed doing. It hadn't taken long to plow through the to-do list Pastor Mussing left for her.

She glanced around the Wabash Congregational Church office reception area. Even the plastic philodendrons had been wiped clean. Still, Tracy didn't need to know she'd knocked out her work already. So, if she were honest, technically she did have time, but rather she didn't want this discussion.

The voice on the line acquired a lofty air. "Let me put this so you will understand. Your arcane attitude is bumming me out. I want to have some fun with my best friend. I've let you have space to pull yourself together, but now it's time to get off your callipygian and party hardy with me."

Sue snorted. "A pretty pukka effort. Do you have your thesaurus open next to you?"

"Nope, you aren't the only one who attended college. Besides, having roomed with you for so long, I've sort of absorbed your vocabulary." Tracy paused and her sigh came through loud and clear. "Please? The only thing we ever do together is work with the girls on Wednesday nights. I have tomorrow off, and I promise we'll be home tonight by ten-thirty, eleven at the latest. C'mon, whaddya say?"

It was Sue's turn to sigh. They hadn't gone out for fun in forever. Which was fine with her. If she didn't see another soul, it would be pukka with her. Visions of becoming a hermit in the remotest regions of Alaska flicked through her brain. Wearing all her big bulky, non-shape-revealing sweaters. If only she enjoyed the cold.

Tracy, however, had been there when she needed a friend and offered her sanctuary. Even helped her find this job. She owed her friend. "Okay, but we stick close to town or head toward Galveston. Nothing south or west. Got it?"

Tracy squealed, and Sue pulled the phone from her ear as the chatter turned high-pitched. "Yay! I can't wait. I'll see you when you get home. Oh, we're gonna have some fun. Bye!"

The line clicked before Sue returned her bye. Stuff like that happened when Tracy got excited. That girl never had a down moment, never met a stranger, and doubted no one's story. Gullible and dewy-eyed, that was her roomie. Made it easy to give Tracy enough story without a lot of details to convince her to let them room together again. Out of the way. No one from Alto knowing where she was.

Sue picked up the stack of finished folders on her desk and tapped them straight before setting them right back where they had been.

What else needed doing? Everything from her in-box was completed, her out-box emptied. Sometimes it was a pain to be so competent.

Boredom is a state of mind—repeat this fifty times.

Then she realized that if she didn't keep busy, her brain would be creating what-if scenarios about this evening. Like what if she ran into someone she knew from Alto? Oops, she'd mused herself into exactly what she wanted to avoid.

However, what if she did? What if someone saw her out tonight? What would she do? She needed a plan.

Hmm, perhaps head for the restroom and lock herself in until Tracy found her? Or play dumb, like the person was mistaken. She'd changed her appearance enough that it was possible. Sue shoved the black cat-eye glasses with nonprescription lenses up to the bridge of her nose. Maybe she shouldn't go.

Yet she'd promised Tracy, and she owed her roommate more than she could repay. Still that happy, squealing face manipulated even when she was miles away.

Okay, what if she dressed frumpy? Would Tracy let her out of the apartment raggle-taggle?

Absolutely no. She'd take it as a personal affront to be seen in Sue's company when not presentably coiffed and appropriately styled.

Great, now what did she do?

"Sue, would you do me a favor?"

She pulled herself away from her concerns to find the pastor's wife, Gloria Mussing, standing at her desk. When had she entered the room? Mercy, this day was growing obdurate about giving her a hard time.

"Of course, Mrs. Mussing. I'm happy to. What can I do for you?"

The woman held a basket of cards and envelopes with a list poking out the top. "I just got a call and need to run an emergency errand. These cards are for the hospital, nursing home, and shut-in visits this Saturday. Would you please get them signed and in the envelopes with the person's name on the front for me? I'll group them by who is taking them out once I'm back. Thought I'd get this done today because the rest of the week is stuffed full, but now this." Mrs. Mussing shook her head.

"I'll do it for you. In fact, I was trying to think of something else to work on."

Surprise raised Mrs. Mussing's brows. "I saw the list Jim left. You finished it already?"

Sue nodded, then added a smile to keep it friendly.

"I can honestly say we get our money's worth out of you. My goodness, you not only work hard, but fast. I told him it would take you three days to get all that done."

"It wasn't so much." She shrugged, hoping it didn't sound boastful. The truth was, the training she received in college prepared her for much more than the simple filing and typing this job required. In fact, the hardest part was keeping the smile on her face when people arrived. It would be so much better if she didn't have to deal with the public or even the congregation. Was she a misanthrope? Maybe a little bit.

"Well, I'm glad you're here with us and that you'll take this off my hands. Good to know we've got someone we can trust to get things done." The pastor's wife set the basket on Sue's desk, waved, and headed out.

This time, her smile was genuine. Sue heard little praise as a rule, and Mrs. Mussing's words felt like Noxzema on a sunburn—only without the sting. Just the cooling sensation that made her want to say "ah."

She pulled out the list of names and began by addressing the envelopes. It'd be nice if her old church did something like this. Then maybe someone would be filling out a card for her brother while he sat at home. Sue didn't recognize any names on the paper. True, she hadn't been attending all that long, only since she'd started her job. But there was no way she'd be going back to her home congregation, and since she hadn't found another place to attend, it only made sense to come here on Sundays. Plus, it turned out Pastor Mussing was not only a great boss, he knew a thing or two about preaching sermons.

Once she had the envelopes readied, she checked the name on the list, noted if the person was in the hospital or a nursing facility or was simply homebound, and chose an appropriate card, signing it with her best penmanship. Blessings from Wabash Community Church.

Mrs. Mussing hadn't said how to sign the cards, so Sue spent a moment considering the best message to write. After completing a couple, she picked up a rhythm and soon had the lot filed back into the basket in three stacks and in alphabetical order. All done.

She stood and stretched and paced the room. If she couldn't do her exercises, she could at least move. After developing the habit, her body itched to stay active, so she counted off steps and made several circuits of the lobby.

Despite the ease of the job, it had a peaceful setting, kind colleagues, and a safety that made it all worthwhile. No one around her recognized her. She could stay cloistered in this office until… Until she didn't have to.

Ten minutes later, she settled back at her desk and decided to start a list of jobs she could get done if Pastor wanted her to. Keeping busy helped, and it was no trouble. She'd gotten to number seven when the notion about the safe and serene nature of this place shattered.

The church office door opened, and he walked in, causing her to retreat behind a personal loup of efficiency.

She wasn't sure if she was repelled or attracted, only that he turned her stomach to flying confetti and her pulse rate to a jackhammer's pace. Either way, he was definitely male. That scared her, and it wasn't good. With effort, she kept that professional mask in place.

Sue noted a slight shuffle to his gait, and he pulled off his motorcycle helmet to reveal a matted, beach blond mane and full beard. A guitar case hung from a strap over his shoulder as he approached her desk.

No, this wouldn't do. He made her too uneasy.

"Is Professor Day in?"

Sue swallowed hard and found her voice. "Um, who shall I say is calling?"

"Just tell him Mac is here for the appointment." The guy glanced around the room, spotted the couch next to the potted fern, and headed that way.

The space between them increased, granting her more breathing room. Not that he smelled bad. She hadn't noticed anything like that. Just that his mere presence made her nerves take up conga lessons. She called into the music director's office. "Mr. Day, Mac is here for an appointment." An appointment for which someone had neglected to inform her.

"I'll be right out." *Click.*

"He's on his way."

She recalled Pastor Mussing's verbal list of her duties. Should she ask if she could get him something to drink? However, starting a conversation meant acknowledging his presence again, and she wasn't sure if that was such a wise idea. Still, part of her job was to be the office hostess. A part she had hoped she would not have to often deal with. But then, Pastor Mussing had emphasized that she was the first impression visitors got, so it was important that she be hospitable. And it was getting summery outside. Logic, and his shaggy pate, told her his head had gotten warm riding with that helmet on. Fine. She'd play Jackie Kennedy. It might not be the White House with thousands of live TV viewers, but she would be as gracious a hostess. No matter if her fingernails dug canyons into her palm.

"May I get you something to drink? We have water or coffee." Should she suggest that the church stocked powdered Nestea for the summer months?

He glanced her way and flashed a touch of a smile. "No, thank you."

Well, that was that. She'd tried.

Had she really? "What about a magazine?"

He shook his head, and the matted, probably sweaty, clumped strands swung a little. "No, but thanks."

At least he was polite. Even if he merely sat there, not trying to talk with her.

That hadn't happened in a long while. Recent history had proven that, given the chance, a man would try to start a conversation with her whether she wanted to talk to him or not. And boy, had she heard some lines.

Well, not extreme recent history. Not since she'd changed her appearance.

So maybe it was working. The thought tickled at the corners of her mouth, and she caught a genuine smile trying to sneak out. But it was followed with a little sadness. Did that mean she'd never again get attention from a man? Never again experience that moment of inner confidence when she knew she looked appealing?

Part of her wanted to cheer that notion across the finish line. Still, another part wondered if she'd always feel this way, and if she'd sliced off her proverbial nose to spite the face that had brought her such heartache.

Mac ran his hands over his jeans, wiping the sweat away again. Despite the air conditioning in the office, his nerves were outdoing his deodorant three to one. He couldn't imagine why Professor Day had asked him to come see him at a church of all places.

He moved his guitar from leaning against the couch to laying across his lap, needing the physical touch as if it were another appendage.

Music had always interpreted Mac's life.

He'd spent adolescent summer days under the boardwalk and nights up on the roof with Ben E. King. Then he moved to the dock of the bay to hang with Otis Redding.

But at graduation, his Uncle Sam sent him on an exotic all-expense paid trip that cost him dearly. Eric Burdon spoke truth to him—he had to get out of that place.

It was bad. So bad.

Especially those first few weeks in the hospital.

Then came the recent years of trying to resurrect his life, of learning who he was.

These days, though, more often than not, he found himself with Doby Gray, grateful for the songs that helped him drift away.

Music. The balm that poured out a measure of peace amid a chaotic world.

Speaking of that, why was this office silent? This was not good. He needed sound.

"Sorry about the wait, Peter. Or do you prefer Mac?" Professor Day stood in front of him, hand outstretched.

Mac rose before meeting the handshake. Didn't do to let anyone assume he couldn't stand on his own. "No problem, sir. And it's Mac. Thanks for asking."

Professor Day held a carton under his left arm. "Give me one more second and we'll go back to my office." He turned to the secretary. "Sue, would you please run these over to my daughters at Ferguson House? They need them before four, but they have a customer until after three, so don't leave before then. They made sure I realized not to interrupt their important meeting, but that the next client needs these reel-to-reels."

"Happy to take care of that, sir." Though she sat there ready to do his prof's bidding, Mac had the impression the woman was a lot smarter than she was given credit for. He took a better look.

"Just Aaron is fine. Do you know how to get there?"

"Yes. Aaron. I'll make sure they are delivered on time." She flashed a smile that seemed rehearsed. Still, it lit her face a little, and two dimples popped like tiny parentheses on either side of her mouth. Maybe they were spotlighting where her real smile should go. She was better looking than she wanted to let on.

"Good, got that out of the way. Come with me, Mac, and I'll explain why I dragged you here." The chuckle floating back was the real deal. Not like Secretary Sue's smile. It was one of the reasons he accepted the professor's request to meet at the church. He liked the guy. Besides, how many advanced music students had a teacher who included sessions with Burt Bacharach, Herb Alpert, Brian Wilson, and Frank Sinatra on their resumes—to name a few? If you wanted to be a professional musician, you should learn from someone who understood the score.

Professor Aaron Day did.

The hallway to his office wasn't all that long, only a couple of doors on either side. The professor stopped at the last one on the left and turned the knob, holding it open.

Mac stepped past him. The room was cluttered with books and instruments and sheet music in piles. Looked like something out of *Goodbye, Mr. Chips.*

"Excuse the mess. Still trying to get organized around here. Splitting my time between the church and the university means I'm never finished combing through to decide what to pitch and what to keep." He lifted a stack from the visitor chair and motioned for Mac to have a seat.

He did, still mesmerized by the sheer musical vastness represented in the small room. "How many instruments do you play?"

"A few. I prefer my guitars, especially my twelve string, and the piano, but I've played clarinet and sax for a few recordings."

Mac would bet there were more than those named. He glanced at his own ax—it was never far from him, like an extra arm. He was self-taught on the piano. Reading music was doable, but playing by ear, that was where he was freest. For the Nam, he'd picked up the harmonica because it would carry in his pocket. That particular instrument he hadn't played since he got home.

Professor Day cleared his own chair and dropped into it as if finishing a race. "So, I'm sure you are wondering why I asked you here."

Mac nodded and kept a tight button on his lip. Too often he'd let the wrong word slip at an equally wrong time.

"If you read the class syllabus, you're aware you must put together a recital of your own compositions to be played by other musicians. You can choose what instruments, but there needs to be a mix of at least three. Most of your classmates will be scheduling use at the IUK auditorium, but I've been thinking. This congregation might enjoy a music night, so I'm offering you a chance to do your final project here. You'd need to present before Labor Day. I'm acquainted with a few performers who attend Wabash Community, and I'll be happy to help you with contacts. The thing is that you'd want to have a theme that fits a house of worship."

Mac mulled the man's words a moment. "What does that mean? Only classical or hymn-like pieces?"

Professor Day shook his head. "No, it only needs to be God-honoring. Even some rock does that. Think of the songs from *Godspell*. There are several that fit that category."

"Are you requiring words for all the music? I'd have to locate a singer." Where would he find one? And no, he was not going to sing them himself. Sweat returned to his palms while his deodorant gave up the ghost. This final project was a giant enough step for him without that added feature of him performing.

"Only one piece needs lyrics, but you can add them to the whole recital if you choose." The professor chuckled, and Mac realized his eyes must have spoken for him about the viability of that ever happening.

"As I looked over the roster for this class, I really felt moved to make you this offer. You don't have to do it." He paused, like he was waiting for Mac to give him direction on what to say next.

"Professor Day—"

"Aaron. As long as we are outside of class, it's fine. Go on."

Mac cleared his throat and tried again. "Aaron, I'm not a super religious guy. I do believe in God, and I've got reason to be grateful. Still, I might not be the right person."

"I think you are. I also believe that as you work, if you pray and ask for guidance, you might find this is more for you than for your audience."

Whatever that meant. "I don't know any singers. Do you have a name or two to go along with the other musicians?"

Aaron grinned. "Do I have a name? Mac, you've come to the right place. The best pianist in town happens to be my youngest daughter. All three of my girls, as well as my wife, have beautiful voices. Sounds like nepotism, I'll bet, but facts can't be denied."

"Oh. Okay. Think they'd be willing?"

"I've got a feeling at least one might be persuaded." Aaron scribbled on a notepad. "Just to make sure I remember to speak with them. Now, before you go, I'd really like to hear you play."

"Um, so it's decided?" Mac suddenly realized he'd been steamrolled.

"You still want to think about it?"

Mac let his gaze skirt around the room before meeting Aaron's, resigned. "I'm in. This thing is going to stretch me."

"That's the point. Now get out your guitar and show me what you can do." Aaron moved to the piano and set the stack of books covering the seat on the floor before sitting down and playing a quick scale. "Want to try 'Classical Gas'?"

With his guitar out of the case, he slipped the strap over his head and played the opening chords.

Aaron joined in, and soon the tiny room was filled with the jam session.

The door suddenly opened, and Mac glanced up to see a middle-aged guy in the doorway as his fingers slowed to a stop on the frets.

"Keep going, sounds great."

Aaron stopped and spun around on the stool. "Oh, Pastor Mussing, come in. This is one of my students, Mac MacKenzie. Mac, this is our pastor, Jim Mussing."

Middle-aged dude walked on in with an open palm. "Nice to meet you, Mac. You are fantastic."

Mac shook the guy's hand and struggled to get his voice to work. "Um, thanks. Nice to meet you too." He'd been having so much fun that his words tasted like lies. No way had he wanted to meet the guy right then, even if he was all right. Instead, it was about playing and getting lost in the music. That's where Mac was truly free.

But his folks had drilled manners into him, and he used them. Besides, he was in church. Which was worse—to lie to say something polite, or tell the truth and be selfish?

"Sorry to interrupt, I was just enjoying it too much. Hope to see you around, Mac. I'll let you two get back to what you were doing." With that, the pastor closed the door.

"Guess we got too loud?"

Aaron shook his head. "No, these walls are thin. It'd be hard for the sound not to travel. You're pretty good on guitar. How are your piano skills?"

"Eh?" Mac shrugged and wiggled his hand in front of him.

"Try this." Aaron pulled out a couple of pages of sheet music.

Mac started to balk. It wasn't that he couldn't read the thing. He could, but getting his fingers to comply as fast as his brain recognized the notes was another deal. Well, maybe he should make his professor aware of the extent of his skill. Would he rescind the invitation?

He laid aside his guitar and inspected the music. It was for a hymn, "O Fount of Many Blessings." At least the piece was familiar. That should help. Mac sat on the seat, got his feet on the pedals and his fingers over the keys, and leaned in to follow the notes, humming them to himself as he did. He could do this. Okay. Big breath.

The song started, and as music tended to do, it flowed up his hands and arms and straight to his heart where he took hold of the nuances and textures, making it come alive. He played the verse a second time and repeated the chorus before drawing to a finish.

As the last note echoed away, he knew something had happened.

There was clapping behind him, but only one person. Aaron. Professor Day. His teacher. He'd pleased the man. Mac's heart pounded.

Maybe, just maybe, he could do this.

Only, he'd have to use his own compositions—not that he'd never composed anything. He had. Several pieces, some that would actually fit this situation.

No, the big thing was, he'd need to allow others to hear his work. An audience. And that might be the hardest part of this whole process.

Chapter 2

Sue pinched the bridge of her nose, her glasses resting on top of her head, while holding the phone receiver away from her ear. If only she could suddenly go deaf. For a moment, at least.

"And I really think Pastor ought to give more messages on that before our young people are so far gone we lose them."

Mrs. Berkley had been rambling about what Pastor Mussing should be preaching for a good twenty minutes. "Yes, ma'am. I will let Pastor know. Thank you so much for calling. Goodbye." She hung up and realized she hadn't waited for the caller to repeat the closing back before she disconnected. Bet she'd get another earful Sunday morning on how to be gracious and respectful to her elders. Oh, Sue couldn't wait for that. Yeah, that and a root canal.

Enough. She'd tried. Really and truly, she had, but the octogenarian was bent on delivering her own sermon via the telephone to whomever was on the other end. It was simply Sue's misfortune to be that whomever this time.

Or was it? Had the call been a cosmic nudge about her former life?

No. That was behind her, and she'd taken steps to keep it there. As long as she wasn't spotted by certain people, there was no problem.

She glanced at her watch. That phone call had eaten into her day. The only good thing was it kept her from counting the ticks on her Timex. It was already 3:20. Time to get the reels delivered. She pulled her purse from the bottom drawer of her desk, made one more check that everything was neatly in place before shoving her chair beneath, and headed out.

Only the door opened first and Mrs. Hartman—Sue wasn't sure which Mrs. Hartman this was, but one of the two sisters-in-law who attended Wabash Community Church—hustled in. "Oh, I'm so glad I caught you. I need the list of what the songs will be for Sunday. I had it and am embarrassed to say I lost it, and now I have no idea what to practice for the service. You don't have a copy, do you?"

Sue opened her mouth to explain she needed to run this errand but decided it would be faster to just find the list and write it out. Her tongue was going to need stitches with all this biting. After locating the correct stack of pages, she pulled over a piece of paper, jotted down the music choices, and handed it to Mrs. Hartman.

"I'm sorry to have put you out like this." The woman stood there as if waiting for a response.

What was she supposed to say? That this was inconvenient, and a call tomorrow would have sufficed? Sue could have read the list off to her. But no, she had to have a copy right then. "No trouble." She even forced a smile despite the guilt of knowing she had just lied through her teeth and was at church no less. Hopefully, the desk between them would keep the woman safe when God sent down a lightning bolt of punishment.

Mrs. Hartman glanced at the list again. "Thank you." Then she turned and left, giving Sue a clear exit. Finally.

She still was okay. It was only three thirty. Ferguson House was close enough that it would take less than ten minutes if she included striding to her vehicle, starting the ignition, parking the machine, marching to the door, and handing over the tapes. The actual travel time was probably closer to five.

Her green VW Beetle sat parked toward the back so that visitors would have better spots. She put the stack of reels behind her seat and climbed in, placing her purse on the passenger side. After rolling down her windows, she inserted her key and prepared to depart.

Only her ignition did nothing.

Not even a sound.

If her battery were going, she'd at least have noted some clicks. However, the only thing she heard was her breathing, getting more exasperated as the seconds flew by. This was not happening.

"C'mon, c'mon, buddy, don't fail me now." Sweat beaded on her forehead.

Whatever had made her ignition go silent was winning this battle.

She smacked the steering wheel. "Really, God? I'm trying to do the right thing here. Can't You meet me half way?" Ah, now she got it. This was in place of the lightning strike in the office. No need to destroy the whole church, just get her alone, away from things and then punish her for her untruth.

Whether it was the heat rising off the black top or her anger growing hot under her collar, it didn't matter. She shook out her hand and tried again. *You. Will. Start.*

Twist the key. Nothing. Twist the key. Nothing.

Her wrist was going to fall off before the stupid car started at this rate. Oh, she wanted to scream.

Sue climbed out and raised the back-end hood. Right. Like she would know what she was looking for when staring at an engine. The stupidity of her moves only added fuel to her ire and with that rear left tire mocking her, she gave it a swift kick.

Ow!

Now she leaned against the bumper to massage her toes.

"Need some help?"

The understatement of the year. Sue glanced up to acknowledge her rescuer, even if he was king of the obvious.

Motorcycle guy. Peter MacKenzie to be accurate. No way. Was God masochistic?

But she did need help.

Sue squeezed her eyes a moment and breathed. "Yes. I'm supposed to deliver these reels..." Great. Apparently, now she was the queen of the obvious since he was in the room when Aaron Day gave her the assignment. "My car won't start."

She thought he cracked a smile, though she couldn't be sure with all the hair on his face, but she figured that was the result. "Let me look. I used to have a Bug, so I sort of know what might go wrong."

As he moved to inspect the engine, Sue stepped away. Mac, that's what he wanted to be called. Fine. "Mac, I'm running out of time. Do you think you can fix it fast?"

He shrugged, lowered himself to the ground, and scooted under her car.

What made him so willing to get dirty like that? Why was he helping her? She peeked at her watch. 3:43.

There wouldn't be time to walk it at this rate.

She glanced down to tell him so, only to catch sight of his right foot. Or what should've been his right foot. His pant leg had shimmied up to reveal a metal bar. He had a prosthesis.

The shock hit her. It wasn't that she hadn't seen similar, but it was unexpected. The guy moved as if he had his own two feet. Clearly he didn't. That realization opened up something softer, kinder in her attitude toward the man. How had he lost his foot? How far up did the prosthesis go? Was he a veteran? She had a feeling he was. It was in the way he carried himself. She'd seen it before.

"I don't think you'll be going anywhere in this vehicle right now." Mac scooted out from under the Beetle, and she noticed how he used his arms and left leg to compensate while rising.

Smile, ignoramus. Don't let him see that you know. "Thank you for looking. I need to get inside and call a cab."

"It won't be here in time." He was just chock full of optimism, wasn't he?

"It might be. Besides, I haven't another option."

"Sure you do. I'll give you a ride. I'm parked over there." He pointed toward a motorcycle, Harley Davidson boldly emblazoned on its tank.

"I don't think so." No, definitely not. She backed up against her Bug.

"C'mon. You need to get those reels there before four, and you're running out of time."

Wonderful, he remembered her instructions too. She glanced down at her split skirt and sensible shoes. Technically, she could ride, but it still wasn't going to happen. Maybe he couldn't tell the difference with skirts. "I'm not exactly dressed for it."

He shook his head and made a face like she was being an idiot. "You can ride in that. No problem."

Now he was deflating all her excuses. And the clock still ticked. At this point, the cab for sure couldn't make it in time. "I don't know..."

"I promise I'm a safe driver. I'll get you there before four. C'mon, Secretary Sue."

Secretary Sue? That's how he saw her? A simple secretary?

Of course, it's what she wanted everyone to think. *You're in hiding, remember?*

She swallowed. If she screwed up this simple task, which was turning out to be anything but, she could lose this job and then she'd be hunting something else and who knew where that would take her? However, climbing onto the back of a motorcycle, being driven by a guy with only one foot—what was his balance like? —and having to hold on to him to keep from falling off, was causing her to freeze rather than fight or flee. Yeah, freeze. Like an ice cube straight from Antarctica.

What if he were Danny? Would she trust him then?

Her brother wouldn't be so foolhardy as to attempt to ride a motorcycle.

Yet none of these arguments were getting her any closer to Ferguson House. Meanwhile, the clock continued to tick.

"You're sure you can do this?" The added weight, her added weight, wouldn't throw him off?

"I'm sure." He pointed toward his Harley and started in that direction.

Oh, boy.

She followed, checking out his gait as she did. If she hadn't seen it with her own eyes, she'd never have guessed he had a prosthesis. Maybe he had put in the hours of practice needed to make the smooth transition. It would've been a boatload of hours.

"Oh, I need to get my purse and the reels." She grabbed her things and rolled up the windows before locking her car. The movement seemed to break off the last chunk of her frozenness. There wasn't time for it anyway. With the carton clutched to her chest, she ran for Mac and his motorcycle.

He'd popped open a storage compartment. "Drop the box in here so you won't have to worry about losing anything." *Or holding on to them and me at the same time.* Yeah, he managed to get that part of the message across with his eyes.

Mac had amazing eyes. Almost hypnotic. *Snap out of it!*

Sue did as instructed, adding her purse.

Mac closed the compartment and climbed on, giving the starter a kick. At least it looked that way. The engine purred like some giant kitten—smooth but loud. "Hop on."

Hop on. Seriously, like it was that easy to do. Even if she felt comfortable about taking a ride with him, the physicality of climbing behind him gave her pause. How did she lift her leg to straddle the seat?

As if hearing her thoughts, he turned her way. "Hold my shoulders and swing your leg over."

Touch him. Well, she knew she had to in order to ride, but now was the moment. He was a male. Even if he were a nice man, he was still a male. Her heart thumped in her chest. She did not want to be this close to one ever again.

But the reels were not going to get to Ferguson House on time if she didn't climb aboard. That could mean her job. And worse.

Sue gritted her teeth, grasped his shoulders, and lifted her leg like she used to do with bar exercises in her ballet class. One fluid move later, she was settled behind him.

He passed his helmet to her. "It might make you feel more confident." Was that a smirk?

She'd show him. Sue took the hollowed out ball and buckled it beneath her chin.

"Now hold on."

"What?"

The motor revved.

She got the message and wrapped her arms around him in the biggest bear hug she'd ever given.

The whole thing tickled Mac. He stuffed his chuckle down deep, though. This chick's hands would fly if she felt him laugh. He didn't want that. Well, it wouldn't be safe, that's for sure.

How long had it been since he'd had a woman holding onto him? Not that he was complaining. Even if her fear made her hang on tight enough to resurrect his breakfast. He bit his lip to keep that chuckle in check.

The additional weight had him adjusting his balance, but it wasn't hard. Not like learning when he first got back. Now it was second nature.

As he leaned into the turn at Sycamore, he slowed. Ferguson House was just ahead.

Pulling in front of the old mansion, he turned off the engine and set the kickstand. "We're here. You can relax now." Okay, maybe he shouldn't have added that last part, or the smirk that followed, but she still clung to him as if she didn't realize they'd arrived. Kinda nice.

Then, all at once, she peeled away. "I'm, oh, thank you." She even sounded cute when flustered, and since he couldn't catch a glimpse of her face while she sat behind him, he imagined it. Yep, cute.

"Um, I need to get off..."

"Grab my shoulders for support and slide right until your foot touches the ground. Then you can swing your leg off the bike."

She cleared her throat. "Sure." Once she stood beside him, she undid the helmet and handed it over. "Thank you, Mr. McKenzie."

"Mac. And no biggie. You okay now?"

She nodded, but then her eyes grew. "I almost forgot. The reels and my purse."

"Oh, yeah. I'll get them." He slid off the bike and opened the storage compartment, handing out her things. "Here ya go."

She clutched it all to her in a bunch. "Yes. Thank you. Again. Mac." After another nod, she spun and raced for the house.

Then he thought of something. "Hey Sue, how are you going to get home?"

She paused at the porch steps. "I'll walk. Don't worry." With a wave, she tore the rest of the way to the door, pulling it open and marching inside.

Guess that was that. Or was it?

Mac decided to wait and see. It wouldn't take her long to just hand over the tapes. He figured they'd made it on time since it was only now that a car pulled up and parked behind him.

Moments later, the door opened, and Sue came out at a more sedate pace. He knew the minute she spotted him sitting there because her eyes grew and then narrowed to a squint. Must be she wasn't pleased.

Okeydoke. As perverse as it might sound, he was getting a kick out of seeing her riled. Enough to let that chuckle escape.

"What's so hilarious? And why are you still here?"

He simply held out the helmet.

"What? I'll walk now. There's no deadline to beat."

Mac shrugged. "Also, no reason to walk, since I can give you a ride."

"I don't need a ride."

"I don't need a lot of things, but sometimes it's just good manners to accept."

Her face picked up color. "I apologize. No offense intended."

"Great. Stick the helmet on and let's go." He grinned.

Sue tipped her head to the side and studied him. "What would Emily Post have to say about someone forcing another to accept what was not wanted?"

"Never met the lady."

"Obviously." She turned and strode down the sidewalk.

"Look. I don't want to be pushy, but it's hot as blazes out and definitely cooler to ride for a few minutes instead of slogging along for several. Just trying to save you steps and discomfort. Besides, couldn't it be that I'm simply helpful?" He straddled the bike, walking beside her next to the curb. Fortunately, no parked cars barred his path.

"It's nothing against you. I don't even know you."

"I can remedy that."

She stopped and turned on him. "Are you planning to annoy me the whole way back to the church?"

"You're walking to Wabash Congregational?"

"Yes. That's where my car is."

He shook his head. "You aren't going anywhere in that Bug in the near future, not until it has a new starter. So I might as well take you home."

Her eyes grew big again. What was she so afraid of? Finally, she sighed. "You're sure? A starter?"

"Yes, ma'am." He held his helmet out to her once more.

This time, she took it and strapped it on. "But I need to go back to the church. You can take me there."

"You'll be okay? I had the feeling everyone was leaving." He still had to grab his guitar that he'd left inside the office door when he noticed her having problems. Might as well check to see she'd be safe.

"I'll be fine. Do you need to start that thing before I get on?" There was the lightest tremor in her voice.

She might not appreciate knowing this, but Secretary Sue made him smile. "I can do that." He started his bike, then motioned with his head for her to climb aboard.

She grabbed his shoulders and swung her leg out like a trained dancer, bringing it over the back end and down the left side so she sat directly behind him. Sue had some long legs. Mac grinned. He liked long legs on a woman.

"Hold on."

She did. Much to his amusement. Okay, maybe he was getting too big of a charge out of this, but it was really fun to have someone who smelled as good as her hanging onto him like he was a lifesaver.

Mac headed for Phillips and hung a Ralph toward the church. He might have taken that corner a bit fast, but she was hanging on tight, so he wasn't worried. Much. He had to stop acting like it was a game. This was merely doing the right thing, giving her a ride. That's all. The rest, having a little fun and being aware of her cuteness, that was all gravy.

He hung a Louie turning left into the parking lot and came to a stop in front of the church office. "Here you go, all safe and sound." Knocking down the kickstand, he turned off the engine.

This time she'd kept her shoulder bag strapped across her body, so there was nothing to retrieve from the storage compartment. She hopped off like a pro and dashed up the steps to the office entrance. When she glanced back, her expression appeared angry, and maybe a little scared. "Why are you stopping?"

He stepped beside her and held the door. "I need my ax."

She tipped her head to the side, confusion filling her eyes.

"My guitar?" He reached around her to get it. "Would've made riding with me a little difficult." He winked and stepped back to the stoop.

Tension seemed to drain from her ridged stance the further away he moved. "Oh, sorry. You were right. About that and the ride. I would've been dealing with the heat if I'd have walked." She paused. "Thank you."

"My pleasure. See you around."

She stopped with her hand on the handle. "Yes. Bye." Then she disappeared inside.

Mac restarted the engine, turned his bike, and headed to the street, needing to get his thoughts into some semblance of functionality.

His buddy Elmer owned a service station and might be able to order the starter. Could be he even had one in stock.

What was the hurry? Secretary Sue had made it plain she wasn't interested.

Still, that left her stuck for transportation, and if she was working at the church, she probably didn't make a ton of money.

Maybe she had a family to take care of things for her.

Maybe not.

Only showed how little he knew about her. However, he did know she needed a replacement starter, or her Bug wouldn't get her anywhere.

The trip east to the highway didn't take long, and he snagged ol' Elmer before he closed the garage part of the station for the day. Mac pulled up to the building just as his buddy was drawing down the service bay doors. "Hey, glad I caught you."

"Dude, you didn't. Stick a fork in me, I'm done. Got my nephew to run the pumps for the rest of the evening. Headed home to dinner." Elmer came closer. "G'me some skin, man."

Mac did, sliding his hand over the top of Elmer's open palm, and grinned. "I only need a starter."

"What? For your bike?"

"No, for a '64 Beetle."

Elmer squinted. "I thought you got rid of that thing a while back."

"I did. It's for someone else." Mac decided he didn't have to share everything.

Elmer must have noticed something. "Oh, a foxy mama. Figures. How'd she talk you into it?"

"No, nothing like that. She's a nice lady, and I found her with car trouble. Figure I can take apart and put together a VW with my eyes closed by now, so I'm helping her out is all."

"Is all? Yeah, right. Well, you're in luck. I happen to have one in the back. It's been there for ages because I ordered an extra for you the last time you were in need, and then you went and sold your Bug." Elmer shrugged and motioned for Mac to follow him into the office. Then he slipped into a back room where grunts and clunks punctuated each other until finally there was a "Eureka!"

Elmer reentered, holding a bent-up box clearly labeled as a starter for a VW Beetle. "Here ya go." He blew a coat of dust off the thing and polished it with his elbow.

"What do I owe you?"

Elmer gave him a price that made him wince, though he knew he was getting a break. But it took nearly all his ready cash. Sue could pay him back. Probably.

Did he want her to?

No, but he also didn't want her to be nice to him just because she felt obligated.

Thoroughly confused by what rolled through his brain, Mac tugged out his wallet and handed over the bills to Elmer.

"You must really like her."

"What's not to like? But that's not why I'm doing it. Besides, she's good for it."

Elmer's chuckle filled the room the whole time he sorted the money into the cash register. "Keep telling yourself that. I haven't seen you interested in a fox since you got home. Good to see you getting back on that horse." He shoved the drawer closed while the machine dinged.

That comment made Mac think of Rachel. Something he didn't like to do because the thoughts were always followed by waves of inadequacy. He shook her from his mind and changed the subject. "Thanks. Smitty been in lately?"

"No. He doesn't keep in touch much now that I'm a family man. Different worlds, I guess."

"Yeah, I guess. Well, see ya around, buddy." He tucked the part into his storage compartment and started his Harley. He'd only asked about Smitty to change the subject anyway.

Elmer sidled up alongside and stuck out his palm. Mac slid his across, then they bumped fists. "Later, man."

Time to head for home.

Mac opened his front door to his phone demanding attention. He grabbed it on the sixth ringy-dingy.

"Hey, dude, where you been?" Speak of the devil. Smitty.

"Just getting in. What's up?" Did he really want to know? If he was going to fix that Bug in the morning, he better not get roped into one of Smitty's late nights.

"Gonna hang out. Come with me."

"Nah. I've been gone all day." Plus he still needed to make some plans about that independent study offer from Professor Day. With all the Bug and the starter and the reels to Ferguson House and, of course, Secretary Sue, he'd sort of let that tidbit slip his mind.

"Don't be a drag. C'mon. You need this. When's the last time you really howled?"

Mac snorted as the memory unrolled. "The last time I was with you."

"That wasn't no howl. That was a whimper. You gotta cut loose. I'm comin' by for you."

"No. Got some stuff to do. Let me know where you're going, and I'll try to show up." Maybe that would buy him some points.

"Right. Like I believe that."

"No, seriously. I'll give it my best shot, I just got junk to handle first." Like get a shower. Between being out in the July heat and crawling under Sue's car, he was feeling more than groady. Akin to an unwashed pair of gym socks. Curiosity convinced him to sniff his pits. Ugh. Now he wished he hadn't. And Sue cuddled up next to that? Man, no wonder she didn't want a ride back.

"Believe it when I see it, but I'll give you a chance. If I don't find you tonight, dude, you'll hear about it tomorrow at work."

Work. Which was another reason he shouldn't be out late. He needed to get that stupid starter installed before he headed for the steel mill.

"Fine. So where will you be?"

"Scene's goin' down at Woody's. Be there. Don't make me come looking for you."

Mac knew he better cut the call short, but he still let the question fall out of his mouth. "Why are you so all-fired interested in my social life?"

"Dude, someone needs to be. Just sayin'." However, it was the laugh that followed that bothered Mac the most.

Chapter 3

"Thanks for coming to get me." Sue leaned back against the passenger seat of Tracy's Dodge Dart Swinger and closed her eyes. Mac had messed with her mind a little too much. There was danger about the man, yet something that made her feel for him. And it wasn't as if she hadn't heard him playing that music when he was in his meeting with Mr. Day, er, Aaron. Would she ever become used to using the choir director's first name?

"No problemo, Kemosabe." Tracy's voice held too much happy. "Besides, now you owe me."

"I owed you before this, and what's with the Kemosabe? You do realize that is Navajo for soggy shrub, right? Do I need to accept insults too?" Sue glanced at her roomie.

"Oh, c'mon. Lone Ranger? Tonto? It was a term of endearment and friendship."

"Tonto means stupid, so it may have been passive verbal retaliation." Sue returned to her eyes-closed posture only to have Mac's furry face grin at her behind her eyelids.

"Or maybe the writers didn't speak Navajo and just liked the sound of the words, adding their own meaning."

Sue sighed, eyes still closed. "Could be, I guess. But back to this owing thing. I already owe you for giving me a place to stay and pointing me at the job and not getting judgmental over everything. However, guilting me into going out tonight feels a bit nonpareil."

"Let's look at it this way. I care about you and can see what you are doing to yourself. You need someone to point you toward what is better, to entice you from your comfort zone, and to support you in making good choices."

"And that's you?"

Tracy's grin was so wide Sue heard it without peeking at her. "Yep, me. So, when we get home, we're having a quick bite, then get into some fun clothes and go out to make the scene. Plan on great music, dancing, and laughter to lift your weary soul."

Sue groaned. Just thinking about the night had her weary soul begging for couch time with a cold lemonade and a riveting read, like the recent re-release of Agatha Christy's *And Then There Were None*.

Five minutes later they parked in the lot in front of Tracy's apartment in Maple Crest. Sue finally opened her eyes, letting the last vestiges of Mac evaporate. He was replaced by a melancholy over the disappearance of that irritating hairy mess from her mind's eye, leaving her more than a little confused.

"I'll make us a couple of sandwiches while you go figure out what to change into. And let it be known, you will be wearing makeup and a cute sun-dress. I know you have a few in your closet, but if I have to, I'll loan you one."

"Yes, Mother." Sue was too wiped out to argue. Which meant she had another valid reason to stay home. The heat drained her, and overcoming her fear of the motorcycle zapped more energy than she summoned in a week, leaving nothing behind to mount a rousing protest to Tracy's plan. Maybe a shower would revitalize her. It couldn't hurt.

She thought she heard the phone ringing as she stepped under the spray. Unless it was Dad or Danny, it wouldn't be for her. Tracy didn't yell, so she continued to wash up.

Afterward, she pulled out her simplest sun-dress and donned her clothes. Makeup and hair she'd do after dinner, so she wandered to the kitchen, taking a seat at the table where Tracy had set a sandwich and some chips at her place. Sue picked up a wedge and lifted a corner of crust. Ham salad.

"Good, you didn't get started yet. I'll do your hair and makeup after I'm ready."

Sue returned her dinner to her plate without a bite. "Oh, come on. I'm perfectly capable of doing all that."

"It has nothing to do with your ability and everything to do with your stubbornness. Just ensuring you will look presentable."

"You don't want me to embarrass you?"

Tracy blanched. "I never said that."

"You didn't have to." The sandwich lost its appeal. "Finish up and get ready. I'll do what I can, and you'll have the final word. Okay?"

"Fine."

The single syllable capped the conversation, and it grew quiet while Sue watched Tracy relish that last bite. Then she returned to her room and pulled out the cosmetics bag that she'd shoved to the back of her top dresser drawer when she moved in. Though it appalled her roommate, Sue didn't even wear mascara or lipstick to church. God said to come as you were, and Sue decided to take Him at His word. It had been four months since she'd worn any. Not since that day... No, she'd promised herself not to relive it anymore.

A little mascara and lip gloss would have to do, though she knew it wouldn't be sufficient for Tracy. She shook her head at her reflection in the mirror over her dresser. Even that tiny bit made her look too much like her old self. Enough for shame to cause her cheeks to heighten in color.

Tracy burst in. "Ready for me?"

Her roommate was too open to ever consider knocking. "I thought you were going to get dressed first."

"Couldn't wait. Looks like I made the right choice too. Here, you sit on the bed. Let me." Tracy pulled out an eyeshadow brush and dusted blue on Sue's lids followed by liquid liner and two more coats of mascara, plus a touch of color to Sue's brows. "I ought to pluck these, but then they'd be all red when we leave. Hopefully this will help shape and camouflage the strays." She tipped Sue's chin up and rotated her head from side to side. "Guess that's as even as I can get it. The lip gloss is fine. Better add a little blush." Tracy applied a soft pink cream, rubbing it across Sue's cheek bones and up toward her temples. "There. Now your hair."

"Can't I just wear it in a chignon?"

"Absolutely not." Tracy ran her fingers through Sue's mane. "I need my scissors."

"No!" Sue popped up only to have Tracy push her back to her seat.

"You have to trust me. Remember when I got you to pierce your ears?"

Boy, did Sue remember. When her dad saw her on her first visit home from college afterward, he nearly exploded. Even now, he occasionally glanced at her lobes and muttered under his breath. "That might not be your best defense."

"Fine, but I cut a lot of hair in our dorm. I only want to give you some layers, just clean up the ones you have, really. You used to have a great shag."

"I want it to grow out." Sue crossed her arms. "No scissors. That's where I draw the line."

"Fine. I'll see what I can do. Where are your hot rollers?"

"I left them at Dad's." Now could she please wear the chignon?

Tracy played with Sue's hair, picking up sections and pulling them back. "There. That's what I'll do. Hang on, I've got the perfect thing." She raced away, returning to the room in mere seconds. "I'll pull the top and sides in to this. May I please trim your bangs?"

"No scissors."

Tracy sighed but stopped fighting. Instead, she brushed Sue's hair and added an oval barrette. "There now. What do you think?" She pulled Sue to her feet and faced her toward the mirror.

The reflection was the image of her old self. The one she'd been running from for the past eight weeks. "It's too much."

"Wear it tonight for me. Please?"

Tracy was a good friend. And she did owe her. "Fine. Hurry and let's go. I want to get this over with." Sue returned her unneeded glasses to her face.

"Great attitude." Tracy headed for the door. "And you are welcome."

Oops. "Sorry." But her roomie was already down the hall. It was hard to feel grateful for something she wanted to avoid. Hopefully there would be some fun tonight.

Twenty minutes later, Tracy parked her car in Woody's lot.

"Why here?"

"You said not to go south or west. This is the other direction."

True, those were her words, but this was a place with memories she didn't want to recall.

"C'mon, don't back out now." Tracy nudged her with her elbow before climbing from the car.

Sue took a deep breath and followed.

Inside, it was noisy. The jukebox barely sung over the conversations coming from all the booths. Of course, on the dance floor, the music would prove clearer.

They found a booth in the corner. It didn't take long for Tracy to attract someone who wanted to dance. She leaned close to Sue to be heard. "Order for me, would ya, please? I'll be back." And she let the guy lead her to the dance floor.

A waitress came around and Sue ordered a Coke for Tracy and a Tab for herself.

The music changed and the Isley Brothers' voices crooned "This Old Heart of Mine."

Sue squeezed her blue lids closed. Getting out was growing too painful. That was—

"They're playing our song." No, not here. Not now. Not that voice. But it was. Brad.

Her eyes jolted wide open. "What are you doing here?"

"At this moment? Asking you to dance."

This couldn't be happening. "No."

"No? I thought you loved this song."

"Not anymore." Her chest heaved air, in and out. "Leave."

"Can't we talk?" He slid into the booth across from her and reached for her hand.

She pulled away in the nick of time.

The waitress showed up then with the two glasses of soda.

Sue scrambled in her purse, but Brad held up a one-dollar bill while beaming his devastating smile. "Keep the change."

"So you're trying to buy me now?"

"Why do you have to put my motives under a microscope? Maybe I'm a nice guy." He grinned and as the light glinted off his blond 'fro, his curls seemed to glow like some halo in Duccio's Maestà. She could almost believe him to be that innocent.

Only she knew better. "You cheated on me."

Brad sat back, his laugh clawing at her resolve. "That's what you think?"

"That's what I know. I saw you."

"You saw *me*. Maybe. But that's not *what* you saw." He leaned forward. "I didn't cheat on you."

"What would you call kissing another woman?"

"I wasn't cheating on you with her." His grin widened as he leaned closer. "I'd been cheating on her with you."

Breath stopped. She had no voice. All she could do was stare at him as pieces of a puzzle she hadn't even registered she was putting together fell into place. Then the picture became crystal clear. Sue was the other woman.

She stood, knocking her drink over. It pooled across the table, dripping onto her skirt. She grabbed at napkins sopping up the spill only to have him do the same.

How dare he do something that someone could mistake for kindness. Or even mannerly.

She shoved the sticky mess, ice cubes, soggy napkins and all, toward his lap.

He jumped up with a curse.

Great aim. His pants sported a wet patch over his zipper. Good.

She scooped her purse and focused on the door.

Brad grabbed her arm. "Where are you going?"

Somehow, strength she never had a clue she possessed lasered her stare to where he still grasped her elbow. "Let. Go."

He did.

Once outside, the dark reminded her that she hadn't told Tracy where she was going. Nor had she considered how she would get to her apartment. A part of her couldn't even remember how she arrived at the parking lot, but now that she was here, some truths were all too evident. It would be a long walk. Ten miles. Fortunately she'd managed to wear flats, but her feet might be the least of her problems. Walking home wasn't the safest of ideas.

However, it was too late to change her mind. There was no way she'd return and risk another encounter with Brad. The night only got darker.

One foot in front of the other. *Keep going, watch your step. Also, beware of cars or anything else that could signal danger.*

She began to rehearse in her mind what she would do if accosted. Her bag hung with its strap across her chest, making it harder to snatch. Should she look for a weapon? Her keys. They wouldn't help at a distance, but them poking between her fingers would allow her fist to be more lethal.

So focused on ways to stay safe, she nearly missed the sound of the motorcycle until its headlight beamed in her eyes.

And it slowed to a stop.

She squeezed her grip tighter around the key chain as her breath seemed to paralyze her lungs.

"Secretary Sue, is that you?" Mac? Seriously? Couldn't she catch just one break?

"What are you doing here?" Though he might have been safe this afternoon, there was nothing to protect her from him but her own ingenuity, and she wasn't going to allow him to get close enough to have to use it. She adjusted her fistful of keys while her imagination popped in too many possibilities of a next move.

"Just on my way to meet someone. What are you doing out here all alone?" He sounded concerned, but at this distance she couldn't see his face clearly enough to determine if that were true.

"My car isn't working, as you are well aware. So walking is what's left."

"Where are you headed?"

"Wouldn't you like to know?" She shook her head.

"Sue. I won't hurt you. I just don't want to see anything bad happen to you. This isn't your sm—safest idea."

He'd been about to say "your smartest." That definitely would not have been an intelligent remark for him, so maybe he knew a thing or two. Still, that wasn't enough to get her to come closer. "I was out of options."

"Well, now you have one. You know I'm a trustworthy driver. Let me give you a ride." He'd turned his bike around and walked it astride along with her.

"I appreciate your help this afternoon, but I'm fine. Thank you." She picked up her pace.

"Oh, c'mon, Sue. I can't leave you alone out here. It wouldn't be right. Besides, I'd have to worry about you the whole time I was supposed to be having fun, and you know that couldn't work out. My friend would get bent, I'd probably be blamed for something happening, not be able to sleep tonight—Ow!"

"Oh, for Pete's sake. What now?"

"Nothing. Stepped wrong on a stone that poked through to my foot."

Dare she ask which one? Should she? If she didn't, would he figure out that she knew? Great. How did this end up so complicated? Better question—What did she do now?

Mac didn't know if he should help her or spank her as she stood there staring at his foot. Something needed to drive some sense into the girl. What was Sue doing walking alone out here? After their meeting this afternoon, he'd been under the impression that she was a highly intelligent woman, but this was one dumb stunt that could get her hurt or killed or... Okay, he couldn't imagine worse than killed but he could think of other really bad things he wouldn't want to happen to her. What was she using for a brain?

"You can wear my helmet again. You're getting good at putting it on."

"I'm better at taking it off, thank you." She tipped her chin a little higher and kept walking.

Well, if she wouldn't get on, he'd just have to scoot along beside her. No way was he leaving her alone out here.

She spun on him almost as if she heard his thoughts. "Why are you following me?"

"It's a free road. No toll booths. You don't own it, do you?"

Sue smacked her head with her left hand, which was when he noticed her right, drawn into a fist with shiny points sticking out between her fingers. Ha. At least she was smart enough to come up with some protection. Though it wasn't enough to make him desert her.

"You aren't leaving, are you?"

"No, ma'am, I'm not." Maybe now that she understood, she'd stop this foolishness and climb on his Harley.

"You're going to walk your bike all the way to my place?"

"If I have to."

She stopped. "If you have to? No one said you had to do anything. I am perfectly capable of taking care of myself."

He grinned. "Right. You and that handful of keys."

She glanced at her fist and then back at him. "You don't think it would work?"

"It might cause some damage if you had an attacker come close, but what if there was a drunk driving home who lost control of his car? Those keys won't protect you from that."

"Oh." She chewed at her lip.

It was now or never. Mac took off his helmet and held it out to her.

She shook her head. "I'm wearing a dress."

"I noticed. Looks nice."

"Thank..." She stomped her foot. "See? You're confusing me. I don't need compliments. How am I supposed to ride with you while in a skirt?"

"I promise not to look while you get on. Besides, it's dark. The bigger concern is the tailpipe. You want to be careful not to let it burn your bare skin." Oops, maybe he shouldn't have said that. She was so close to accepting the helmet.

Now she took a step back. "Guess I'd better not."

"No, Sue. I didn't tell you that to talk you out of it. I don't want you to get burned. Come on. Just be careful and it'll be fine. Let me take you home."

Her eyes widened. Funny, but they seemed to be emphasized like how his little cousin used to outline all her coloring pages.

"Or wherever you want me to take you. I'm not out to learn where you live. Only get you to the destination of your choice. As long as I have enough gas, that is. So, not Chicago, okay?" He winked at her and tried to hand off the helmet once more.

Finally, there was a peek of a smile before she took it and buckled it under her chin. "Fine. Are you happy?"

"Getting there. Time for me to hide my eyes while you climb aboard?" He grinned back.

She thumped his shoulder before dropping the keys in her bag.

"Ow, what was that for?"

"I'll tell you once I think of something. Now watch the road."

He let the gentleman his mother had cultivated override his urge to catch a peek of just how long her legs were. But in his imagination, those shapely limbs went on forever.

"Okay, I'm ready." She wrapped her arms about him like she knew the drill. Guess she did after this afternoon. Good thing he'd taken a shower. And he still enjoyed sharing the bike with her more than he should have.

Mac revved the motor. "Maybe you should tell me where we're going."

"I'm in the Maple Crest apartments off Washington."

He nodded and pulled onto the road. That would've been a ten-mile hike for her. Good thing he came along.

All at once, he realized she did more than hold on to him. Sue was resting her head against his back. Maybe she trusted him a little. Or she was plain tired. Either way, it was a pleasurable sensation.

Soon, what would have taken her hours got accomplished in a matter of minutes. He stopped at the entrance and turned toward her. "Louie or Ralph?"

"What?"

"Louie or Ralph? Left or right?"

"Turn left."

"Right, hang a Louie."

"Not right. Left."

"Yeah, I get it. Hang a Louie."

He felt the helmet rub against his spine and figured she was shaking her head. It sort of tickled as he followed the narrow street a block or so.

She tapped his shoulder and pointed to the right. "There."

He stopped the bike in front of the unit she indicated and kept his head facing forward while she climbed off.

"Oh!"

"What? Did you get burned?" He turned, despite his promised protocol.

"No. I'm fine. But I felt the heat in the nick of time." She slipped off the helmet and handed it back. "Thank you for rescuing me. Again." Sue spun and made for the door, pulling her keys out as she moved.

He waited to make sure she got inside and then took off.

The last thing he wanted to do now was go meet Smitty at Woody's. Of course, that would mean facing him tomorrow at work. He was tired of confrontation. Mac was also tired of being careful where he stepped so as not to rile his cousin. Mac had seen that vicious temper in action.

Then he remembered what not being careful enough had cost him.

Not that it was exactly his fault. He hadn't been the one driving, the one to trip the device. But he had trained the guy who did, and the poor schmuck got the worst of it, though at the time, Mac wasn't all that positive he believed that.

But this was home, not the Nam. And if push came to shove, he was pretty sure he could take his cousin. He just didn't want to prove it.

Smitty was retaliatory enough to share with work and others what only his family knew. Mac wanted to keep what the family knew quiet, but he wasn't going back to Woody's. He had a five AM appointment with a certain VW Beetle in a specific parking lot that had to get taken care of before he reported to the steel mill at six. He headed for home.

Maybe Smitty would be too hung over and would call in sick to work. That would help. Mac held onto that hope until sleep overtook him.

The next morning, he continued to roll it around in his mind while getting ready and when he worked on Sue's car. The starter slid into place slicker'n snot. And he finished up with enough time to get to work and clock in at six on the button.

He glanced at Smitty's punch card. The guy hadn't shown up yet. But as he breathed out a sigh of relief, his cousin stumbled around the corner.

"Didn't think you were going to make it." Mac handed Smitty his time card.

"Like you didn't last night? You had the right idea. My howl got a little out of control. My head's probably gonna fall off from the noise in there, so no more talking."

That was fine by Mac.

Besides, he'd been doing some thinking. When he left work, he was going to run an errand and then grab a shower before he headed for the church.

It hadn't mattered all that much to him before, but something about Sue made him want to up his game. He didn't know if she'd go out with him or not, but he figured he ought to do whatever he could to put the odds in his favor.

Union rules required he take his lunch break, or he'd skip it in order to split earlier. Just meant he'd have to move faster when work was done.

Today he was back to his rolling machine and the product *du jour* was nails. By the time the break whistle blew, he'd seen enough nails to last a lifetime, but he'd thought the same thing yesterday about wire. It just got monotonous—a typical Wednesday. Still, it paid his bills.

It took most of his lunch hour to psych himself into returning to the job. At least Smitty left him alone, but now he wondered what happened. Usually his cousin was happy to share his exploits, not that Mac was all that excited to hear, but this was unusual. When he clocked in, he noticed Smitty had punched out early. Bet his head succumbed to the noise.

The second half of the day finished a bit quicker than the beginning. Mac couldn't leave fast enough. First stop, his buddy Fred's shop. Of course he'd hear about it, how it had been a long time and all, but it'd be worth the ribbing if it got Sue's attention. Next, he stopped by his apartment for a shower and a change of clothes. Nothing too flashy, but something to show her he had some taste—and not all in his mouth, like Mom used to say.

He walked in the church's office door at 3:58. He wasn't sure if Sue left at four or five as a general rule, so he'd hustled.

There she was at her desk, finishing a phone call. She hung up and peered at him. No reaction. No recognition. Her fake smile said she had no clue who he was, as if he were a stranger. Had he overplayed his hand?

Chapter 4

Wednesday, June 21, 1972

"Yes, Mrs. Chapman, I'll tell him. Thank you, Mrs. Chapman." Sue held in the sigh that would surely set the head of the missionary league off on another tangent. Why couldn't the woman take a hint and end the call?

She'd already had one strike from the pastor's wife about being more patient with Mrs. Berkley. It had been intended as a gentle reminder, but the frustration of it all took any of the intent out and poured an accusatory timbre over the whole message. For that reason, she twisted herself into imaginary knots to keep her tone professional and kind when what she really wanted to say probably shouldn't even be thought on church property.

The front door opened, and Sue glanced up to spot a nice-looking man striding to her desk. Her gut tightened. "I'm glad you made me aware of that, Mrs. Chapman, and I will be sure to let Pastor know. Someone just came into the office, so I need to go. Thank you for calling." She gave the matron a moment to say goodbye, but instead only heard the buzz from the disconnected call. This time, the sigh escaped. She'd tried really hard, but there would be another lecture in her future.

She returned her attention to the visitor, plastering that welcoming smile on her face despite being uncomfortable in his presence. Something about his gait was familiar, and she could swear she'd seen that grin before, but the dimples that accompanied it weren't anything she could recall. If she had previously encountered them, she'd have remembered. On that note, she was absolutely positive.

The more she gazed, the bigger his grin grew until she realized she was staring. And not speaking. She cleared her throat. "May I help you?"

Now he laughed. She recognized that laugh. What she didn't know was the face. Mac?

"I can't believe this is what all that hair was hiding." She caught the corners of her mouth twitching with the semblance of a smile as her stomach relaxed. Some.

"Eh, I got tired of the fuzzy bear references."

"I noticed the homogeneity." This time she flashed him a big one, especially because it was true. Now that she thought about it, he had been a massive ol' teddy bear and quite comforting to squeeze when she rode behind him on that motorcycle. Oh, why had her thoughts gone there? Her face warmed.

"Oo-kay?" He shook his head. "I wanted to say that your Bug is ready. The starter's fixed."

"What? When? Um..." She scoured her brain for the correct response. "Thank you. What do I owe you?"

He shook his head. "It was no biggie. I knew a guy and got a deal. Put it in this morning before work."

He'd already completed a full day at his job? And he fixed her car before that? "I need to reimburse you. What time were you here?"

"Doesn't matter, but I do have a question. Would you have dinner with me?"

The request froze her in her chair. Stomach alarms clanged and knots returned. She'd sworn off men. No more. Mac might be a nice guy, but he was definitely a man. Sue refused to lead him on.

At the same time, she owed him. He'd not only fixed her car, he'd bought the part and installed it at the crack of dawn it seemed. Those puppy dog eyes peered at her. "When were you thinking?" Maybe she could let him down easy by there being a conflict.

"Tonight? I realize it's short notice but hoped being a week night you might not have plans." He held up crossed fingers and winked.

Whew, it wouldn't work. "I don't even go home after I close the office on Wednesdays. We have dinner here at church and then Bible study classes. My roommate and I teach the middle school girls." Then words popped out of her mouth before she thought about them. "You are welcome to come with us."

Her first instinct was to retract the offer, and based on his expression of disbelief, she presumably ought to have. Then her gaze zeroed in on the strap slung over his shoulder. "I bet they'd love to hear you play your guitar."

"I don't know. I've probably never heard the right songs." He sounded so disappointed it played havoc with her resolve.

"I'm sure you're aware of plenty, and I promise, those girls will love you. Please, be my guest tonight?" The more she considered the idea, the more she thought it was brilliant. They'd have a plethora of chaperons. And with this shave and haircut, those prepubescent girls would be going nuts. He hadn't gone GI with his new look, more *Gentleman's Quarterly* with a layered cut of his sun-bleached mane that neatly curled at his collar and over his ears, trimmed sideburns that angled at his lobes toward his jaw and connected with a tidy handlebar mustache that still allowed those dimples to shine through. She hadn't realized how handsome the man was. Maybe that was a good thing.

"Well, I hate to turn a lady down when she says please." He paused. "Okay, but don't build me up too much with your class. I'll do my best, but no promises. At least I'll get to have dinner with you." His grin was back, and she hated how it made her pulse race.

"I need to finish a couple of things here before I lock up. Then we'll walk over to the fellowship hall. I try to pitch in and help the ladies over there who make our dinner. Tonight it's meatloaf." Hope he liked meatloaf. She crossed her own fingers but kept her hand in the pocket of her skirt while she did. Wouldn't do if she got caught looking superstitious in the church office. Probably would be another strike against her.

"Meatloaf is great. Haven't had that in a while. Anything I can do to help?"

She put him to work shutting all the blinds while she organized her desk and pulled her purse from the bottom drawer. Moments later, she led him to where the missionary ladies bustled in the large kitchen.

At least Mrs. Chapman wasn't there. The woman was great at setting up a rotating schedule for the members of her group to oversee the Wednesday night dinners, but she rarely showed until immediately before the classes started. Of course, Sue could just be in the dark about reasons for that, perfectly reasonable reasons. So she shouldn't judge. It's just that sometimes when one tended to get judgmental with another person, that other person often became judgy in return.

Sue introduced Mac to the ladies who oohed and ahhed over him as if he were their grandson. To his credit, he flashed his pulse-thumping grin and said something to each of them to make them feel special. It added to his brownie point account. She didn't want to admit that it raised his value in her esteem, but viewing him in action made her long for him to talk to her that way.

This was not good.

She turned to the nearest lady, Elsie Brown, drawing her focus from Mac. "How can we help get things ready?"

Elsie slowly pivoted toward her, as if not really seeing her at first. Then she shook her head and giggled. "Guess my attention was elsewhere. You've set up the drink station before. Why not take care of that?"

"We'll do it. Come on, Romeo, your fan club needs to get busy." She tugged at the sleeve of his polo shirt.

His face got rosy, and the women all noticed. "Um, I guess I have work to do. It was nice meeting you all." Mac had a good sense of humor.

Sue guided him to where the rolling cart they used as the drink station was kept in a deep pantry-like closet. Metal urns to hold the iced tea and Kool-Aid choices sat on top along with an industrial sized coffee pot. "How are you at making coffee?"

He shrugged. "Fair, I guess. Rarely make it for anyone but me."

"That gives you more experience than I have, so you win. The filters and can of Maxwell House are on that shelf." She pointed into the closet. "You can use the pitcher there to get the water. The wall socket is here." She indicated behind where she parked the cart. "I'll start the tea and Kool-Aid. Then we just fill the pitchers with ice and water and set out the cups."

He tossed her a quick salute and stepped into the closet for his needed items.

Tracy blew in about then. “Are you speaking to me yet?”

Sue had been in bed before her roommate got home and gave her the silent treatment on the way to work this morning once Tracy confessed that Brad had called last evening and begged her to choose Woody’s for their girls’ night out. He’d lied and said he’d tried to apologize, but Sue wouldn’t talk to him. Gullible Tracy had fallen for his act and now felt horrible.

“I guess. You’re not going to do that again, are you?”

Tracy vigorously shook her head before crossing her heart and holding up the Girl Scout hand sign.

Sue couldn’t help but forgive her friend. Her roomie never had a malicious intent, though she did push hard for what she thought was a good idea. “So we never mention that name again. Ever. Okay?”

“S’alright!” Tracy imitated Señor Wence’s Pedro with a guttural voice—classic Ed Sullivan moment.

Sue cracked up. “I can’t stay mad at you. C’mon. You do the tea while I do the Kool-Aid.” One of these days, she might have to share more with Tracy so she’d understand, but there was no way she’d ever tell her or anyone everything.

Tracy dropped her stuff on the nearest table, then jumped as Mac exited the closet with a filled coffee filter. “Oh, didn’t see you there.” She stuck out her palm. “Hi, I’m Tracy.”

They shook hands. “Mac.”

Sue glanced between the two of them, noticing in particular how Tracy continued to hold Mac's hand longer than needed. She also took note that it bothered her more than she wanted to admit.

Then another thought shoved its way to the front. Tracy was one of the sweetest people Sue knew, but she never had a steady boyfriend mainly because she couldn't connect with a truly nice guy. Mac was as close to truly nice as anyone she'd ever met. Why not help steer them toward each other?

The idea took root and possibilities bloomed. If Mac became interested in Tracy, then it would get rid of those worrisome concerns about him wanting to build a relationship with her. And if anyone deserved a nice guy, it was Tracy. Yes. This could work. She just needed to keep pointing the two of them in the right direction.

And ignore the tiny bothersome niggle that wasn't on board with her idea.

When the urns were filled, Sue passed out pitchers to Tracy and Mac and led the way to the ice machine where they packed them with the cold cubes before topping them off with water from the faucet. They continued to make trips until a pitcher sat on every table.

Last, she dug in the closet for the cups and handed them out for Tracy and Mac to set next to the drinks on the cart. "I think we're pukka. Let's go find seats, maybe toward the back."

Tracy scooped up her belongings.

"Pukka? What's that mean?" Mac stood staring as if they suddenly spoke gibberish.

Sue glanced at Tracy before they burst into giggles. "Pukka is English, but Indian English. It means genuine or reliable—"

"It basically means good or proper." Tracy grinned at Sue like a student showing off for the teacher. "Sue here is a professional grade wordsmith. Know how some women collect salt and pepper shakers? Sue collects words—interesting, multisyllabic, and rare words. So don't be surprised if she drops one or two into your conversation."

Sue wished the floor would ingurgitate her.

Mac swiped his guitar from where he'd propped it, and the three of them made their way to the far end of the fellowship hall. It would be a little quieter in this corner, so maybe Sue could nudge the conversation in the right direction.

"So Mac, how did you and Sue meet?" Tracy barged in before Sue got a chance. Typical.

But Mac was just Mac. "I had a meeting with Professor Day. I guess he's your choir master or something? Anyway, I'm taking a summer class with him at IUK, and he asked me to meet him at his church office."

"What kind of class?"

"Mac plays guitar." Sue nodded toward the case he'd stood against the wall. If she didn't say something, who knew where this conversation might go? She had to keep it on the right track.

Tracy leaned on her fist, elbow propped on the table, and eyes glowing with interest. "You do? That's wonderful."

"He's agreed to play for our girls tonight."

"You did?"

Mac shifted in his chair. "Um, maybe. We'll see. I'm not sure I can pick out the songs you all would want."

"Oh, play anything. They'll love you." Tracy jerked, her eyes big. "I mean, they'll love the music. Right, Sue?"

Sue smiled. "Right." This was going to work.

Sure, Mac knew he wasn't the sharpest tool in the box when it came to women, but was Sue trying to set him up with Tracy?

It was like she was singing his praises to her friend. The worst part was, Tracy seemed to be interested.

This was so not what he'd planned. And he shaved for this?

The whole thing made him uncomfortable, as if it were possible to become more uncomfortable after agreeing to play his guitar for a bunch of middle school teen-wannabes. *God, if You're up there, I could really use some help about now.*

A dinner bell clanged, and everyone stood. The pastor guy who'd come into the professor's office yesterday—what was his name? —had everyone bow their heads while he spoke a prayer over the meal. Then, all at once, a mad rush raced to form a line by the kitchen window that opened into the big room. Sue nudged him while Tracy led their small group to join at the tail end.

"Think there will be any left when we get there?"

A school-aged boy in front of Tracy turned around and captured his gaze with a serious one of his own. "There's always enough, mister. Even for seconds."

Tracy grinned back at him while Sue leaned close to whisper. "Looks like you got told."

"Guess I did." Would she please say more to him in his ear? The sensation of her breath made his heart beat faster, and the scent of her perfume was a sudden, tantalizing jolt against a space filled with delicious dinner smells.

The line moved forward at a steady pace. Though there were conversations around him, neither of the girls did much talking except to answer greetings from other folks. They each introduced him a few times. Hopefully, there wasn't a test because his anxiety over needing to play his guitar to an audience had taken charge and not a lot of retention remained for outside details.

When he got to the front of the line, the kitchen ladies all grinned at him. As his plate was passed from server to server, he noted that his helpings were on the heaping side. Plus, as each woman doled out her item, she made sure to wink at him. At least he wasn't going to starve anytime soon.

Maybe he shouldn't have gotten that haircut.

Tracy led them back to their table in the far corner. Only now, a young family with three kids had joined them. All the extra ears made having a private conversation with Sue a bit difficult, but he might suggest that he needed to set up in their room before the girls arrived and that would give them some time.

What would he say if they did have that moment alone?

That he wasn't interested in her roommate?

That this wasn't the date he'd had in mind?

That if this was all the chance he got, he'd still take it just to spend time with her?

Right. Mac liked to believe he'd get those syllables out of his mouth, but he was no silver-tongued devil with the perfect phrase. Being honest, words came hard.

Maybe that's why Rachel stopped waiting. No, there was more. He knew that. Even so, he'd never even tried to tell her what had been in his heart.

"I'd say someone behind that counter likes you, Mac." Sue winked at him. "Or maybe several someones."

"She's right. I saw how the helpings grew when it was your plate going down the line." Tracy giggled. "What did you say to those sweet old gals?"

Mac shrugged. "No idea. I'm afraid to leave a morsel for fear of insulting them."

"Oh, no, you don't want to do that. There's no telling what they'll dip up for you next time if you do." Now Sue chuckled along.

"This is more food than I eat all day. If I finish, I'm afraid I won't be able to move." Or was this his out? He was too full to play guitar for the girls? Nah. The gleam in Sue's eyes told him she wasn't going to let him off the hook. Besides, now that she'd dragged Tracy into it, he'd have to fight them both. There was no winning here. "How about you two help me?"

"Nope, can't do it. Look over there."

Mac followed where Tracy pointed. Elsie was wheeling a cart piled high with servings of some kind of cobbler—peach maybe? And there was a tureen filled with something white and fluffy—whipped cream? Oh, not fair.

He groaned and glanced at Sue. She hadn't eaten but a few bites. "Are you feeling okay?"

"Sue's like that. Only eats small portions. She's careful about her weight." Tracy made a face at her roomie who gave her a laser stare at the comments.

"You mean you're going to pass up dessert?"

"She never has dessert. Won't risk a single pound. Sue is the most determined person I know."

"Excuse me." Sue gathered her things and headed for where the trash barrels had been set up.

"Don't mind her. She's sensitive because she used to have a weight problem, but she worked hard to get past it and now won't take a chance of it ever getting the best of her again. I shouldn't give her a tough time, but I worry about her not eating enough." Tracy shrugged.

"Do you think there's a problem?" Mac sincerely hoped not and now studied Sue while she dumped her paper plate and plastic utensils. She was slender, but was she too thin? He couldn't tell.

"Not sure. Probably not yet, but if it continues, there could be. She is strong willed and could sit in a room filled with chocolate and never eat a morsel."

"Any idea why she's like that?"

"Got more than ideas. I know the whole story. I think." Tracy paused as if reflecting. "I don't share her secrets, but I will tell you this much. Sue's sworn off men. I'm amazed you've gotten this close."

Someone had hurt her. That was clear without Tracy's confirmation. "I'd like to get closer, but from what you're saying, if I try harder, I could push her away. Do you have any suggestions?"

Now Tracy grinned. "That I do. Just listen to my advice, and I think you might be what our girl needs."

"Okay, then, oh wise one, what do I do first?"

She tapped her chin a moment before her eyes widened. "Your guitar. Oh, yeah. She loves working with the middle school girls group. If you would come each week and play for them, make it a regular thing, she'd get more used to you. Feel safer. You'd gain a lot of points that way. Of course, I'll need to figure out more stuff, but that's where you start."

Ugh. Not just one time, but every week? In front of an audience? Please let the class be small.

Sue came back. "Want me to show you where you'll be? We'll walk you over if you're done, and you can get comfortable."

Like that would ever happen. Comfortable? In front of an audience? Even if they were pint-sized women, they were still people. Still, he nodded, too full to indulge in dessert.

Tracy looked put-out but gathered her things when he did, and they walked together to dispose of them. "Seriously, just because she doesn't want cobbler doesn't mean we don't."

"Actually, I'm too stuffed to even think about it."

"Oh." She dropped her mess into the trash barrel. "Then I guess she figured right. Like I need it anyway."

Sue picked up his guitar and handed it to him.

He knew she was being helpful, but no one touched his ax. Time to shove those irritations down and deal with them later. When he could be more rational and not anxiety riddled.

Tracy looped her arm through his, making him stare at her. She winked and leaned her head against his bicep. Perhaps she should have shared more of her plan because even though he got that Tracy wanted Sue to feel jealous, he was sure his reaction didn't help with her end goal.

Sue led the way without looking back. Down a corridor to a room on the right. Slightly bigger than an office, it had a circle of folding chairs set up in the middle—about ten seats. If that included places for Tracy and Sue, then there were only eight girls at the most. Eight. That wasn't so much, right? He needed to keep telling himself that.

"Sit anywhere you want. There are usually extra chairs." Sue had no idea how that helped.

He took her advice, tuned his six-string, and gave it a strum. A song he'd heard on the radio recently came to him and he picked it out.

Both Tracy and Sue stopped setting papers on the chairs and looked his way. Before he knew it, they were singing that melody from *Godspell*. "Day By Day." It was a simple melody and easy enough to play. Good, one song down. But he didn't want to change songs. Sue's voice surprised him, and he was afraid she'd stop if he did.

Eventually he had to as preteen girls began entering.

"Cool, what all can you play?"

Sue put her arm around the girl and guided her away from him and to a chair. "We'll tell you all about it when the others get here. Maybe you could think of a song we could sing?"

That's what he was afraid of—the girls coming up with tunes he'd never heard of. Made him wish he'd paid better attention when he attended youth group back in the day.

A few minutes later, Tracy started them off with prayer—mentioning him and his playing for the group tonight—and then Sue introduced him.

"Hey, all. I won't guarantee I know everything, but if you want to take turns suggesting something, I'll give it a try."

A girl in white shorts and a daisy-covered top waved her hand, so he pointed to her.

"Are you married?"

"What?" Mac was not ready for that question. No way. No how. Where did that come from?

"Dionne, that's not a song suggestion."

"Yeah, but how else am I to find out?" Now all the girls were giggling.

Mac cleared his throat. "Well, I'm not married. Never have been. Hope that answers your question. Do you have a song we could try?"

Sue pointed to another girl who'd waved her hand. "Lynnie?"

"Can you play 'House of the Rising Sun'?"

In church? What was going on here?

"Are you sure that's appropriate, Lynnie?" Tracy stepped closer to the blonde.

"Yeah, it's appropriate. You just don't use the words. Instead, you use the melody and sing 'Amazing Grace'."

"Oh." Mac checked for a cue from Sue, who nodded. "Okay, then, I can play that. You all sing." He finger-picked a short intro and soon all seven females in the room were singing the old hymn with a different tune. He had no idea how many verses there were, but after the fifth, Sue motioned that he should wind it up.

"One more song before we start our lesson. Leslie?"

"'Kumbayah'?"

Mac glanced at Sue, hoping she'd rescue him. That was one he didn't know.

Instead, she came next to him and hummed.

The melody was simple, and he was able to pick out the chords. But what should have been easy was harder than it needed to be. With Sue's voice coaching him, he had trouble focusing on anything else.

And he was going to do this every Wednesday? Heaven help him.

Chapter 5

Thursday, June 22, 1972

"Ay-yai-yai! What a day!"

Sue watched as her roommate added drama to her stretch with a big yawn. What was Tracy up to? "What kept you so busy?"

Now home from her job with Kokomo Opalescent Glass Company, Tracy plopped on the sofa across from Sue and kicked off her sandals before massaging her foot. "I must have run errands for half the glass-blowers today. Changed to my boots while there, of course, to keep my tootsies safe, but getting back into my Birkenstocks was too little too late for comfort. I covered the front office, the gift shop, and played go-fer. Just a long, hot day. How about you?"

Sue squished her lips toward the right while she analyzed her roomie's demeanor, doing her best Popeye thoughtful expression. What was Tracy's stratagem? How did she answer without inadvertently giving the girl added ammunition for something? "It was a normal day. Not enough to do and more than enough encounters with parishioners to last me a good long while."

Tracy released her foot and leaned forward. "Sue, why do you keep everybody at arm's length? Seriously, not everyone has a motormouth.

More people than not are predisposed to kindness and empathy. Really, to misquote John Lennon, you should give trust a chance."

No, Sue had seen what trusting could do. She shook her head, knowing she'd dropped into the trap but wasn't sure where this was headed. "Not ready for that. Wounds are still too fresh."

"Not so fresh that you can't have a conversation with Mac." The girl waggled her eyebrows.

Aha. Despite the poor grammar, now Sue realized where Tracy was trolling. "I saw something." Sue shrugged. "Made me sort of let my guard down. A little. Okay, but that doesn't mean I'm ready for a new relationship or that I trust him completely." An offense is often the best defense. "However, you two looked cute together."

Tracy snorted. "Yeah, right, but hey, whatever floats your boat." She stood and swiped her sandals as she padded for her room. Just as she reached the hall, though, she called over her shoulder. "You have my permission to get to know him better. The adorable couple was the two of you."

Her bedroom door closed before Sue got out a retort. Drat!

A relationship with Mac? Well, he was thoughtful and sort of vulnerable. Not to mention extremely good looking. Okay, hot was more like it.

Oh, who was she kidding? She'd thought Brad was kind. He seemed almost angelic. Too bad his appearance had nothing to do with his character.

There was no way Sue would be lured into something again because of some idealization that turned out to be merely a mirage.

She set aside the book she'd been trying to read. She'd even dissected the first paragraph about a bazillion times, but she couldn't remember a thing about it. *Watership Down* was supposed to be brilliant, but she was stuck on page one. It had nothing to do with the story. Of this, she was aware. Instead, it had everything to do with her own inability to get her mind off of her churning emotions each time Mac's face flitted through her brain.

Before Brad, she wouldn't have had a problem speaking with Mac, getting close to him, maybe even flirting with him. Definitely flirting. She probably would have scared him spitless. That made her chuckle a moment.

What if she tried to become acquainted with him now? Wouldn't that mean that he'd get to know her as well? If that were the case, what would he say if he learned of her past? Could she bear to see the same look in his eyes that she saw in her father's?

Enough of this. It was her turn to fix dinner anyway.

With all the heat, she'd decided to try gazpacho and salad. Healthy and cool on a summer's day. While she dropped tomatoes, cucumber, garlic, red bell pepper, and red wine vinegar into the blender, she came to a decision. Even if Tracy couldn't see it, Mac was the perfect guy for her. The bonus being, if he were paired with her roommate, Sue wouldn't have to worry about him being attracted to her. She hit the high-speed button and blended the veggies smooth as her emotions tried to follow suit. A touch of olive oil drizzled in for creaminess gave an example to her heart to add a tad of balm to her feelings. This was for the best. For all concerned. After including a bit of lemon juice and Worcestershire sauce, she set the blender pitcher into the refrigerator to chill while she made homemade croutons. None for her, but plenty for Tracy. Then she tossed together a simple garden salad. A little bit of this, a little bit of that. Just the right amount of things to make life bearable without falling for a specific ingredient and it becoming a craving. Green Goddess dressing for her roomie, oil and vinegar for herself.

Tracy emerged from her room and began setting the table. “More healthy eating, huh? It’s okay to indulge every so often as long as you don’t go crazy. Just sayin’.”

“I’ve already been to Crazyville and won’t let myself go there again.” Though why she still clung to keeping her figure when she didn’t want any man to pay attention made no sense. Even to her. However, throwing away all her hard work because her life headed down a different path made less sense. Therefore, she would stay determined and maintain her perfect weight.

After pouring the gazpacho into chilled bowls, Sue brought the food to the table, and they said grace.

Tracy sampled the cold Spanish soup and grinned. “Okay, so healthy can taste good, and the croûtons on top add the perfect crunch. Hey, where are yours?”

Sue waved the question away. “I don’t need any.” Though it would be satisfying to grind on one of those beautifully toasted, buttery treats coated in gazpacho. No, there will be no letting guards down at this table.

“Seriously, I admire your resolve, but a tiny cube of toasted bread won’t destroy what you’ve accomplished.”

“Are you sure? Think about what one teensy bite did for Eve. I don’t need to take that chance. Besides, I made them for you.”

Tracy huffed, setting her spoon back in the bowl. "So you're saying it's okay for me to fluctuate a few pounds, but not you? I thought you were the one who'd sworn off men."

"I'm not doing this for a man, though maybe in the beginning that motivated me. You are active all day long and not an ounce has ever stuck to you. Besides, you have a better figure than I do, and it doesn't interfere with you talking with men. You look adorable no matter what you do."

"Gee thanks, I think. Seriously, Sue, you need to relax. It's not as if you're going to inhale all the food in the place or stop your workouts. And, to bring up that sore subject, I still don't understand why you and Brad couldn't work it out. I am totally on your side whether you explain or not, but he didn't seem like such a bad guy. I mean, if he's sorry for whatever he did, doesn't it count?"

Sue breathed in slowly and held it a second while she set her fork on her plate and dabbed the corners of her mouth with her paper napkin. "I appreciate your concern." Another breath. "I'm not ready to talk about it." She squeezed her eyes closed, wondering if she could get anything out that would help her roommate understand without having to confess her own guilt. "Um, it involved his cheating, and he isn't sorry. Now if you'll excuse me?"

Sue stood and carried the majority of her meal to the trash can and scraped her plate before sending the gazpacho down the sink and rinsing her dishes. The act gave her a moment to calm down, so she turned back to Tracy. "It's complicated and painful. Please don't ask about more details. If I could tell someone, it would be you, but right now, I can't even think about it."

With that, she retrieved her unread paperback from the coffee table and barricaded herself in her room.

On her bed, book in hand, she tried again to be master of her mind and force herself to immerse into the *Watership Down* world of Fiver and Hazel and their warren problems. She got enough out of the story to realize they would do the hard thing—act on the truth.

Could she? Was she able to clearly view her life and choose to act on what she knew in her heart was true, even when it was difficult? Even when it meant no more hiding?

What would that look like?

She laid the open book page-side down on her chest and closed her eyes.

Immediately Mac's face with his smile and dimples and the bluest oculi she'd ever encountered materialized in her mind.

What would it be like to take a chance and explore if there was something to the attraction? And yes, there was attraction. As much as she hated to admit it.

Was he a little attracted too?

She had a feeling that the answer was also affirmative.

But what if she let her guard down and got to know him and he rejected her? Could she withstand that? Or would it be the kill shot to her soul?

Setting *Watership Down* on her nightstand, Sue sat and pulled her knees to her chin, wrapping her arms around her shins. *God, I know You're out there and that You already are aware of how bad I messed up. I'm trying, Lord. Trying so hard. I don't want to mess up again. But I could use a little help here. Am I supposed to be single for the rest of my life to atone for my stupidity and ego? Or may I have a second chance at being who You created me to be? Please show me, God.*

There was a knock.

Sue swiped at her face. "Come in."

The door creaked open, and Tracy peeked around the edge. "I'm sorry I upset you. I won't pressure you to talk, won't even ask again. But remember, I am here, and I love you, my friend. No matter what. I do know you are hurting, and I miss my fun-loving pal. Hoping she'll come back soon for more escapades." She winked at that. "Is there anything I can do?"

The tears increased from trickling down Sue's cheeks to pouring as sobs escaped and her lungs heaved to capture air. There was no way to force out words.

Then she didn't have to as her friend's arms suddenly enveloped her, rocking her back and forth while soothing shushes whispered at her ear.

It wasn't that Sue hadn't cried over the mistakes she'd made, but this was the first time it all had burst out of her like a breached dam. Maybe it was because Tracy was there. Without judgment. Or possibly it was she'd finally turned back to learn what God wanted of her. But whatever the reason, this uncontrollable storm pouring from her was what she needed. She knew that.

It might not be all she needed, but it was a step.

The sobbing slowed to hiccups and Tracy pulled back, wiping her fingers over her own eyes. "Stop making me blubber too. We're such shambles."

Sue snorted. Well, actually she'd tried to laugh, but a hiccup grabbed her and for all intents and purposes, a snotty snort emerged sending her grappling for the Puffs box on her night stand.

Tracy understood and giggled. "Yep, down-right shambles." She helped herself to a tissue as well.

"So, what do we do about it?"

What were they to do?

Tracy held her gaze. "If you think trying to set me up with Mac is the answer, you've got another think coming. The guy already knows who's sparked his interest. So, the big question is, are you interested too?"

Was she?

Yes. She was.

But what was she going to do about it?

What was she willing to do?

That was the real query. And Sue didn't have an answer. At least, not yet.

The horn blew. Mac paused his machine. After grabbing his lunch box, he met up with Smitty in the corner of the steel mill's break room and settled in to hear the latest about his cousin's adventures.

"Tried calling you last night, but now that I see you today, I know what went down." Smitty snickered.

"What do you think happened?" Mac bit into his sandwich. He was getting tired of PB and J. Time to run by Mom's and ask if she'd fix him a meatloaf to use instead. The one the church ladies served put him in mind of his mother's.

"W.O.M.A.N. You fell for a chick, and now you're on her scent."

Mac choked and grabbed for his thermos. Once he was breathing again, he stared at Smitty. "What in the world are you talking about?"

"You." Smitty waved his hand in front of Mac. "You got all prettied up. No more hermit-man look. Bet you flashed those dimples and the babes lined up around the block."

Suddenly, the ladies from the church kitchen blinked through Mac's mind, bringing a smile. That definitely wasn't what Smitty meant.

"There. You're remembering. I nailed it."

Mac shook his head. "Nope, not even close. Just met some grandmotherly types who were very kind to me. They sorta liked how I cleaned up." He took another sip, for thirst reasons and not for anti-choking ones.

"Seriously? You wasted all that on old ladies? Dude, you got most of the looks in the family but none of the brains." Smitty picked up his sandwich and chopped off half in one bite.

"Always thought you said you got the looks in the family, with all those blond curls the girls go for."

Smitty chuckled, grinning with a mouthful of bread before swallowing. He wiped his hand over his mouth. "I said most. Not all. However, it's obvious I came out ahead on brains if you're spending your evenings making up to old ladies." He shook his head. "Such a waste." He returned to the rest of his sandwich.

Should he tell Smitty about Sue and Tracy? He could mention that he had an interest in someone and that she had a friend. Hmm. A double date. Except Smitty was supposed to be in a relationship. Not that he acted like he was. That pinched a nerve, as he had a fleeting thought of Rachel.

No, Mac was not going to be the one to introduce his cousin to someone who might cause a break up. Something told him that Smitty wouldn't worry about cheating on Rachel if the opportunity presented itself.

No, he'd keep the reason for his new look to himself. Why get involved in that potential mess?

Still, if Smitty blew things with Rachel, would she be interested in getting back together with Mac? Did he want that?

A week ago, he might have given it a moment's consideration. However, that was before he met Sue.

Now, even Rachel paled in comparison.

He took another thoughtful bite from his sandwich while Sue's smile replaced Rachel's. How was he to keep that shining in his direction?

If you would come each week and play for them, make it a regular thing, she'd get more used to you. Feel safer. You'd gain a lot of points that way.

Tracy's words echoed, making him cringe.

"What are you thinking about now?"

Mac glanced at his cousin, who'd finished his meal and was reaching for the apple Mac had tossed in his lunch box. Didn't matter what he said or did, Smitty would still get that apple, and Mac realized it from the moment he added it to bring, though he didn't want to admit that. So he just shrugged.

"I don't know. Thought you had a babe on your mind, but then you got this look. Sort of terrified but resolved." Smitty bit into the apple and spoke around the mouthful. "I don gitchoo."

"What?"

Smitty chewed and swallowed. "I don't get you. You could be having the time of your life, but you just exist. The war is over, at least for you, bro. Let it go."

"I wasn't thinking about the Nam, but thank you for mentioning it in case I forgot about it for a millisecond. Look, dude, I am grateful you didn't get called up. Truly grateful. Coming home was a luck of the draw. Besides, if you make it, there's no telling how much of you makes it. I'm not talking body parts here. The things it changes, it kills that part of who you were back in the world before..." Mac shook his head again. This time because he couldn't come up with words to help his cousin understand. "No one has come home the same, and the world we left disappeared, so we returned to something foreign. You're the one who doesn't get it, and I thank God you don't." Mac stood and packed up. He needed a few minutes alone to gather himself.

Fortunately, Smitty didn't follow.

Mac stepped outside into the June heat. Not as hot as the room where he was running wire, and the tiny breezes reminded him there were open spaces here. Only the noisy echoes of the machines inside followed him. He wasn't surrounded by walls that could close in if he allowed himself to think about it.

A different line of thought was in order, and of course, Sue came to mind. She tended to do that often these days. Boy, he had it bad, and she was so out of his league. He ran his fingers through his trimmed up hair.

When his clock-in time arrived, he hadn't come to any solution.

He could say the same thing when he clocked out for home after four more hours of work. What was he going to do about Sue?

He climbed on his bike and started the ignition as Tracy answered him again—as if she was listening into the radio station in his head. *If you would come each week and play for them, make it a regular thing, she'd get more used to you. Feel safer. You'd gain a lot of points that way.*

Still, Mac didn't want to strum his guitar for a group of almost teen-aged girls every Wednesday. Not because of them, but because playing in front of anyone set his heart to pounding like walking in the jungle. In both situations, it was vital not to be seen, not to have a target painted on you. That's how you survived.

Of course, it made no sense, then, that he'd signed up for a class where he needed some sort of spotlight. That he only had to write the scores and not perform them helped. Music was a very personal thing for Mac. There was something intimate that touched his soul when he played. Usually. In front of an audience, he didn't have it in him to be that vulnerable. He'd rather streak through the steel mill buck naked while sparks flew than agree to play in front of those girls week after week.

Yet he was able to do it last night, and the world didn't crash in on him. He survived and people were smiling.

If it were anyone or anything other than Sue, he'd walk away and not worry about it.

But it was Sue. That was the point. Could he do this? Was he willing to try if there was a chance to get to know her better?

God, you see how I feel about this and about Sue. I'd sure like to learn if there might be something there with her. And while I'm bringing this up, please don't let me raise my hopes only to have her not be interested. I don't think I could handle it.

Mac pulled into his parents' driveway and shut off his bike. Though her meatloaf was his excuse, his real reason for stopping was Mom's advice and encouragement. He needed all of that.

"Hey Mac, how's it going?"

He glanced up to see Rachel waving at him from next door. The reason he'd not been home in a while came rushing back.

"Hey, Rache, doing okay. You?"

She started to chew her lip, a sure sign something was wrong. "Have you seen Smitty lately?"

Great. She wanted him to be the go-between. "He was at work today." Do not ask why. Do not offer her a shoulder. Be strong.

"Oh. I was just wondering..."

"He's Smitty." Mac shrugged. That should end the conversation.

"Would you—"

"Don't ask me, Rache. I don't want to be involved."

She seemed to shrink in front of him. "I'm sorry, Mac. You're right. I'll see you later."

"Wait a sec. Look, we're still friends. If you need someone to talk to, I'm here. But delivering messages..."

"I get it. Don't mind me. I'm probably worried about nothing. It's been one of those days, ya know?"

He forced a smile. "I hear ya. You okay?" No matter what had happened between them, he still cared about her. How could he help but care?

"Yeah. I'm good. You go in and hug your mom. She's been missing you. I'll catch you later." Her smile didn't reach her eyes, but she waved and plodded back into her house.

Funny, but the sadness he felt was more empathetic for her than brokenhearted for himself. Maybe he was healing.

"Mac, is that you?" Now there was a voice he'd never tire of hearing. His mom. That was true music. He shouldn't have avoided home for so long.

"Yeah, Mom. Missed your cooking." He grinned as she greeted him with a big hug and kiss that she planted on his jaw while she stood on tiptoe.

"Well, it's about time. I've got some lemonade and an hour before I start dinner for Uncle Frank and Aunt Gracie, so let's go sit on the back porch." Mom took his hand and gently pulled him through the living room and kitchen. "So how have you been, sweetie?"

"Mom, we just talked on the phone Sunday."

"That is not the same. I've needed to see your face, and you accommodated me by shaving all that scruff off, thank you very much."

"You didn't like my beard?" He pretended shock and stroked his bare chin, as if he wasn't perfectly aware of how she would react.

"Oh, sweetie, I get that it's a guy thing to let your face go *au naturel*, but seriously, I wondered if I'd lost you under all that hair." She gave his hand a squeeze. "So tell me what brought you here. And don't say you've a sudden hankering for my pot roast."

She knew him. "Yeah, well, more like meatloaf. PB and J is getting old for lunches."

Mom leaned forward in her chair, capturing his gaze. "Mac, what's going on?"

"I can't believe I'm here needing to talk to you about this. Good grief, I'm twenty-five. I shouldn't need my mom's help."

"I wish your dad were here." Great, now he'd made Mom tear up.

"No, that's not what I mean, Mom. I'm too old to be struggling to start a relationship—"

She was out of her chair and hugging his neck before he could finish.

"Mom, Mom, c'mon." He disentangled her arms from around him. "I take it something has you excited."

"Oh, you!" She smacked him on the chest. "I was beginning to wonder if you would ever..." Mom jumped back, her hands over her mouth. "Oh, honey, I didn't mean..."

"It's okay, Mom. I get what you mean. If you'll sit, I'll tell you all about her. And then I need your advice."

She hustled to her chair, scooted it until their knees touched, and folded her hands in her lap while leaning toward him. "I'm all ears and promise not to interrupt. Just don't leave out a thing. I've been waiting on this a long time, son."

"Well, you may still because I'm not sure if I can do what her roommate says will work. I don't even know if I should."

"Start at the beginning. You've got—" she glanced at her wristwatch, "fifty-seven minutes. Go."

So Mac took a breath and obeyed like the good son he wanted to be. Before he finished, and before she could advise him, he knew what he had to do.

Chapter 6

Wednesday, June 28, 1972

It had been seven days since Mac had dropped her off at her apartment, and that bugged Sue to no end. It was as if his absence brought him to her thoughts on a regular basis. Last week he had turned up so often she'd worried he might become part of her life and now, poof! He'd disappeared from the face of the earth.

Okay, maybe it wasn't that dramatic. She hadn't gone out of her way to find him, that's for sure. In fact, other than work or church, she never left home.

Still, it was starting to niggle at her, and that had to stop now.

Might be easier said than done since there was nothing here to keep her mind focused on work. She'd finished every to-do list shoved her way. Maybe news had gotten out that Wabash Community's secretary was a bit blunt—for lack of a better expression—because the visitors to the church office had dwindled to zero. Zip. Nada.

That should've made her ecstatic, but instead it caused her to worry that she'd been overly gruff while trying to be efficient.

The phone rang, and Sue nearly jumped on it. At least it was an action she could take.

"Wabash Community Church, how may I direct your call?"

Someone sneezed, then coughed. "Sue?"

"Tracy? What's the matter?" Her roomie's voice was husky and weak.

"I should've known something was wrong when I woke early this morning with a headache. Whatever this is—" she hacked again—"I shouldn't be near the girls, or anybody for that matter. I'm sorry to bail on you—"

"Don't think a thing about it. Consider it handled. Just get better. Spray some Lysol around the apartment if you are up to it."

A scratchy laugh was her answer. "I'll hibernate in my room so you won't come down with this. Thank you. I'm really sorry."

"It's fine. I've got it. Rest, and I'll check on you once I'm home."

They said their goodbyes, and Sue hung up. Sick. Her roommate was sick. Without thinking, Sue raised her fingertips to her forehead.

Way to go. Thinking about yourself instead of praying for your ill friend.

Sue squeezed her eyes closed. That's exactly what she'd done, and the shame scraped her tongue like a mouthful of sand. How had she become so self-centered?

Before she dwelt on that to the point of forgetting to pray for Tracy, she stopped and folded her hands.

Afterward, she contacted Hazel Norman, who was at the top of the phone prayer chain, reminding Sue of her novel at home. She started to imagine the list as Hazel's warren. Oh, her thoughts were taking her down another rabbit hole. No. Focus. She added Tracy to their prayer concerns.

That action improved things. However, she needed to plan what to teach tonight. She'd always let Tracy run the class and simply helped as needed. Now it was on her, and that was more than a little intimidating.

Why didn't she ask what the next lesson entailed? Should she call back and risk waking Tracy? And if Sue did let on that she didn't know the curriculum, what would her friend say?

What if it meant she ended up subbing more often in order to carry her weight as the co-teacher? Tracy was the queen of fairness and justice. Helping was one thing, being in charge was something else. What could she do? What should she do?

A Bible lay on the coffee table where visitors waited when they arrived for appointments, and it drew her like a magnet. Holding the book close to her chest, she closed her eyes and lifted yet another prayer. *Lord, please show me something in Your Word to help me with the girls.*

She returned to her desk, setting the Bible on her blotter. After a moment, she closed her eyes and slowly reached out, opening it, and placing her finger on the page. It revealed Romans 3:23. *For all have sinned, and come short of the glory of God.*

Sue didn't know if God pointed straight at her or if this was an assurance that she wasn't alone. Maybe both? She read the whole paragraph beginning with verse twenty-one continuing through verse twenty-six.

For someone who loved big words, this was a treat. But it took longer to really let the full meaning settle in. Everyone had sinned. Yet everyone had the same chance at righteousness—right standing with God—because of Jesus and through His sacrifice. Everyone. Not everyone except Susan Marie Mitchell. Just simply everyone. However, it required dependence on Jesus, surrendering to Him and allowing Him to handle it for her and everyone so all can stand in His righteousness.

Another verse came to mind. Psalm 51. *Have mercy upon me, O God, according to thy lovingkindness: according unto the multitude of thy tender mercies blot out my transgressions. Wash me thoroughly from mine iniquity, and cleanse me from my sin.*

Within seconds, it became the cry of Sue's heart. *Have mercy, Lord Jesus. Have mercy.*

Her tear ducts welled until she suddenly remembered where she was. Digging in her purse, she found a tissue and dabbed at her eyes. Sue knew as well as she knew her name, the second she left her desk to run to the restroom, someone would come in. On the other hand, anyone coming in would notice her blotched face if she didn't.

In desperation, she pulled a file folder from her out box and began fanning her cheeks. Those Scriptures wouldn't hit her so hard if she'd just forgive herself. If she could do that, she wouldn't waver so much about Mac.

Would the girls ask for him? This would be the night for him to show up if there ever was one. Not that she wanted to be alone with him, but he'd be backup support for her first solo mission into leading this class.

Should she call him and see? His phone number was most likely listed in the White Pages, if Mr. Day, er, Aaron, didn't have it, but what excuse would she use to ask him?

The White Pages it was.

Sue set aside the file folder and pulled out the phone book, flipping through fragile sheets until she found the M's. Then she ran her finger down the lists of names until she hit MacKenzie. What was his real first name? Oh, right, Peter. Peter MacKenzie.

There it was. Neatly typed with his address too. He didn't live all that far from her apartment. Hmm.

Well, was she going to stare at the entry all day or act on it?

Sue shook herself out of whatever had magnetized her gaze to the listing and dialed, letting it ring at least seven times before settling the receiver in the cradle as defeat washed over her.

Maybe it was a good thing he didn't answer. What would she have said? She stared at the phone as if could magically respond.

"Got a minute, Secretary Sue?"

Sue snapped her head up to meet Mac's gaze. How in the world? She could feel her cheeks flame as she stuttered for words.

"I'm sorry, I didn't mean to scare you. Just wondered if I could play guitar for the kids tonight."

Play guitar? Had God really listened to her?

"Yes! Yes, you can. Sorry, I didn't hear you come in. Believe it or not, I just called you to see if you might want to."

"You did?"

All she could do was nod with a silly grin on her face. "Yes. You didn't pick up, so I was trying to figure out what to do, and in you walked. Tracy is under the weather, and I'm it. I was hoping you might come, and..." She shook her head and stared at her shoes. How pathetic she must sound.

"Actually, I almost never play in public, but it seemed to go well last time, so I figured it was a safe place." He paused a second, so she glanced back at him. "Sort of helps me get used to performing in front of people. But, hey, do you need help getting the office closed down?"

"Yes, please." She shook her gaze out of his laser beam and scanned her desk. Everything was in place but for the phone book, which she quickly put away. When she glanced toward him, he was closing the blinds. "Thank you."

Why was it suddenly hard to speak with him? She didn't know what to say and everything that swirled in her mouth was either cliché or obvious.

He finished the shades and returned to stand before her desk. "Anything else I can do?"

Stop making my pulse dance the cha-cha might be a start. But then, did she really want him to? His very presence poured life back inside her, something she hadn't felt in a long time. Still, it scared her. Dead to her feelings was safe. This euphoric animation was dangerous. Like sitting at the top of a roller coaster. With no brakes or seatbelt. And no way to tell if part of the track had been destroyed. Who needed King's Island with Mac around? She couldn't deny the electrical thrill that tingled through her when his gaze joined with hers.

"Sue?"

"Um, yes?"

When she refocused from her mind wanderings, she realized he was staring at her.

"Is there anything else you need me to do before we leave here?"

She shook her head. "No, nothing more."

"Then we should head over?"

"Right." She nodded and cleared her throat. "Let's go." After grabbing her purse from the bottom desk drawer, Sue led the way to the front door, locked it, and then they exited through the back way that took them to the kitchen entrance. She stopped before entering and turned toward Mac. "The dinner ladies are sure going to be happy to see you again."

He blushed, making her heart go "aww."

It also caused her to chuckle as she twisted the knob, pulling the door open. "Hey, guess who I found."

The dinner crew all stopped what they were doing to stare Sue's way.

Sue stepped into the kitchen, revealing Mac, who trailed behind.

"Oh, you're back!"

"Knew you couldn't resist our cooking." That was followed by a wink from Delores Burns.

Elsie just gave him a giant motherly embrace. It must have been a little tight as his eyes got big.

Sue stood in back of Elsie, catching the "Help me" message Mac mouthed to her over the woman's shoulder, but it was too fun to pretend she couldn't understand. Eventually, though, she decided to rescue him. "Mrs. Brown. Elsie. You need to let him go. He's here to help, but he can't while you have him locked in a bear hug."

The elderly woman released her hold and giggled. "Oh, oops, sorry. Good to have you here, Mac." She patted his arm, giggling again, and returned to mashing her potatoes after tossing a wink his way.

That exchange was the funniest thing Sue had seen in forever, but she didn't dare laugh. "We'll take care of the drinks." Locking arms with Mac, she dragged him to the closet where the cart, urns, and pitchers resided. Once there, she pulled him inside, glanced out the door to make sure no one was near, and then they locked gazes. And laughed. Together. No words, simply laughter.

The closet, or walk-in pantry, was good sized for its intended purpose. However, with two adults inside, it was definitely close quarters. As the laughter ebbed, Sue grew more and more aware of how tight the room was.

She turned, apparently at the same time he did, and they were face to face. Very close. Enough to affect the air in her lungs. Was she even breathing?

He was aware of it too. She could tell by the way his pupils dilated and he seemed to hold his breath. Then her name floated on his exhale. Velvety. "Sue."

It was as if she'd been touched with a cattle prod. She jumped for the door. "I'd better pull this cart out. Can you find the coffee and filters? We've got to get the tea and Kool-Aid made. I'll fill the pitchers." The words poured from her mouth, building a defensive barrier. She swiped up the two nearest containers and raced for the safety of the sink.

What just happened?

Mac watched Sue retreat from the closet where she'd dragged him. He'd scared her. That he knew. Maybe even himself a little.

Or maybe a lot.

There was the moment, a split second, where his head abdicated to something basic inside him and he'd nearly kissed Sue. Just thinking about it made him question who he was.

Forcing himself on a woman was not his style. Okay, he hadn't forced himself, but he had stepped out of his comfort zone and took a chance he never knew he could.

Sue wasn't ready, and he'd frightened her.

How stupid was he? Wait, he didn't need to know that.

Instead, he found the coffee and filters and got to work doing the same job he'd performed last week. At least it was something familiar.

Unlike this feeling trying to take over his life.

He had loved Rachel. Until things went south, it had been easy, simple, like they were fated for each other. Maybe that had been the problem—everyone assumed they were. Only Rachel figured out the myth first. Perhaps if they'd concluded that together, it might have been less painful. If they'd gotten there before... Well, he wouldn't have blamed that reason for Rachel breaking up with him.

Could this actually be true?

Great. How much coffee had he measured in while his brain ran amok? Mac removed the filter and carefully funneled the grounds back into the canister before remeasuring correctly.

Sue returned with the pitchers and silently filled the urns for iced tea and Kool-Aid. Looked to be grape flavored this evening.

He borrowed the now-empty containers and meandered after the water for the coffee maker. Mrs. Brown offered him a grin. That woman knew what she was doing, but he realized it was only for fun. He tossed her a wink and a smile before filling the pitchers.

Back at the cart, Sue was already collecting more jugs for the ice water to go on each table. He should talk to her. Explain. But she kept so busy. Probably to stop any effort to discuss what happened. Should he honor that or try to clear the air? Maybe let God get the timing right? There was a novel thought to have in church. Mac shook his head and poured the water into the industrial percolator.

"Hey Mac, good to see you here."

He turned to spot Professor Day. "Hey, yeah, I've been helping with the middle school kids."

Professor Day glanced from Mac to where Sue was returning with four pitchers of water. The corners of Aaron's lips rose as if he approved of the idea. "Great. Glad you can do that. You're helping with music?"

Mac nodded. "Did it last week, and it went well." He was running out of things to say.

"Have you started on your assignment?"

Oops, guess there was more to discuss. "I'm still working on a theme. You'd mentioned it needed to be God-honoring. I have to narrow that down a bit."

"You'll get there. I have confidence in you." Professor Day stuck out his palm.

At least someone believed in him. Mac shook the man's hand while his brain admonished him. His mother believed in him too. And there were more who would if he gave them the chance. "Thanks. I'd better get this finished." He nodded toward the coffee pot.

"Of course. I'll see you around." The professor walked away only to be summoned by someone else across the room.

Mac got the contraption brewing before collecting several pitchers and heading for the ice machine. Sue was already there, filling her last container. She turned and sort of smiled, like she was uneasy but didn't want anyone to know. Had he made her nervous on top of everything?

Man, he'd really stepped in it.

This wasn't the place for a clear-the-air type of discussion. He'd have to wait until the jobs were done. Maybe he could find enough alone time to apologize.

Ten minutes later, the drink cart was ready, and every table had a pitcher of water. Sue motioned toward the back corner, and he followed with his guitar.

He waited until they were seated across from each other before diving in. "I need to apologi—"

"Don't." Sue held up her hand like a traffic cop. "You didn't do anything wrong. It's me. I..." She focused on the table, tracing the pattern scuffed onto the surface while her voice grew softer. "I can't. I'll be your friend, and even that breaks the rules of my life. But anything more, I just...no."

"It's okay. Don't worry. I'm honored to call you my friend, Secretary Sue."

Her head popped up, and she studied him while he grinned. Tension left her face and shoulders as she flashed a smile his way.

If she preferred friends, then friends it would be. He wasn't ready to rush into anything anyway.

The dinner bell rang, and this time Professor Day spoke the prayer over the food. Then the line magically formed, and Mac and Sue joined at the tail end. Tonight's fare was beef stroganoff with potatoes and peas. Again, the ladies were generous with their portions. Mac was going to get fat eating this way, even if it was only once a week.

Then he got an idea. Was it possible to save some for tomorrow's lunch at work? Had to be worth a try. He divided his food in half, and after enjoying the first part, took the rest to the kitchen to see if they had a way to preserve it.

Doris and Elsie came to his rescue and soon he had a well-protected to-go plate, folded and secured like a taco, so it fit into the storage compartment on his bike. Now that would taste great tomorrow, even cold.

By the time he got back, Sue had cleaned up and was ready to head for the classroom. At least she'd waited for him.

The chairs had been set up, and there was little else to do other than tune his ax and be prepared. He'd talked with his mom about other songs he could play, and she gave him some great ideas, so he wasn't starting out so much in the dark.

Sue paced while waiting for the girls.

He wanted to ask what was wrong but figured that would only make it worse, so he kept to himself and allowed her the freedom to do what she needed to do.

Minutes later, the first girl, Lynnie, came in. "You're here again. Far out." Then she leaned out the door. "Hey, Dionne, he's here." She turned back around and grinned as Dionne ran into the room and skidded to a stop. "Hey."

Mac waved. "Hey." So grammas and preteens liked his company. Too bad Sue didn't fit into one of those categories. However, if she did, he wouldn't be interested either, so there was that.

"You're going to play again?" Dionne had moved closer to him.

"No, dork, he's gonna whistle. Whadya think?" Lynnie made a sound that only females seem to be able to make that left no doubt a stupid remark had been uttered.

"Yeah, I'll play. Hope you know some songs that I've been practicing." He started to cross his fingers to emphasize that hope, but remembered where he was.

"Let's just come in and find seats until the whole class arrives." Sue guided the girls to the other side of the chair circle, and Mac relaxed a bit. Sue had his six. But then she'd wanted him here to have *her* back. He could do that.

Soon everyone who was coming had arrived. Turned out that they were having a small class tonight. Looked as though more than Tracy had come down with the latest bug.

"Let's open in prayer, and then we can sing for a few minutes. Leslie, would you please lead us?"

The girl nodded and started to pray. She hadn't even seemed nervous about doing it in front of everyone. The idea startled Mac, and the simple prayer was finished before he'd had time to listen to the words.

"Okay, does anyone have a song suggestion? And remember where we are, keep things focused." Mac appreciated Sue's instruction. He wasn't ready for off-the-wall questions like last time.

Lynnie raised her hand. "How about 'Spirit in the Sky'?"

Mac began to strum when Sue stopped him. "Let's slow down a second? Does anyone know the words to that song?"

All four girls lifted their hands.

"Okay, let's go through the lyrics before we sing the song. Dionne, tell us about the first verse. Can you recite it please?"

Dionne did.

"Does anyone have a problem with those lyrics?"

"Miss Sue, they're just words."

"You're right, Dionne. Just words. Yet words have meaning and power. If you say something enough, it can become true to you, even if it is a lie.

Think about where we are right now. Do you want to sing words that are untrue in this place? Or any place, for that matter?"

Dionne shrugged, and the others shook their heads.

"So is there anything wrong with those words based on what the Bible teaches?" Sue seemed on point with something.

Lynnie waved her hand. "It calls God a spirit and the Bible agrees that He is. It says He's in the sky, and the Bible tells us that's where heaven is. Plus it says that we want to go to the best place when we die and that the place is with God. So those words work."

"Good job, Lynnie. That's what I was after. Yes, those words match with the Bible. Next verse. Who wants to try?"

Leslie shot up her hand, so Sue motioned to her.

After she spoke the lyrics, Sue asked the same question about them and how they related to the Bible.

Again, Lynnie chimed in. "This time it is saying we need Jesus, or we can't get to the best place. The Bible says Jesus is the way, the truth, and the life. So that goes together too." A tiny smirk appeared on Lynnie's lips.

"I agree, Lynnie. The main question is does the Bible agree? And so far, it does. Sharon, how about you share the last verse of the song?"

Sharon was new to Mac since she hadn't been there the previous week. She was also quiet, so he wondered about Sue putting the girl on the spot, but Sharon came through, reciting the lyrics verbatim.

That's when Mac heard it for the first time.

Oh, he'd listened to the song on the radio a lot, even picked it out once or twice. But he'd never really thought about the meaning. Until now. He had a feeling that this was the whole point of Sue's questioning.

"So does the Bible agree with this verse?"

Lynnie was slower to shoot up her hand, but she finally did. "The words say that the singer doesn't sin and has never been a sinner. I don't think that matches because only Jesus never sinned."

"You're right. Jesus never sinned. Even more importantly, please open your Bibles to Romans chapter three, verse twenty-three. Does someone have that?" Sue paused until all hands were raised and then called on Dionne to read it aloud.

"'For all have sinned and come short of the glory of God.' Oh, now I get it."

The rest of the girls nodded before Lynnie lifted her hand. "Couldn't we just sing the first two verses?"

Sue shrugged. "I guess so, but let me tell you about something that happened when I was in college. First, I need you to promise me you will never try this."

All the girls agreed.

"I knew this person who got upset with a guy who'd been bothering her. He wouldn't take no for an answer when he kept asking her out. So she made a batch of cookies and let him think he was finally getting his way. She delivered them to him and afterward she never saw him again."

Leslie blurted, "Did she poison him?"

"In a way. These were chocolate chip cookies. But instead of using Nestle's chips, she used pieces of chopped up Ex-Lax." Sue paused, and one by one the meaning settled on the girls while they covered their mouths, and their eyes grew wide. "So there was only a little bit of Ex-Lax in the cookies. The rest was good stuff. Do you think they were okay to eat?"

The girls silently shook their heads in unison.

And somehow, Mac finally had a seed of an idea for his project.

Chapter 7

Sue unlocked the apartment, coming in as quietly as possible, and took her things to her room first before cracking Tracy's door a smidge to peek in.

Her roommate lay in bed, propped by a couple of pillows, with a washcloth over her eyes. No way to tell if she was asleep.

"How did it go?" Tracy's voice was froggy and weak.

Since she was awake, Sue pulled the door wider and stepped inside the room, keeping her distance. "Mac showed up, and I put him to work. Probably not the lesson you would have taught, but we muddled through. How are you feeling?"

"I've got chills and my eyeballs want to burst. Haven't been this sick in a long time." There'd been no rush for Tracy to get her words out, and Sue could tell her throat must hurt along with everything else.

"I can call in tomorrow for both of us and then arrange a doctor appointment for you."

Tracy groaned. "Don't want to even think about it. I hate for you to miss work, but..."

"So it's settled. Grab some sleep. I'll see you in the morning." Sue blew her a kiss and stepped out, keeping the door cracked enough that she could hear if Tracy needed her.

Back in her own room, she changed into her pajamas before settling into bed with her Bible. This time she wanted to study the verses in her own Good Book, not some stranger's. It wasn't as if she never read Scripture, but if she were honest, she'd have to admit it had been a while since she'd cracked hers outside of church. She ran her hand over the onion skin page. So fragile, yet so mighty, bold. Life changing but easily discarded. Filled with wonder and mystery, still it often sat on a shelf. She remembered a verse, something about foolishness to the wise yet lifesaving to those who heeded. Where was it? She turned to her concordance and searched.

There it was. 1 Corinthians 1:18. *For the preaching of the cross is to them that perish foolishness; but unto us which are saved it is the power of God.*

Yep, couple that with *The fool hath said in his heart, There is no God,* and she could understand why someone would think he was wise in his own eyes and yet be a perishing fool. She definitely didn't want to fall into that category.

However, God gave her a brain. Why would He do that if He wanted her to play dumb? In fact, that was a pet peeve—females who hid their intelligence just to get a man to pay attention. What if the pendulum swung the other way? What if women, or anyone for that matter, got so smart they forgot Who gifted them with that wisdom? Who offered them avenues of learning? What if they—she—became too wise in her own eyes and took credit for all the blessings God poured out?

No. She might be the one using her brain, but it all came from God—*All good gifts come from the Father of lights*. It was a matter of gratitude. An attitude of gratitude.

When was the last time she'd said thank you?

Sue couldn't remember, but she could remedy the situation. Rolling to her side, she turned off the light on her nightstand, wrapped her arms around her Bible, and prayed a prayer of thanksgiving until she fell asleep.

It was the first good night's rest she'd had in months. And apparently she hadn't thrashed about because when she opened her eyes, she was still clutching her Bible to her. That brought a smile. "Thank You, Lord."

Minutes later she checked on Tracy who seemed to have not been as fortunate. With red-rimmed, swollen eyes and a hacking cough, the poor girl appeared as miserable as she sounded.

After retrieving the thermometer from the bathroom, Sue came closer and checked her friend's temperature. 102.8 And that was under her arm, not tongue. She definitely had to get Tracy into see Dr. Schwartz. "Want to try some juice or tea with honey?"

Tracy only shook her head, then she put her hands on either side of her face. The movement must have hurt.

"Then you sleep until I come help you get ready for the appointment. I'll call the church and the shop for us. Don't worry. Just rest."

This time Tracy didn't acknowledge anything as her eyelids slid closed.

Sue took the cue and left to make her phone calls. Everyone on the work-front was understanding. Dr. Schwartz's office sounded as if they'd seen this scenario before and offered advice on giving the patient some comfort before the three o'clock appointment, which was the only opening available. A summer cold was one thing, but this sure seemed to be something else.

The rest of the morning passed in quiet solitude. Sue checked on Tracy periodically but let the poor girl grab as much sleep as she could until close to two. Then, with all the gentleness she could muster, she helped her roomie wash up and dress. Besides the fever and sore throat, there were no gastric symptoms, though Tracy showed few signs of hunger since swallowing caused torture. Still, she needed fluids to fight off whatever this was, so Sue pressed the honeyed tea.

A little before three, they pulled into the doctor's parking lot and settled in the sick waiting room. The hacking and coughing and sniffling made a macabre sort of symphony, and Sue fought the urge to wait in the car. Still, whatever this was, she'd already been exposed by caring for Tracy. She might have become infected at the same time as her roomie since there were girls from their Wednesday night class out ill too. That thought just thrilled her to no end. Oh, goody. Add in a burst appendix and they'd really have some fun.

Dr. Schwartz was running behind, but with the crowded waiting room, it was no wonder. Still, the nurse called Tracy back after only twenty minutes. Tracy motioned for Sue to come with. Once Tracy laid on the examination table, though, the wait was longer. When the doctor finally showed up, Sue wondered if he'd be the next one seeking medical help. The poor guy looked done in.

"So, you've got it too, Tracy? What about you, Sue? Have you shown any symptoms?" He'd brought both girls into the world and handled all their illnesses.

"No, I'm healthy as a horse."

He coughed into his sleeve. "Just take precautions. Lots of washing your hands, and keep the Lysol handy. Now, let's get a look at you, Miss Callahan." After the usual check of her ears, nose, throat, and eyes, he referred to his chart where the nurse had recorded Tracy's current temperature and blood pressure. "Yes, ma'am, you've got this bug."

"What is it, doctor?" Though a name wouldn't change anything, Sue needed to know.

Dr. Schwartz shoved his glasses to his forehead and met her gaze, his tired eyes revealing how worn he'd become. "It's a virus. No epidemic of a known disease. Yet. Simply a widespread bug, making many people miserable. Imagine a sinus infection and strep joining forces. I started seeing this not quite a week ago. The good news is that it hits hard for about two days and then eases up. My first cases are about ready to return to work or school."

"What about you?" Sue couldn't help but be worried for him.

"That's not your problem. I have it covered, but thank you for your concern. Now let me get a prescription for Tracy for amantadine, but first, you both need shots of gamma globulin just to give your immune system a boost." He prepared the injection.

Sue winced as the medication went beneath the skin of her arm, but it was a small price to pay if it meant not getting this virus.

Dr. Schwartz then wrote on his prescription pad and tore the piece away, handing it to Sue. Tracy followed with her eyes but remained silent.

"Is this liquid, Doctor? She's having a rough time swallowing with her sore throat."

"Yes. I figured as much. Do you have a humidifier?"

Tracy shook her head, but Sue thought she remembered one from her childhood. It would be at her dad's...

"Gargle with warm salt water every couple of hours. Tea with honey will soothe." Sue gave Tracy an I-told-you-so glance as Dr. Schwartz continued. "Just don't do it right after taking the medication."

Tracy slid off the exam table and started to offer a handshake but pulled back with a sheepish smile. Then she sort of cleared her throat, winced, and mouthed "sorry."

Dr. Schwartz patted her shoulder as he ushered them toward the receptionist. "Nothing to worry about. Call if things worsen, but you should see relief in twenty-four to forty-eight hours."

Sue walked with Tracy to the desk where she paid for her shot while her roomie pulled some cash from her purse for her part. Then they headed for the car.

"Can you handle my dropping off your prescription before I take you home? Then I can swing around and pick it up after you're back in bed."

Tracy nodded. This was the quietest she'd ever known her roommate to be, and it was oddly disturbing.

Sue pulled into Hooks Drug Store and Pharmacy parking lot. Tracy was already half asleep with her head lolled toward the passenger side door. It was growing warm outside, so this would have to be a fast trip, or the poor kid would bake while waiting.

Five minutes later, she'd dropped off the prescription and was back at the car. Six more minutes saw them opening their front door with Tracy wobbling to her bedroom. When Sue passed the doorway seconds after, her roommate had face-planted on her bed, still fully clothed, including her shoes, which dangled over the edge.

After shaking her head, Sue came in and helped get Tracy back into the comfort of her pjs and covers. She then made a new cup of honeyed tea for the girl and set it on her nightstand before returning to Hooks. She was on a mission in her mind, trying to figure out the best way to ask Dad to borrow the humidifier.

Sue parked in the same spot, this time making sure to roll up her windows and lock the car first. Then she marched into the drug store toward the pharmacy counter where they had promised to have the medication ready when she returned. They'd better keep that promise if they knew what was good for them.

"Secretary Sue."

Only one person called her that. No matter the urgency of her mission, just hearing his voice made her breathing change rhythm, like that second before coming downstairs at Christmas. Only the more she thought about it, this was not a good thing. "Mac?"

"What brings you here?" He was in no hurry it seemed. How she wished she weren't.

"Um, need to pick up some medicine for Tracy. She's really sick."

He's demeanor changed, the smile leaving his face and his eyes glowing with compassion. "I'm sorry. Is there anything I can do?"

She shook her head. Maybe she should've shaken harder since a crazy idea popped into place. No, she couldn't ask. It would be stupid. Nonsensical. Irrational even. However, coward that she was, it might be what she needed. "Would you be willing to go with me to pick up some things for Tracy at my dad's house?"

"Sure. Happy to help."

He had no idea what he'd just volunteered for.

Thursday, June 29, 1972

What just happened?

All Mac planned to do was grab a fountain drink and bug-out for home to work on his project. Then he heard his mouth agreeing to go with Sue to her dad's house. What was he thinking?

Well, he wasn't, at least not with his brain.

However, if she was asking him to meet her folks, maybe she was ready to take another step in their relationship. Right? It was a logical conclusion. Could be she wanted to see if he could get along with her family.

Did that make this a test? Oh, great. He'd just thought himself into another wave of panic. His brain and his mouth were spending way too much time letting his heart take point on this mission. And he knew, deep down, that he needed to go slow if there was a chance of Sue choosing to try more than friendship.

He shook his head, realizing she was waiting for more. "I was going to buy a phosphate. Would you like one?"

"No, that's fine, thanks. I do need to take the medicine to Tracy first and give her a dose before we leave. Get your drink. Want to follow me home?"

"Sure, how about if I drive?"

"Arriving at my dad's on your motorcycle? Um, I don't think so."

Mac chuckled. "Not to worry. I've got my truck today. It's starting to get a little warm, so thought I'd switch it out."

Sue paused, and he could almost see the wheels in her brain processing this new development as she cocked her head and rolled her lips between her teeth. Finally, she sighed. "Fine. Okay. Meet you in the parking lot." She headed to the pharmacy counter while he took off for the soda fountain to get his drink to go.

Soon they were outside in front of the store. "I'll follow you."

"Well, you know where I live in case you lose me."

"True. See you there." He waited until she was in her Beetle before climbing into his Ford F-Series and pulling behind her at the parking lot exit. He'd realized when he took her home the other night that she lived in his neighborhood. At least within a six-block radius.

Mac pulled up in front after she parked and waited with his radio playing background music while she ran the medication inside. It gave him a moment to think about what he was about to do. Had he read too much into this? Wouldn't be the first time he'd built up some idea in his head only to be on the wrong track.

Since he would be meeting her father—he was about to meet her father, right? Whatever. He'd just be the accommodating friend. Be polite, use the manners his mother taught him, and see where this led. Could it be leading somewhere? If things went well, would Sue agree to go out on an actual date? One without the teen-aged chaperones. Would she—

The passenger door pulled open. "All set. Made her take her first dose, and now she'll sleep the whole time I'm gone." She gazed at him. "You all right?"

Mac shook the craziness from his brain. "Yeah, sure. Which way?" He pulled from the curb as she gave him directions toward Alto. A little burg he'd visited often to hang with his cousins. So that's where she was from. Wonder if she went to school with Smitty?

He punched a preset button for WLS and twisted the volume knob on the radio. Gilbert O'Sullivan bemoaned his single life in "Alone Again, Naturally", and Mac noticed Sue grew quiet while staring out the passenger window. The Main Ingredient's "Everybody Plays the Fool" came next, and tension radiated off Sue. Was she having a hard time with the songs? He glanced at her hands that were balled into tight fists in her lap. Something was definitely wrong. Should he ask?

Then Beverly Bremers began to sing "Don't Say You Don't Remember," and Sue switched off the radio. "Sorry. I'm not big into scorned lover ballads."

"Okay. What type of songs do you like?"

She shrugged. "Ones without words, I guess. That's what always seems to create the problem."

"What do you mean?"

Sue turned toward him. "It doesn't make much difference what type of music. Rock and roll, bubblegum, Broadway, opera, country—they all end up with words where someone is hurting someone or begging someone to come back. You've got Barbra Streisand singing about her man that she loves so much no matter what he does to her. You just heard three songs in a row about unrequited love. Plus, you remember what they say about country music. The only way to make it happy is to play it backwards. Then you get your dog back, your truck back, and your girl back. I simply don't agree that singing about all the pain is helpful."

Mac kept glancing between her and the road ahead. "Want to tell me how you really feel?"

Her eyes widened, and he was afraid she might be angry, but then she snickered until it turned into a giggle and then an all-out laugh. He joined her.

"Guess I got carried away. But honestly, I'm done with those love songs that only talk of heartache. The ones where the couple is so sickly happy? Well, that doesn't happen, so..." She wasn't laughing anymore.

"You don't think there are couples who love each other and are happy?" The only way she could be that jaded is if someone deeply hurt her. No wonder she'd sworn off men and only agreed to friendship.

Sue shrugged, never answering his question.

"Instrumental it is, then." Only Mac didn't have a preset that would bring up anything like that. So they continued on with small talk while he tried to imagine who could have been so cruel to her.

"Turn at the next left." She snapped him out of his mind wanderings.

"You mean hang a Louie?" He flashed her a grin and was rewarded with one from her.

"Right, hang a Louie."

"Oh, no, right is Ralph."

She punched his arm and he relaxed. Sue's sense of humor had returned. At least until she directed him to park in front of a small white bungalow. "This is it." Now she was more nervous than she'd been in the church pantry closet.

That made him apprehensive. "You okay?"

She nodded. "We won't be here long. I just need the humidifier for Tracy. That's it." He wasn't sure if she was talking to him or herself.

Mac hopped out and came around to get her door, but she'd already climbed out and was shutting her side as he got there.

"I ought to..." Sue shook her head then raised her chin a notch. "No, there's no way to prepare, so just be ready for anything."

That sounded like something his sarge said his first time in country. Did not bode well for meeting Sue's father. He followed her up the cement steps to a small porch where she knocked on the door.

Sue knocked.

What was wrong with this picture?

He always walked right in at his mom's. For Pete's sake, didn't she grow up in this house? Maybe her dad had other rules. Or maybe there were other people who lived here, so she didn't want to walk in on them. Still, no matter how he tried to justify it, this just seemed weird.

The door squeaked as it was pulled open, but it was hard to see a person doing it. Then Sue bent over and hugged someone, and Mac noticed the wheelchair.

Oh, not good. His entire nervous system flew into a frenzy while his body froze in place. How did he escape? Could he just wait in the truck? The questions pounded his ears like someone had put an album on the 45 speed and even the Chipmunks spoke slower than that and was he breathing?

"Mac?"

He shook his head. "Huh? I'm sorry..."

"I said, this is my brother Danny." She stepped to the side.

Now Mac had a full view of the guy in the wheelchair. With no legs below his knees. Who had his hand outstretched to him.

Please don't let me do something stupid.

It took his entire focus, but Mac shook hands with Danny and even choked out what he hoped sounded like, “Nice to meet you.”

“Come on in, you two.” Danny maneuvered his chair with practiced ease, turning a one-eighty and leading deeper into the house.

Mac followed Sue who trailed her brother.

“I just need to get that old humidifier. Tracy’s really sick and her doctor suggested she use one.”

Danny wheeled into the kitchen. “Want something to drink?”

“No, no thank you. I’m good.” Mac glanced at Sue who stared back with questions in her eyes.

“I just need that humidifier. You haven’t seen it have you, Danny?”

“Nope, but Pop might’ve. He’s in the den watching his show.”

Sue turned to him. “He has to watch Vin Scully each afternoon.” Like she didn’t want anyone to think her dad watched *The Secret Storm*. “I guess I’d better go ask him. Hang out with Danny. I’ll be right back.”

Mac stared as she left the room. She was deserting him? Wasn’t the point for him to meet her father? Nerves pounced and pinged throughout his body, and it took everything not to stare. But he should make eye contact, right, but could he? And how soon would Sue be back? Would she hate him if he ran out?

“Have a seat, dude. No worries. I realize I don’t make the best first impression. But hey, you could probably outrun me.”

What?

“Only way I know to cut through the awkward. Seriously, dude, you need to lighten up. So how long you been going out with Sue?” Danny had pulled up to the table and was cracking up.

This was not how Mac had figured things would go down. True, he hadn't really come up with an idea of how they might, but this? Definitely not on his radar. He pulled out a kitchen chair and sat, putting himself more on eye level with Sue's brother. It helped keep certain things out of sight. "We're not going out. We're just friends. I play guitar for her class at the church."

"She's going to church again? That's great."

"Had she stopped?" Was that the right question to ask?

"When she moved out I wasn't sure she would go, at least for a while."

"Well, she works there, so I guess that's why she attends." Or was it why? There was a lot about Secretary Sue Mac didn't know, and he was just starting to figure that out.

"Oh, I hadn't heard that's where she was working. Huh. With her degree and all, I figured she'd be at one of the museums there in town, you know with Seiberling Mansion now on the National Register of Historic Places and the Elwood Haynes museum there. Sue'd be in her glory with all that old stuff."

"I had no clue. She digs antiques?" This wasn't anything they'd talked about.

"You really are new on the scene. Yeah, she's got her master's degree in museum studies. Thought for sure she'd use it. In fact, she finished out her bachelors in less than three years and completed her thesis work before her twenty-second birthday. Sue definitely got the brains in the family." The pride in Danny's voice was hard to miss. "I'm glad she's involved at a church, and you seem nice enough even if you are clueless." Danny chuckled again.

Mac had to agree. "True. I'd like to get to know her better, but she says friend is all she's willing to do. Who doesn't need more friends, right?"

"So I've figured out the nice and clueless part. Tell me more about you, Mac."

The guy had no filter, or maybe he just had what his sarge used to call chutzpah. "I'm into music. That's what I do for Sue's class. I play guitar."

"Cool. I always wanted to learn to do that. How long have you played?"

Had there been a time when he didn't? Well, there must have been, but Mac was hard-pressed to remember. "I started pretty young, I guess. My granddad taught me on his. Eventually I saved up and bought my first one. It's like a part of me."

A shout came from another room followed by Sue charging in carrying a big box. "Let's go, Mac."

She caught her brother's stare. "Sorry, Danny. I love you." Sue leaned over and kissed his cheek. "Gotta run." Then she raced for the door.

Mac met Danny's gaze and shrugged.

"Take care of her, dude."

"I will." Then Mac followed Sue out to the truck, glad to be out of there.

Chapter 8

Sue gripped the humidifier box to her as Mac drove from Alto. The scene with her father replayed before her.

Dad had already finished off a couple of bottles of Pabst Blue Ribbon. "So you found another one. Brought him home this time. What are you trying to do to this family?"

"What do you mean? Mac is a friend from church who offered me a ride."

"Your car doesn't work? Are you playing up to him to get him to fix it?"

Sue shook her head. Why couldn't he recognize she wasn't the same person who'd done all that? "Tracy is sick. That's the only reason I came here. I know you don't want to see me, that I embarrassed you."

"You just take all that sashaying around, flitting from one man to the next, out of here and out of our town. Got plenty of men at work telling me about you."

She'd rushed out with the humidifier then, but now, looking back, she realized something that she hadn't before. Her own father not only believed the rumors, he didn't stand up for her. He was more worried about his reputation than hers.

That point was more painful to bear than her mistakes that had brought her to this moment.

"We're here." Mac jiggled her elbow. The Stylistics "Betcha by Golly, Wow" was just ending on the radio. When had Mac switched it on? She'd been so in her head, she never heard it.

He'd let her stew in her own mind all the way home and hadn't pressed. Now he looked concerned, kindness making his eyes bright, but he wasn't being nosy. Instead he smiled and hopped out of the truck, coming around to her side.

She could open her own door, and she did. No need to depend on him. Or any man. She still owed him, though. "Thanks." With the box cradled to her chest, she raced to her apartment but turned back. "I really do thank you, Mac."

He tossed her a languid salute and headed to his truck, though he didn't move on. As she watched him sit there with the motor running, she realized he wouldn't pull away until he made sure she was safely inside. That small gesture touched her.

If he only knew the woman she was, the person she'd become when she returned home from college, he'd have no inclination to associate with her.

Sue slipped her purse from her shoulder and dropped it onto the sofa before tiptoeing to Tracy's room to check on her. Gently pushing the door wider, she took in the sleeping form of her roommate—disheveled, sweaty, and snoring. The sooner Sue got the humidifier set up, the better.

Only she'd forgotten how noisy it could be. Not super loud, but enough that when she started it up, Tracy stirred and crack a lid. The one-eyed stare came from a glassy and bloodshot orb. That poor thing.

“I’m sorry it woke you. Are you feeling any better yet?”

“Dunno. Water.”

Sue handed Tracy her cup from the nightstand, and she took a sip before handing it back. “Throat still hurts. Need time.”

“Yeah, you’re right. Only been about a couple hours. Can I get you anything else?”

Tracy gingerly shook her head and leaned against her pillow.

“You sleep and I’ll check in on you later.” Sue pulled the door to a crack so she could still hear if there was a problem. But with how quick the snoring returned, she doubted there would be.

She wandered to the living room, noting her purse, and made a decision. Pulling out the White Pages, she double checked her memory. Yep, she’d remembered. Then she swiped up her keys and bag and headed for her car.

Less than five minutes later she pulled up in front of a tiny craftsman. It looked as if someone had built two structures on one parcel, and now she needed to figure out which belonged to Mac.

Sue sat behind her steering wheel, mentally reviewing what to say. Say and go. He wouldn’t want her staying anyway. Might as well get it over with.

A tap on her passenger door made her gasp.

Mac peered at her through the open window and grinned. “Want to come in out of the heat?”

With her hand to her heart, she calmed herself enough to nod before climbing out. “I wanted to explain.”

"No need. I figured out that something upset you, but it's none of my business. You can still come in if you want." He held out his hand. Mac might as well be holding out an anchor line.

Sue took it and let him lead her to his slab porch. "Here is fine." Loggins and Messina's "House at Pooh Corner" drifted through the open door.

"Pretty warm out. I've got the window fans running, so it's definitely cooler inside."

Sue shook her head. She wouldn't give him the bad reputation by going in his house unchaperoned. "The porch is good."

He unfolded a couple of white and green webbed chairs and set them up before motioning her to sit.

Sue scrunched her purse in her lap, searching for the right words to start. "I used to be fat. Oh, not morbidly obese, just what my mother called pleasingly plump. I think she wanted me to feel better."

"That's hard to picture."

"Trust me, I've got the photographs. I didn't date throughout high school, and when I arrived at Radcliffe, I threw myself into my classes. After a bit, I realized I was losing weight from not stopping for meals and getting in lots of walking." She risked a glance at Mac. He had leaned forward a tad, giving her his full attention.

"So I decided to help myself. I added ballet lessons and watched my food intake. The pounds fell away, and for the first time in my life I felt pretty." Heat warmed her cheeks as she admitted such a thought. "I learned more about how to dress and do my makeup. I hadn't been home in a couple years. I needed to work every break to supplement my scholarships, and my folks couldn't afford the plane fare. So you can imagine what it was like when I came home."

This time he offered a smile and nod, so she kept going. "Danny was back from Viet Nam. Not in as good of shape as now, but he'd come home alive, and that was the main thing. My mom, though, had become ill while I was away. She'd had a heart attack that had made her bedfast, and she continued to grow weaker. Nobody told me, and then she had a fatal attack about two months after I turned up. Our whole family got thrown into a tail spin. I think Danny actually handled things better than anyone. He turned to God and was determined to become mobile to help. My father, though, seemed to have crawled into the coffin with Mom. Me? Well, there was this guy who worked with Dad who came by to check on him. Apparently, he appreciated what he saw when he noticed me and asked me out. I was so hungry for attention and missing my mother so much. Missed Dad too, I guess. Anyway, I enjoyed the spotlight. Then everywhere we went, I realized something. Men liked looking at me. If I flirted a little, I got lots of notice. So I dated other guys, never getting too attached."

Now she didn't want to meet Mac's gaze, but she needed to evaluate how appalled he was. So she peeked.

His expression hadn't changed. It gave her courage to continue. "There'd been one guy in my high school that I'd had a crush on since my freshman year, but he never noticed me. That is until I altered my appearance. I was finally getting what I'd always wanted—attention from, well, from that secret crush. We dated and I thought we were serious. I was, at least." Sue paused as Brad's smirk from when he informed her she was the other woman flashed in her mind. She winced. Still, she had to keep going. "Then I found him with another girl. I was so destroyed. That triggered a spiral of dating every man who looked at me, simply to prove I was desirable. A couple of guys tried to take it too far, but I was able to escape. That's when the male employees where my dad worked started giving him grief. Not to his face, exactly. They'd make comments they knew he'd overhear. Called me a tease, and worse. Guess I embarrassed him. Small towns have few secrets. He made sure I heard all the names from him, and he never asked for my side. Instead, he ordered me to get out. I did. Today was the first day I've been back."

The air grew quiet but for another Loggins and Messina song. Uncomfortable. What was Mac thinking? Would he now view her the way her father did?

Sue couldn't bear to know. She stood and headed for her Beetle. Before she got two steps, though, he captured her hand. Did she dare to glance at him?

"Sue, we all have a past. We all have scars. I don't see you that way. Please, sit. Please?" He guided her back to her chair.

"I can't be that person ever again, Mac, but I don't want to be the overweight, invisible wallflower either. I'm trying to find my equilibrium, and the only place I feel safe now is at church. Only I'm so terrified someone will recognize me and they'll all discover who I really am and kick me out." She buried her face in her hands.

Mac scooted his chair closer until their knees touched and drew her fingers gently away, making her focus on him. "Makeup and hairstyles might enhance, but your beauty shines from the inside. That is the woman I'd like to know better. If you would trust me, I won't push you faster than you want to go. And if you prefer to stay only friends, I can do that. You didn't scare me off, though. Believe me."

As she scanned his face for the truth, his gaze gleamed with genuine compassion. Not pity, not judgment. Just compassion. "I believe you." She dug a tissue from her purse.

He took it from her and dabbed at her eyes, making them well up again. "I wasn't trying to make you cry."

"I'm not sure I can deal with that much tenderness."

Mac grinned. "Then wipe your tears, Secretary Sue, while I search for my macho side."

That made her giggle. "I don't think you have to explore far."

"Are you flirting with me, Secretary Sue?"

Her heart stopped. *No, please I didn't mean to.* "I'm sorry. I—"

"I'm just having fun with you. Stop barricading yourself behind your fears. I should have used a different word, but between you and me, a little innocent flirting isn't a bad thing. Okay? I'm a big boy, dealt with enough stuff on my own that I'm not going to have a problem if you say something flirtatious today and not tomorrow. The bottom line is we're friends. If we test the waters to see if there's more, that's fine too. But our foundation is friendship. I'm always here for you. Got it?"

"Yes, sir." She paused as a question tickled its way to her tongue. "Did you serve in Nam?"

Mac pulled back as his thoughts convulsed over his face, making him squint and wince.

"I'm sorry. I shouldn't have asked, but I wondered. There's so much I don't know about y—"

"Yeah. Yeah, I did." He paused, and she waited to see if he'd elaborate. About when she'd given up and formed her apology in her head, he spoke. Softly. "Not today. I will tell you, but I'm not ready right now."

Sue nodded. She'd put her foot in it this time. "Guess I should be leaving."

As she rose, he did too, and he took her hands. "Sue, I get this is all confusing. I want to know you better because I'm attracted to you. If getting closer means revealing more of myself, then I guess I ought to not be so private. Holding all that in has made life easier but very boring and monotone. You've brought harmony into my recent days that I had no idea I'd been craving. You were brave enough to share with me, and it only heightens my opinion of you. Your worth has nothing to do with cosmetics. Now I need to summon up some courage. Will you give me time for that?"

Sue's hands trembled in his, and as she fought to form an answer, her lips quivered as well, so she nodded.

He released her fingers, and before she knew what he was doing, he stroked her bottom lip with a feathery touch of his thumb, sending shivers to her toes. Then, leaning close, he brushed a kiss to her cheek before walking her to her car.

Once Sue was on her way, Mac meandered back to his house. His entire world grew emptier with her gone. However, it was time he got busy, no matter what his thoughts were doing to his brain.

Inside his front room, he shut down his turntable and settled into the old chair Mom had found for him at a garage sale, propping his ax into position. Holding it, strumming it, that was the only time he felt complete.

When someone watched him, though, that all changed. He was suddenly vulnerable, naked, and all his secrets danced around to the beat of the music for anyone to admire or criticize or steal. It paralyzed his soul.

So how did he get over this for his project?

He knew if he did well that Professor Day had contacts who could give him a step up. No guarantees, but definitely more of a chance than if he didn't make an attempt. But if he was so afraid of playing his music in front of people, why in the world had he bothered to sign up for the class?

Because he had to. If he hadn't, he would never try again. It would all remain in his mind and fade away there. His soul might have to die for his gift to live. He'd known that the instant he applied for the class. However, that was head knowledge. Now was the moment of truth, of action. Reality. It was far scarier than what he'd imagined.

Mac strummed his fingers over the strings once more, then reached for the phone. He needed a dose of courage.

"Hello?"

"Hey, Mom, what's happening?"

"Mac? Oh, sweetie, it's the same old thing. How are you?" It was like she could tell though she didn't point that out.

"Um, I'm working on my class project."

"How's that going?" She'd drag it out of him bit by bit, which was exactly why he'd called and what he hoped would happen, even if it wasn't fun. At least Mom was gentle.

Mac sighed. "I have an idea, and a few of my pieces should work, but I have to write one with lyrics."

"I see. Will you have to play them yourself?" She knew his fear.

"No, I just compose and give the musicians the sheet music."

"That should help, I'd say. Lift some of your anxiety. So what exactly is getting to you, hon?"

Mac paused to put words to what he feared. "I think it's that when it is only the music, the hearer interprets any way he wants, but when I add lyrics, now that's my interpretation."

"Feels revealing?"

Mom nailed it. Perfect pitch. "Yeah."

"Can you pick a subject that is fun or lighthearted so you don't need to dig as deeply?"

Okay, that had never crossed his mind. "I guess so. That could work. Only..."

"Only what?"

"That would change the rest of the program. I started thinking about how one little thing can turn what was good into something contaminated."

Now Mom was silent. Then he heard her breathe. "Is it possible to show that one good thing can conquer the bad?"

That was a new twist. "I, uh, yeah. That could work. Then the lyrics should be simple and easy. Like you said, lighthearted. Mom, you're a genius."

"Well, I try. Remember, though, I've known you an awfully long time."

That made them both chuckle.

"Ready to try again?"

"Yep, I think I've got an idea. Better go."

"Love you, kiddo."

After he hung up, a melody started in his head. It wasn't exactly what Mom called lighthearted, but it had a brightness. He fingered the frets, finding the right key, then began to hum while he strummed. As much as he tried to pick up the tempo, it remained slower, more ballad-like. The notes held sweetness, but it wouldn't be something people would dance the Jerk to. Did anyone still do the Jerk?

It'd been a long time since he'd tried dancing, and he never was good at it anyway. Slow dancing? Mac could sway with the best of them back in the day. But even in his prime, he didn't have what anyone would call moves.

So why did he think this needed to be a dance number?

Go with what comes to you.

Fine. Mac tried the song again, getting a little more depth, more layers. It developed complexity on his third attempt, and he knew it was time to begin notations on his pad of sheet music.

An hour later, he'd added some harmonies, but he needed to use a piano to get what he was aiming for. Maybe Professor Day would let him work at the church after punching his card at the steel mill. He'd stop by on his way home and see.

Should he clean up first, just in case?

In case of what? Running into Sue? Would she even spend a moment with him now? He'd probably gone too far and scared her off. He ought to give her space.

He still needed the piano though.

Calling to talk to Professor Day wouldn't work. She'd answer the phone. Stopping by had the same outcome, only in person. Even if the point were to connect with his teacher, she might take it that he was pushing her. Or would she feel disappointed he hadn't called her?

These thoughts were going to tie his brain into knots.

Stop being an idiot.

Mac needed air, despite the window fans' best attempts. He jumped on his bike and headed toward the highway.

Without trying, he ended up at Elmer's station. His friend was balancing a tire in the shop.

"Hey, Dude, what's shakin'?" Elmer never looked up, he knew it was Mac.

"Not a lot. Just wanted to get out. Need any help there?"

"Nah." He attached a weight to the rim. "I'm 'bout done with this one. Been slow for a Thursday, so planned to let my nephew take over while I close the shop and beat it home. Hey, wanna come for dinner?"

"Misty won't mind?"

"No way. She'd be thrilled to see your ugly mug. Speaking of which, what did you do? Got yourself all spiffed-up." Then he cackled. "That's right. The lil' lady with the VW."

Mac knew his cheeks were gaining color when Elmer pointed and laughed harder. Then he rested his arm across Mac's shoulder and turned him toward the office. "Let me scrub the top layer off so Misty won't kill me, and you can follow me home."

Five minutes later, Elmer had removed some of the black streaks from his face and changed out of his coveralls. "Let's go."

Elmer slipped around the side and reemerged, wheeling a 1960 Triumph Bonneville.

"You got it finished. Nice." Mac glided his fingertips over the trademark pearl grey fenders with the azure blue center strip outlined in gold.

"And she purrs so sweet. Listen." Elmer climbed on, started his motorcycle, and revved the engine.

"Definitely sweet. What are you going to do with her?"

"I'd keep her, but Misty says we need to sell. She worries about me riding it."

Mac grinned. "Didn't she first like your Harley before she gave you a chance?"

Elmer shook his head. "When chicks turn into moms, they suddenly get safety conscious. Guess she don't wanna be no single parent." He shrugged. "Come on. She hates when I'm late gettin' home too."

Mac followed his buddy, now worried Misty might not be cool with Elmer inviting him. Maybe he could talk his way out of it so the guy wouldn't be in hot water.

However, Misty was on the porch, bouncing their baby on her knee when they pulled up. Handing the tiny girl off to her daddy, she gave Mac a big hug. "If Elmer hasn't invited you to dinner yet, I'm doing it. You'll stay, right?"

Mac glanced at Elmer who stopped blowing raspberries on his little one's belly long enough to give him the I-told-you-so look. "Sure, thanks. Has to be better than anything I'd fix."

"Knowing you, you'd have a bowl of popcorn or Captain Crunch."

"Now don't go putting down the Captain. He's not such bad company." When Misty punched his arm, he rubbed it like crazy. "Ow! Hey, call off your woman. She's got a mean right hook."

Elmer laughed while the baby grabbed at his hair. "You walked yourself into that one, bud. Can't help it if your mouth got the rest of you in trouble."

"Fine friend you are." Still, Mac joined the laughs and followed the family into the house.

"Hon, the grill is all set for you, and the coals should be just right. I'll get the hamburger patties out. Oh, Mac, do you like your buns grilled?"

"Sure. What can I do to help?"

Elmer handed his daughter to him. "Keep her happy and safe while her parents prepare your dinner. And medium-rare is all I do." He followed Misty toward the kitchen.

Mac turned the baby so she faced him. "Good thing that's how I like mine. Hm, I guess I should introdu—"

The baby squealed.

"What? What was that about? Hey, we can be friends, right?"

Misty peeked around the living room doorway. "Cindy does that. Usually it means she's happy."

"What else does it mean?" Cindy took that moment to grab his nose.

"It could mean she's displeased because she's wet, or hungry or just feeling irritable." Misty grinned.

"What did she mean this time?" He nodded while Cindy held on to his face.

"I think you're cool this time. In fact, you're doing great. No worries. I gotta go help Elmer get dinner on the table. Good luck."

"What? Wait." Mac held the baby up high, then brought her back to eye level. "I'm new to this. Guess you can call me Uncle Mac. Should I confess that I don't have a lot of experience with babies? I can keep you safe, though I doubt I'm that good at entertaining."

She grabbed his nose again and twisted.

"Whoa. Hey, let's not hurt the newbie babysitter. You take after your mom, don't you?"

Cindy shrieked once more but seemed content.

Mac backed up to a chair and sat, seating the baby on his knee, and bounced her while humming "My Pony Boy." "But you are a young lady. What tunes work for that?" He tried to remember the songs his mother sang back in the day. "Hickory, dickory, doc. The mouse ran up the clock. The clock struck one—" Cindy squealed and waved her chubby hands. "Oh, you like that, do you?" Her gummy smile lit her eyes, making Mac think, for the first time in a very long while, that he might want to be a father. If there were a guarantee that his child would be as adorable as this little cutie pie, he'd give it serious thought.

On the sixth repetition of "Hickory Dickory," Misty returned. "You did surprisingly well there, Mac. I might need to introduce you to a few of my friends." She took her daughter and led to the kitchen where dinner was ready.

Mac chose to ignore the comment. Too much acknowledgment, and the woman would be sure to fix him up.

Baby Cindy was placed in her highchair and Elmer entered from the back door with a plate of char-lined patties and golden-grilled buns. "Let's eat."

Misty elbowed him. "We say grace first."

Elmer took on the proper chagrined look and reached for his wife's hand. "You bless the food."

She did and then everyone sat, and the food was passed. "Hon, you should have seen Mac in there with Cindy. He'll make a great dad. Oh, I know, I should introduce you to Anna. She's just the sweetest."

Mac choked.

"Hey, you okay there?" Misty jumped up and pounded his back.

"Yeah, fine." Mac glared at his buddy.

Elmer's eyes grew wide, and he shook his head while keeping out of Misty's line of sight. "Um, hon, I think Mac might already have a girlfriend."

Misty, in her chair again, peered at Mac and then Elmer and then Mac. "You do? When did this happen? Who is it?"

Mac telegraphed Elmer with his eyes. He'd be getting even with his buddy, that was for sure. "Um, it's pretty new. I met her at church. Yeah, at church."

"Where does she attend?" Misty turned on her best Perry Mason parody, digging for every piece of information she could. This was not how Mac saw tonight going.

"She's the secretary at Wabash Community." Maybe he should check in with Sue to see if she was ready to take that step and be his girlfriend.

Chapter 9

Friday, June 30,1972

Sue smacked her steering wheel. Still so caught up analyzing what happened on Mac's porch yesterday, she'd driven past the turn to the church's parking lot. Stupid!

The whole thing made her brain behave like a phonograph needle, stuck in a groove, playing the same section over and over. Repeatedly. Ad nauseam. To the point she couldn't even hang a Ralph.

Great, now she was using Mac's jargon.

She might as well. What she'd once considered to be a massively impressive lexicon of her own was wiped clean, as if someone took an eraser to the chalkboard dictionary in her mind.

How was she to function like this?

Perhaps she was catching Tracy's infection. That might explain it. Maybe it was affecting her thinking skills.

Right. Mac winked at her in her mind's eye.

This was not happening. She must not fall for that man. It would pull her back into that spinning vortex of male interaction that hurt feelings, destroyed families, and isolated her.

And it would ruin Mac.

If she cared for him, she'd better make darn sure they were never alone together.

So why did she so want to have him touch her face like that again?

And why was her hand resting on her cheek?

God, help me. Please!

Sue pulled into her parking spot and turned off the engine. There was work to be done inside, even if her brain was MIA. She needed to at least appear to be doing what she was paid to do. With a sigh, she rolled up her windows, leaving them opened just a crack, and locked up. The walk to the front door had never seemed so long.

What was she doing here? That was one more reason to add to her list of why she shouldn't get involved with Mac. The church. Sue would never risk putting it in a bad light. Besides, she'd lose her place of refuge. Okay, two reasons. Great, now she'd lost her math skills.

Inside, as she stashed her purse in the desk drawer, a piano melody filtered into her office space. It wasn't familiar, but there was something about it. Plaintive and sweet, the notes wound their way through her soul, doing a dance around her heart. She followed the sound to locate the Pied Pianist down the hall to a rehearsal room.

Standing outside the door, she closed her eyes, transfixed by the melody. She'd never heard anything so beautiful, so pure. *If there are words, please don't let them be of broken trust and unrequited love.*

Sue leaned her head against the jamb, but it made a small thud. The music abruptly stopped.

Run. You'll get caught.

However, her feet were cemented in place as the door opened.

Mac appeared startled as he ran his fingers through his hair. "You were listening?"

She nodded, unable to trust her voice.

"It's for my project. I needed a piano to find the harmonies." He paused, as if giving her time to reply.

But words still failed her.

"Um, I didn't see you in the office. Aaron told me it was okay to use the room. Said you had to go home to check on Tracy. Is she all right?"

The change of subject did the trick, and Sue's vocal cords remembered how to work. "Yes, she's much better today. She'd been asleep when I came here, so I've gone home a few times to see her." She nodded to make sure he understood. Then wanted to slap herself for acting like such a buffoon.

"So you're cool with me working here?"

Was he serious? Where did he get the idea she had any power to approve or deny his request to use a rehearsal room, especially if Mr. Day gave permission? "Um, sure. Not my job to keep you out."

"Well, it sort of is. You're the gatekeeper, right?" He winked at her.

All semblance of intelligence vaporized as heat roared its way up her face.

"Are you okay there, Secretary Sue? Looking a bit flushed." He touched her cheek, and electrical voltage brainwashed her.

He took her hand and led her to a folding chair. Once she was seated, he set up another one and joined her. "Hey, I'm getting worried about you."

Suddenly, Sue looked around the room. They were alone. The door was open, but there was no one else in sight.

Danger, Will Robinson!

She popped to her feet. "I need to get back up front." Fast. Her heart raced like a freight train on a straight stretch of track.

He stood too. "Okay. Are you sure? I mean, we haven't talked about yesterday, and now you're acting sort of peculiar."

Peculiar? He called her peculiar? "How dare you."

Mac's eyes widened, but he remained silent. What was there to say? Then that little voice in her head spoke up. *You're not acting exactly sane at the moment.*

"I need to go." She plowed for the door.

"But we will talk about yesterday. Right?"

Sue spun toward him. "I said all I want to say on the subject."

"I didn't."

Great, now he was going to tell her what a wanton woman she was. It was bad enough to be embarrassed around him because of her confession, but she'd thought he'd let it go, especially after his reaction yesterday. Maybe with time to think about it, he'd changed his mind.

However, she wouldn't hide. The truth was, even though he didn't know everything, he still had enough of the story to find fault with her morals, and she deserved every righteous justification he might hurl at her. It was the hair shirt she wore. So she'd stand and take it. Still, she tipped her chin in anticipation of the first verbal blow.

"I meant what I said yesterday. I just wondered if you'd reconsider going on a date with me. The Fourth of July is next Tuesday, and I get off early. I thought maybe we'd take a picnic and go watch the fireworks out by Stellite."

Sue blinked. What did he say? "Um. After I told you all that, you still want to ask me out?"

"Yes."

"You realize if someone from my past sees us, you will have ruined your reputation."

"I doubt that, but who cares? I'm not worried what others think of me."

She couldn't help the smirk. "Right. That's why you hate playing your guitar in front of an audience."

That shut him up, and he broke eye contact. For a moment. Then he recaptured her gaze. "Okay, you got me. When it comes to my music, I'm very private. It's personal. As for whether people consider me Don Juan or Prince Valiant, like we used to say in the Nam, it don't mean nothing."

"That's what you said?" Did her brother think that way?

His voice dropped. "Yeah. We had no control, so it was a way to keep the fear from overwhelming us."

He'd shared something about his tour. Maybe he would eventually tell her the rest. Even about his leg. If she didn't push.

"I wonder if Danny ever said that."

He sort of smiled, though it was more grim than happy. "I guarantee he did. It was key to survival."

"Would you talk with him?" The words were out before she finished formulating the idea. Just because her brother was doing better than the rest of the family didn't mean he was good as new. Who lost both their legs and remained happy and innocent?

"I..." He took a step back, running his hand over his mouth. "Sue, I don't talk about that. I promised you I would let you know some of my story. Eventually. I'll keep my word, but seeing your brother brought back a lot that I can't relive. I'm discriminating about what I choose to remember, or rather, dwell on. The rest can go bury itself in the deepest recesses of my mind and never show up again." Mac straightened and his eyes grew steely.

"I won't ask. At least not for me. But Danny could use a friend. Someone who might understand him better than Dad." Dad being understanding? That was a laugh. Everything was about how it affected him.

Still, Mac softened a little. "I'll think about it." Then he smiled. "On one condition. You go out with me next Tuesday."

"That's extortion."

"Nope, just a deal. You do something for me, I'll do something for you. And, considering both requests stretch us out of our comfort zone, I think it's fair."

She wanted to disagree. His talking with Danny wouldn't ruin his reputation or possibly start a downward spiral where going out with Mac could set all sorts of things in motion that could potentially wreak havoc on many innocent bystanders. Tracy, the pastor and his family, the church's image. Why couldn't he see that?

"C'mon, Secretary Sue, it's one date. Just once. I promise to be a gentleman."

"I don't doubt you would be." *Just once*. How those words raked over her heart with their sharpened claws. If he only knew. "You've no idea what you're asking."

"Sure I do. One picnic, some laughing, some pretty sky art, maybe a flirtatious word or two—hey, being honest here. I will be on my best behavior. You can trust me." He stroked her jaw.

Oh, how she wanted to lean in to his hand, feel his fingers cupping her cheek. This is where the danger lay. "Okay." Yeah, right. That and how her mouth formed words before her brain could veto them.

What a minute, what had she just agreed to?

"Good, we have a deal." He grasped her right hand and shook it.

She needed to get out of there before something worse happened. At this point, she couldn't imagine anything worse than the catalyst that had just set in motion the potential dismantling of her life. Not to mention the fallout on everyone else. Especially Mac.

She'd attempted to warn him. Had she tried hard enough? Was he simply that stubborn? Plus he'd come up with a condition she was hardly able to refuse—talking with Danny. Her brother was her blind spot. She'd walk through fire for him. But go out together?

Mac's voice singsonged in her head. *What harm could one little date do?*

That was just it. He didn't know. It had only been the one time, and everything in her life fell apart.

Just once.

Those words were the kiss of death. She was pretty sure the serpent even whispered them in Eve's ear while she examined the fruit that caused her ruin—and the downfall of every man, woman, and child ever born.

What about Jesus?

A single good thing in a mix of evil. He didn't stand a chance.

He conquered sin and death.

Then why was there so much suffering, so much evil in the world? Huh?

No response.

Sue didn't have one either.

The insistent *br-r-ring-br-r-ring* of the phone broke through the notes playing in Mac's head, like it wanted him to bring his body over to the kitchen wall and pick up the receiver. Someone's timing was way off, chasing his musical thought out the window.

He swiped up the handset. "What?"

"Is that how you answer a phone these days?" Mom was only half teasing, and Mac knew it.

"Sorry. I was working on my project and, well..." No need to make Mom feel bad because he'd lost his train of thought. "What's up?"

"I was wondering if you have plans for the Fourth. Hoped you might want to come by. We can grill some hamburgers and hot dogs and sit on the roof to watch the fireworks."

Something about this sounded suspicious. Was she trying to set him up again? Even after he'd told her that little bit about Sue? "Who is we?"

"Oh, just the royal we, for now. I could invite Rachel if you want."

And there it was. "Nope, I've got plans. I have a date, in fact."

"You do?" There was too much excitement in those words.

"Yeah, Mom, I do date on occasion. For the record, it's the girl I was telling you about. I took your advice, and she's agreed to go out with me for Independence Day."

Independence Day? Sue was the queen of independent. Now there was some irony.

"Would you bring her by?"

"Mom."

"Oh, honey, I'm just tickled my son is dating someone, and I'd like to meet whoever sparked that interest. Is it such a bad thing for a mother to want?" Her sigh came through loud and clear.

"No, Mom. It's not. However, it's also our first date. I'm not sure taking her home to introduce her to my mother won't add some pressure. Besides, I promised her a picnic."

"Oh, I see." The disappointment had even more clarity than her sigh. "Well, some other time."

"Wait." He was going to hate himself, he knew that. "I'll ask her if she's okay with it. Maybe having others around would help."

"I'll keep my fingers crossed. Let me know what she says. Love you, sweetie."

"Love you too, Mom." He hung up, knowing his mother was the only person who could have talked him into that.

It also meant he needed to call Sue.

Or he could go to church Sunday morning and maybe catch her there.

Would that feel like pressure to agree to something she didn't want? He'd already applied enough by getting her to comply with his deal. Though, truth be told, he'd almost prayed she wouldn't accept so he wouldn't have to talk to her brother again. Not that the guy was bad or anything. He was simply a reminder. A Technicolor, in-stereo, neon-string-around-his-finger reminder of things he never wanted to remember again.

So if this caused her to back out of their deal, there was the unspoken gift of an out for him as well. Only what he would lose bothered him more.

That was surprising.

He found Tracy's number in the phone book—good thing he remembered her name and address because there hadn't been a listing for Sue Mitchell. He dialed and waited for her to pick up. It took several rings before anyone answered, and then it was Tracy, or at least he figured the froggy rasp belonged to Sue's roommate.

"Hello?"

"Tracy, is that you? It's Mac."

"Oh. Yeah. Wanna talk t'Sue?"

"Yes, please." If that's how the girl sounded when she was getting better, he couldn't imagine how bad it had gotten.

A moment later, Sue picked up. "Mac?"

"Yeah, it's me. My mom called to invite us to her house for a barbecue on the Fourth. I told her I would ask you, but we don't ha—"

"Yes."

"You're sure?" That came out mighty quick.

"Yes. I'd like to meet your mom."

She would? "You would?"

"Of course. What time should I be ready?"

She was really willing to do this. Hot diggity. Then it hit him. Sue probably figured it would ensure his good behavior, what with his mom looking over his shoulder. Should he be insulted?

Did he want to go out with the girl or not?

Yes, he did. In fact, several times, lots of dates with her. So, yeah, he'd take what he could get. Plus, if it made Mom happy in the process, all the better.

"I'll be by around three. Will that work? Mom will have some games out, and she'll want to talk with you too."

"Oh." Now she wants to back out?

"Nothing intense. She'll probably ask how we met, that sort of thing. She gets curious, but she's never super nosy. Not a thing to worry about." He reassured himself along with Sue.

"Okay. I wasn't worried. Not much, anyway."

"Good. So, three then?"

"Yes. I'll be ready."

He finished the call and returned to his guitar and music stand, just in time for the phone to ring again. Seriously, could he catch one break?

"Hey, cuz. Whacha doin' home on a Friday night?" Smitty.

"Waiting on you to call, I guess." Only seven thirty, and the guy was snockered.

Smitty giggled. "I shoulda called sooner. I'll 'member dat."

Mac doubted the guy would remember much at all tomorrow. "What do you need, Smitty?"

"Aw, now, don't git thadaway. I's only thu-inkin' a you. Cross m'heart."

"Sorry. I'm working on something."

"Ya need t'spot, uh." Smitty giggled again. "I mean s-s-s-s-stop and come join me. Les have sum fun. Whadya say?"

"I gotta finish this. It's for my class."

"Whya doin' that? Dincha get 'nuff sch-ool back ina day? C'mon. Be a pal."

Mac pinched the bridge of his nose where the headache had started. He needed this time to work, but what would happen to his cousin if he didn't go? Would he try to drive in his condition? Then all the possibilities of what might happen with that decision played through his brain.

Crud. He had to go. Smitty left him no choice. If the idiot killed someone on his way out, it would be on Mac's head as much as Smitty's because he'd chosen to not intervene. "Fine. Where are you?" The noise in the background only meant it could be any number of places.

"The O-aces."

The Oasis. That was one seedy place. "I'll be there in ten minutes. Don't go anywhere."

"Where'd I go?" More giggling. "Nah, I'm ri'here."

"Well, stay there. I'm not going looking for you.

"Yehsir." The line disconnected, followed by the dial tone. Hopefully Smitty passed out by the phone, and he could just carry him out and dump him at his apartment.

True to his word, Mac pulled into the three-quarters-full lot and locked up. Now to find his blotto cousin.

Turned out, it wasn't that hard of a mission. Smitty had his hands against the paneled wall on either side of an equally drunk girl, essentially trapping her in place. "Aw, c'mon preddy mama, ya know ya wanna."

“Hey, Smitty.”

His cousin spun around and crashed into the girl who slid down the paneling into a heap.

“Oh, no. Lookie whatcha made me do, Mac. Is she dead?”

Mac highly doubted she was, but she might have been hurt by the klutz. He checked her pulse. It was fine. Then he snapped his fingers in her face.

Her eyes popped open. “Wha?”

After helping her to her feet, Mac turned his attention on his cousin. “Let’s go.”

“G’where?” Smitty swayed even while using the wall for support.

“Hey!”

Mac turned to the female voice behind him and walked into a fist. That cold-cocked his nose. “Whad you do dat for?” Blood seeped between his fingers.

“You touched me.” He did what? And how did her speech suddenly get so clear?

“I hepped you up affer you fell.” Oh, yeah, his nose was broken. For sure.

“I was pushed.”

Smitty stepped forward. “Tha’ be me, preddy mama. Sorry ’bou tha.” He took on a leer that he must have mistaken for sexy. “Can ya forgive me?”

“Sure.” She wrapped her arms around Smitty’s neck, then got a weird expression on her face. All at once, she turned and ran for the ladies room.

Mac tapped Smitty’s shoulder. “C’mon. I need da get you ’ome so I can go do da ER.”

"Okay." It was a word Smitty rarely used. Then he even helped Mac to his truck. However, when he tried to get Mac into the passenger seat, that came to a screeching halt.

"Sorry, pal, I'm driving."

"Okay." Where was the demanding, I-know-what's-best Smitty? This was way out of character.

Mac stopped trying to stop the blood. His shirt was already ruined. He climbed in the driver's seat and turned the ignition.

Smitty sat with his head back against the seat rest, his eyes closed. But when they hit a hole in the blacktop, the jolt jarred him awake. "Where are we?"

"Aboud a mile from your place."

"Hey, what happened to you?" He'd slept it off that fast? No way.

"I gah decked for saving your honor."

"I ain't got no honor. Ask Rachel. She'll tell ya."

Mac grimaced. "I don see Rashel."

"Yeah. I forgot. Sorry. She's been pushing to get married now that she's back home. I said we should live together, but she's got that antiquated notion about waiting. For what? I don't wanna wait. No piece of paper's gonna change anything."

Mac was in enough pain without this. All he tried to do was his good deed for the day and possibly save some lives. Instead he had a broken nose, a throbbing headache, and now had to listen to Smitty talk about sleeping with Mac's ex-fiancée?

There was no justice in the world.

If there were, Smitty would have the broken nose. Rachel would have married someone from Ball State and settled in Muncie where he wouldn't have to see her or hear about her from his cousin who couldn't keep it in his pants if he tried. Just because Mac was over her and learned that his feelings for Sue were stronger than they'd ever been for Rachel didn't mean he hadn't felt anything.

"Maybe I oughta marry her and shut her up. I'm sure not having any fun going out these days."

Aw, you're breakin' my heart.

Mac kept his lips zipped and his thoughts to himself. It was safer for all concerned.

He pulled in front of Smitty's place, halfway to Alto. Well, it made sense, since his parents still lived in the tiny town. "Can ya make it from here?"

"Yeah. Sorry about your nose. Thanks for the ride." Smitty closed the door, then leaned in at the open passenger window. "Did you see my car in the parking lot?"

"Lass time I look, it was still dere."

"Thanks, man. I'm really sorry."

Mac waved him off and flipped a Louie. It would take him fifteen minutes to get to St. Joe's. The bleeding had only slowed, not stopped, and he was pretty sure they might have to reset his nose.

It had happened once before, back when he and Smitty were kids. The funny, not ha-ha-funny, part was that it had been Smitty's fault as well, though he hadn't touched him then either. A bully came by while they were deep into their cowboys and Indians horseplay. Smitty was smaller and an easy target with his big mouth. So when his cousin looked to be about to get creamed, Mac, the older and larger of the two of them, stepped between and the bully popped him in the nose.

Of course, Smitty saw his chance and decked the bully who was shocked at what he'd done to Mac. Looking back now, Mac was fairly certain that the bully was less the instigator and more trying to stand up to the guy who'd been bad-mouthing him. Smitty. All these years, and this was the first time Mac had ever realized this. Smitty was the real bully. Plus, he was cheating on Rachel to get even with her for her morality.

The picture was anything but pretty. It was time Mac faced the fact that Smitty had basically bullied him his entire life.

Chapter 10

Sunday, July 2, 1972

"You have a what?"

Sue winced as Tracy's voice rose higher.

"With whom? Oh, I know!" Her roommate bounced like Tigger. "It's Mac, isn't it? It is, I can see by your face."

Sue found herself swept into a bear hug that Smoky would've envied. "Tracy, you're wrinkling my clothes."

Still, Tracy continued to hop and twirl and embrace until Sue had no recourse but to push away and do her best to smooth out her church dress. "Don't get so excited. We made a deal."

"Deal, what deal?" At least Tracy had stopped causing the floor to jump.

"Danny needs someone to talk to who understands, though Mac doesn't really want to." Her voice trailed as wonderings wandered into her thoughts. Why couldn't Mac feel safe talking with a person who understood? Danny lost more than Mac, and if she hadn't noticed when he was under her car, she'd never have known he was an amputee. Of course it had to be traumatic, but Danny's was more so, a much more severe loss. Wasn't it? Why was a conversation with her brother hard for Mac?

"I can see you are over-thinking things again. What's the problem?"

Sue sighed. "It's just" ...No, she couldn't reveal Mac's secret. She was sure she wasn't supposed to know, and to tell someone else, it would be a betrayal. "They were both over there, but Mac has a hard time talking with Danny. That's all. I don't want to hurt Danny's feelings."

"Danny has it together better than most people. I wouldn't worry about him, but that's why you agreed to a date? So Mac would talk with your brother?"

Sue nodded. She hated to disappoint—

"Yay! I was praying for something, no matter what it would take, to get you back out there, and look how God answered my prayer! Thank You, Lord! Whew!"

"That's what you prayed?"

"Well, I had plenty of time in bed and no energy to do much else, so I prayed for you and a lot of others. This is so exciting. When are you going out? Do you know where? What will you wear? Can I help? Please, please, please."

Ack! "I suppose I'd better let you, or I'll never hear the end of it. Only promise me you won't go overboard."

Tracy held up three fingers, tipped her chin, and stood straight. "On my honor. You can trust me. I was a girl scout."

That made Sue chuckle. "Of course I trust you. I wouldn't be here if I didn't. We'd better get moving or we'll be late for church." She reached for the doorknob.

"Fine, but I want the rest of my questions answered in the car. I'll drive." Tracy probably needed the chance to do something other than hibernate at home. Besides, it would save Sue some gas if Tracy drove anyway.

But once they'd backed out of their spot and turned onto the street, the interrogation started in again. "I need to know everything. I'm entitled since I did all that praying."

"Is nosiness a theologically sound doctrine?"

"Oh, of course it is. You know, after a miracle, the women would be asking all the pertinent questions that none of the men thought to consider. However, I'll be kind and ask one at a time. Let's start with when you are going out."

Sue let the passing landscape send her back to Friday in the rehearsal room where the chemistry had been almost combustible. Just remembering sent tingles down her spine. "The Fourth of July."

Tracy squealed. Was it safe to drive and get that excited? "You will have a blast. Bet you're going to some celebration, maybe out at Stellite? Anything else?"

"I'm meeting his mom. She's having a barbecue and then we'll watch the fireworks."

"You're meeting a parent? He's serious, kiddo. That's huge." Tracy kept glancing at her while driving.

"Keep your eyes on the road. He was sort of stuck. We already had the date when his mom asked him, so he told her he'd see if I was willing."

"You could've said no."

"True, or I can be more comfortable while not being alone with him."

The light turned yellow, and Tracy gunned it to get through the intersection before glancing over again. "Seriously? You're going to meet his mom to avoid being with Mac? That is so wrong."

When she put it that way, maybe her roomie had a point, but then Tracy still didn't know the whole story, and it was really for Mac's own good. "It's fine. We'll be just fine."

"Sure you will. Well, at least I have an idea of how to dress you."

"What am I? Your personal Barbie doll?" Sue was ready to escape this vehicle. Thoughts of jumping out at the next stop light and walking from there started to appeal.

"Never thought of it that way, but I'm down with that. You are gorgeous and have the perfect figure. I could dress you up and do your make up any day. Just another art form. I love color and design, so sure. You can be my Barbie."

Sue gritted her teeth, only allowing a hint of what was going on in her head out her lips. "I am not a Barbie." Then she clammed up for the rest of the ride.

At least Tracy got the warning and stopped pushing. Instead, she turned on the radio. Roberta Flack and Donny Hathaway were crooning "Where is the Love."

Sue sat on her hands and mentally chanted na-na-na to drown them out. Except it didn't work. It took all her resolve to not switch stations, but if she did, the cross-examination would resume.

Tracy turned into the parking lot and braked into a space before shutting off the engine. "There. Made it in one piece."

"Thank God for that." Sue climbed out and slammed the door harder than intended.

Tracy joined her, linking arms. "That was supposed to be a joke. Don't tell me you were worried."

"Who me? Just remind me to make sure my life insurance policy is up to date." But to soften her words, Sue winked. "Let's get inside where it's cooler."

Tracy grinned and practically pulled Sue into the narthex where Rob Crawford handed out bulletins. Sue was not fooled. Her nosy roommate simply wanted to get her seated where she could continue the pumping. After a few smiles and good mornings, they settled on a pew close enough to the back for Sue's comfort but on the aisle for Tracy. Sue became engrossed in the bulletin to hold off the questions.

Tracy found another person to engage. Whew.

Today's scriptures came from Romans 6:4 and Lamentations 3:22-2 3..Sue already knew that but now realized she'd messed up. She should have written them out in the bulletin. So much for setting her high standard in efficiency.

She decided to look them up before the service started.

The Romans verse read *Therefore we are buried with him by baptism into death: that like as Christ was raised up from the dead by the glory of the Father, even so we also should walk in newness of life.*

Newness of life. Sounded so simple. However, her past didn't appreciate being left behind.

She looked up the Lamentations verse. *It is of the LORD's mercies that we are not consumed, because his compassions fail not. They are new every morning: great is thy faithfulness.*

New every morning. Each day was another beginning to get it right. When she failed, and she always did, she could start again because His compassion was new every morning. Why hadn't she seen this before?

Because she forgot to do this part of her job. Or maybe God needed her to see it now.

Could that really be true?

The organist began and everyone stood. The first hymn was, of course, "Great is Thy Faithfulness."

Today was just for her, it seemed. Well, she'd wanted some answers, and it looked like she was getting them. Only she hoped Pastor Mussing wouldn't be so punctiform. She suddenly had an image of a dartboard, and she was the bullseye. Sue shuddered.

Though it was more on-the-nose than she cared to admit, the sermon was full of grace. Pastor even quoted Martin Luther about how believers should remember their baptisms every morning when they washed their faces. That newness in Christ, that was fresh every morning because of His mercy, gave hope to the hopeless, energy to the weary, direction to the lost, and refreshment to Sue.

Yes, she'd made a mistake. A bad one. However, she had asked forgiveness and had taken to heart Jesus's admonition to the woman caught in adultery to go and sin no more. Now she needed to embrace the newness He gave her.

Could she do it? The mental record album of how bad she was chose to play at the worst moments. How did she flip it over to loving affirmations? Ones that reminded her that it wasn't anything she did, right or wrong, but that she was loved no matter what. Her chest ached to believe it.

By the time the sermon ended, and the organist played the intro to "Just as I Am," Sue was undone. She'd used every tissue in her purse and her glasses were too splotched to see through. She slipped out to the restroom to clean up and gain some control before the postlude.

The woman staring back at her from the mirror had red eyes and a redder proboscis. Cleaning her glasses would help conceal the first part, but she had nothing to take the heightened color from her nose. After holding cool wet paper towels to it, she finally gave up. Tracy would be looking for her and other women would be coming in. Someone might notice and then there would be the awkward questions because this was a kind congregation.

Then again, would they? Had her reserve, her aloofness even, pushed people away enough that no one would care? Or worse, figure she had it coming from somewhere?

That struck home and nearly started the waterworks again. Instead, she bit the inside of her cheek to gain some control. Not too hard, just enough. She needed to exit and find Tracy and escape.

Only the first person she ran into was Mac.

When had he started attending Wabash Community?

And what on earth did he do to his nose? Next to him, no one would notice hers. "Mac, um, hi." Dare she ask him?

"Hi." His voice sounded like he had a head cold. "Guess you're wondering what happened."

"Yes, I'd be lying if I said I hadn't observed there was something different." She raised her fingers to her mouth to camouflage the grin that wanted to peek out.

He must have caught it because he had one of his own. "Got this trying to be a good Samaritan. My cousin is always getting me into some kind of trouble."

"Sounds as if you should stay far from certain relatives."

"I'm coming to that conclusion. Hey, would you like to catch lunch?"

Sue's heart thudded. She needed an excuse. "Um, I rode with Tracy today. I need to find her."

"She's heading for her car."

Oh, she wouldn't. She couldn't. Sue hustled to the big glass windows overlooking the parking lot, just in time to see Tracy driving toward the exit. She even spotted Sue at the window and waved.

Sue spun around and nearly landed on Mac who caught her.

"Whoa, there."

She shoved her hair from her face. "Did she talk to you?"

"She only said to tell you that she needed to get home, that she'd overdone it and needed to rest. I didn't know you hadn't driven."

Sue shook her head. Tracy was more devious than she'd figured. "But my sweet roommate did. She probably saw you and came up with the plan."

"Seriously?"

"Oh, yes. In fact, if I hadn't gone to the doctor with her and taken care of her myself, I'd be wondering if she fabricated her illness just to bring us closer."

Mac stared. "She'd really do that?"

"I wouldn't put it past her." Great. Now she needed to ask Mac for a favor. Unless she could spot someone else who would take pity on her. However, no other woman even looked her way. It was time to set her pride aside. "It seems I need a ride home. Would you be willing?"

Mac's grin glowed with neon intensity. "Only if you're willing to have lunch with me. How about Krieg's?"

Mac realized he had Sue over a barrel, though he'd take her home even if she said no. However, why confide that now?

"Yes. Krieg's is fine." She didn't look like it was fine, what with her pinched lips and narrowed eyes.

"Look, I won't force you. I just figured you have to eat and so do I, so why not?" Mac shrugged, hoping to add a more noncommittal atmosphere to the conversation that was suddenly spiraling out of control. If she'd said no and stayed true to her stubborn self, he'd been ready. However, this resigned yes made him want to retract his offer. "If you prefer to go straight home, I'll take you."

"I apologize. That was rude of me. I would enjoy having lunch with you at Krieg's." She even tossed in a small smile that seemed genuine despite its size.

"Then my chariot awaits, m'lady." Mac exaggerated a bow, and she smacked his arm.

"Fine, goof ball. Let's go."

He stopped himself from reaching for her hand. Improving her mood was hard enough without ruining things. However, he did get the door and opened the passenger side of the truck for her. That should only be interpreted as good manners.

As Mac walked around to the driver's seat, he heard someone call his name.

"Yoo-hoo, oh, Mac." Miss Elsie motioned to him.

He waved back, and she giggled before climbing in a car with another lady. She was sweet, but he was glad there were five parking spaces between them.

Mac shook his head and got behind the wheel.

"She's totally smitten by you, you do realize." Sue's smirk was hard to read. She couldn't be thinking what she was thinking.

That was ridiculous. "I'm the age of her grandson, *if* she has one."

"Oh, it's not romantic or anything. That being said, I wouldn't put it past her to try to adopt you."

The idea cracked him up. "She can do that any day of the week. Between you and me, though, I'm not sure I'd survive her python-strength hugs."

Now Sue laughed too. "Wait until Christmas. Oh, I wonder if she's figured out when your birthday is?"

"Have you?" He glanced her way before putting the truck in reverse to back from the space.

"Um, I haven't investigated, so that'd be a no."

"Do you want to know?" He might as well egg her on.

"Do you want me to know?" Oh, she was good.

He grinned, glimpsing her expression as he looked both ways before proceeding past the stop sign. "Only if you want to know."

"Just spit it out. You're dying to anyway."

"Oh, so you do want to learn when my birthday is? I'm not so sure I should tell you."

She turned to face him better. "Why is that? Is it a national security issue?"

"Maybe. I mean, you could find out and then feel obligated to get me a present. I'm not sure what your budget is, but I would think you would choose something nice for me. What if the gift is too expensive and then you couldn't pay your share of the rent or groceries, leaving poor Tracy to foot your share of the bill?"

"Poor Tracy, my dear Aunt Fanny. *Fttt.*" Guess Tracy really was in the dog house.

"Now hear me out. What if Tracy can't manage paying for everything? She might not simply fall behind on bills. Maybe she even has to declare bankruptcy." He gasped to get his point across.

Sue shook her head, her smirk growing.

"Then comes the day when her boss gets word that she's in financial trouble because her creditors are calling her at work, so he has to fire her, leaving him shorthanded, right when they're working on a major project for the White House."

"Now really."

"You see where this is going? Because her boss couldn't meet the deadline and he'd signed all sorts of paperwork that he'd keep this hush-hush, the government had to do something so he and the whole business disappear." Mac snapped his fingers for added emphasis. "All because you just had to figure out when my birthday is. So you'll understand if I don't tell you, right?" He'd timed it to perfection, braking into the parking spot at Krieg's as he finished.

Sue stared. Then applauded. "That's some imagination you have there, mister. I bow to your prowess." Only then she gave her self away with a snort that escaped while her quivering lips attempted to hold back a grin.

That did it.

Now both of them were laughing.

"Pretty good, Mr. MacKenzie."

"Why thank you, Miss Mitchell. Shall we?"

"Indeed we shall." She turned to open her door, but he was determined to get there first.

Only as he raced to her side, he noticed at the last second bits of gravel peppered all about the painted lines. Just as his right foot skidded over one. Mac slipped. Lost his balance. Landed on his keester. Stupid, stupid, stupid. His face heated worse than the blacktop.

Sue charged toward him. Great. And then he noticed his leg sprawled out in front of him. With his bellbottom slacks flipped back. Enough that his prosthetic rod was visible.

Mac quickly straightened his trousers and used the bumper of his truck to hoist himself up. However, there was no way he could look her in the face.

She knew.

He knew that she knew. She'd seen it. How could she miss seeing it? His prothesis had been uncovered for the entire world.

"Mac?"

"Don't say anything."

"Mac." She touched his hand. Wonderful, now she pitied him.

"I promised you lunch. Let's go inside." And never speak of this again.

"Hey. You are still you. I see you. Isn't that what you told me?" Her fingers exquisitely burned his skin with pain and longing.

Somehow, he threaded his own between hers and caught her peering at their hands before her gaze met his. "I like this." The words escaped his heart and were the complete, honest truth.

"Me too." Her voice was a whisper only for him.

He swallowed. "I promised I won't push, but this feels right."

She nodded and for a second, leaned against his arm. If only he could capture that moment, freeze it, and never let it end.

But it did.

"Are you ready?" She sent a squeeze to their clasp.

"If you are." He dusted his backside with his free hand. At least he hadn't torn his pants.

She still held on as they moved toward the restaurant entrance. He wondered how long they might keep it up, but once they were shown to their table, he had to let go.

Mac didn't want to let go of anything. Except his stupid blunder. Thankfully, she picked up her menu without any questions.

However, now he absolutely had to tell her. There was no getting around it. He'd promised he would one day, but he'd hoped that day would be further off.

The waitress arrived, shifting him from his dread of the future to her need to take their present order. Mac had only stared at the menu without reading it.

"I'll have a salad, Italian dressing on the side, and a Tab, please." That was it? That's all Sue was getting?

Mac cleared his throat, stalling, and then dove in. "I'll take a T-Bone, medium rare, baked potato with butter, sour cream, and chives, and let's start with a shrimp cocktail." He handed the menu over, feeling pleased he'd pulled that off. At least something went right.

As soon as the waitress left, Sue leaned forward, her voice low. "You can eat all that?"

"Uh, yeah. Besides, I skipped breakfast, so I'm starving." He smiled, grateful that was what she wanted to talk about.

"No way are you starving. You don't have an emaciated hair on your head. Now, I'll give you hungry if you've neglected the most important meal of the day. However, starving? Not buying it."

"You really want to go there? Fine. Just to inform you, if I don't get fed in the next, oh, let's say, twenty minutes, you may have to carry me out to the truck and drive me to the nearest hospital. I am that weak from lack of food."

"Oh, really. You are something, Mac MacKenzie. Knowledge of your birth date can cause a federal disaster in which people vanish, and if you miss one meal you become as feeble as Samson without his hair. Are you sure it's safe for me to be around you?" She sat back and crossed her arms.

"As long as you feed me regularly and don't peek at my driver's license, I think the world is secure."

Sue blinked, her eyes growing wide. "The world?" Did she just sputter? "As in the whole wide world? That is some massive ego you've got there, buster. I'm flabbergasted."

"Told you we ought to get better acquainted."

That elicited a chuckle from her. "You did at that. Okay, without revealing any classified secrets, what is the strangest thing that's ever happened to you?"

"You were there."

"When?"

"When the ladies, especially Miss Elsie, took a shine to me. I've never experienced anything like that in my life. Definitely on my *Ripley's Believe It or Not* list. So, how about you? What's the strangest thing to ever happen to you?"

Sue closed her eyes a moment, then a smile came to her face. "My mom loved ice cream, but towards the end, she wasn't eating much of anything. Of course, I was trying to think of something that would tempt her, and finally she suggested an ice cream cone. I wanted to kick myself because I'd not picked any up at the grocery. Before I said anything, there were these bells. They rang outside toward the street and got louder as whatever it was grew closer. Then I realized that—it was the ice cream man. His truck slowly cruised the neighborhood. I ran outside and stopped him, asked for an ice cream cone. As he dipped it up, I explained it was for my mother and what was going on. He handed it over, not taking a penny from me. Claimed it was his gift to my mom. I never saw that truck in our area again. That ice cream cone was the last thing she ate before she... she died."

Mac reached across the table to stroke her hand, as she had done for him moments ago. "I'd say that was strangely wonderful."

Sue blinked a few times. "I agree. Let's talk about something else. What is your favorite, oh, how about movie?"

"You'll laugh."

"No I won't." She looked so solemn, holding up the Girl Scout hand sign, but he figured she would.

"Okay, just remember, you promised." He paused and leaned in. "*Snow White*."

There was no hiding her snicker. "*Snow White*?"

"Yes, ma'am, *Snow White*. You're laughing."

She covered her mouth. "No, I'm not."

"Right, well, no matter. *Snow White* has it all. Adventure, intrigue, a daring rescue, the best kiss in cinematic history, and the business of the dwarfs is outstanding. I mean, when they have that scene where they find her sleeping and one by one their noses pop up over the foot of the bed? That's priceless. How about when Dopey gets in line twice for a kiss before work? Bet you laughed, didn't you? It's classic."

Sue shook her head and stared. "The best kiss in cinematic history? I beg to differ."

"Name a better one."

"I will. *Cinderella*."

"*Cinderella*?" She had to be kidding.

"Yes."

The waitress arrived with their orders, so Mac decided to gather proof. He checked her name tag. "Marsha, we can't agree on something, and I hope you will help me, er, us out with it."

"If I can." Marsha's brow furrowed with skepticism.

"What movie is the best ever made? I say *Snow White*, but my friend here says *Cinderella*. So, you tell her, er, us what the definitive answer is, please."

Marsha glanced between the two of them, back and forth, several times before she must have decided the question was on the up and up. "Sorry, but *Pinocchio* is my choice." Then she moved to the next table to take their order.

"*Pinocchio*? Is she for real?" Mac couldn't believe it.

“But it doesn’t even have a kissing scene.”

“Right.” He nodded in agreement.

Then Sue’s cheeks grew pink and her eyes rounder. Her thoughts might as well have been written across her face. She was sitting in a restaurant comparing cartoon kisses with him, and now she’d figured it out.

He wanted to kiss her.

Chapter 11

Sue touched her face. Her cheeks must be cherry red, considering how hot they were. Why did her thoughts go there? They were simply talking about cartoons.

And great kisses.

Right. Someone just cranked up the thermostat in her head even higher.

"You okay there, Sue?"

"Yes. Um, if you'll excuse me a moment." She swiped her napkin across her lips that seemed plumped and over ready. Time to get out of here.

Where? Where could she go? It wasn't as if she had her car. Sue scanned the restaurant, searching. The ladies' room?

She hightailed it, colliding with a waitress and a full tray and only nearly averting an impossible scene. "Sorry, so sorry."

Flying through the restroom door, she remembered too late about the possibility of someone being on the other side. She smacked a blue-haired lady in the head with a thud.

"Oh, no. Let me help you."

The elderly woman dressed in her Sunday best rubbed her forehead. "No, that's okay, dear."

"Are you sure? May I see?" What if Sue had given her a concussion?

"I'm perfectly alright but for being startled. I'm more concerned with you. Something drove you here in a hurry. Are you sick? Should I find help?"

What kind of person gets smacked in the head and offers assistance?

Sue stepped to the sink. "I just needed a moment to compose myself."

"Did someone get fresh with you out there? I can give him a talking to." The lady squared her shoulders. This feisty gramma-type would do it too, and poor Mac wouldn't see it coming.

That squeezed a giggle out of Sue that surprised them both. Instead of looking confused, the sweet woman opened her arms to give a hug.

That was all it took. Crybaby Sue lost it again. "I'm sorry. I don't even know you."

"I'm Elenore. Don't you worry about it. Want to tell me what happened?"

No, it would be too embarrassing. Apparently, Sue's mouth had another idea. "My name's Sue and we were talking—me and this young man who brought me here. It was silly stuff, the best movie ever. We got into a humorous disagreement before I realized that the criteria we were using..." Saying it aloud only made it worse.

Elenore's gaze bore into Sue's, not letting her glance away.

"It was which movie had the best kiss. I suddenly thought about kissing him. Then I could read in his eyes, he knew what I was thinking. I had to get out of there." Sue reached for a paper towel to mop up her face.

"So you haven't known your young man very long then, I take it."

"No, not long, but I like him. I've had, well, let's say my experience with men until now hasn't been all that great. This one might be different, but I'm—"

"Scared?"

"Terrified. I've been wrong before. Very wrong."

Elenore squeezed Sue's hand. "You could be right this time."

"You think so? Is it possible?"

"I don't see why not. It's worse to hold back from an opportunity because you might get hurt than to take a chance and learn something. Only those who keep rising when they're knocked down ever find success. I have a question." Elenore peered at Sue with her blue eyes that matched her hair.

"What's that?" This encounter had gotten personal awfully fast.

"What movie did you say had the best kiss?"

That's what she wanted to know? "I said *Cinderella* and he said *Snow White*."

"Oh, honey, you grab hold of that fella. He's a keeper." Elenore patted Sue's hand.

They both giggled.

"Now I'm going back out there before my dinner gets cold. You look just fine. Follow me and get this thing started."

What?

However, Elenore had already linked her arm with Sue's and was headed for the door.

Sue inhaled and blew it out. Might as well not fight it.

When they got to Elenore's table, a couple away from where Mac sat watching, the woman introduced Sue to the others seated as her new friend. No mention that she'd almost been taken out by a door. Fortunately, there wasn't even a mark on Elenore's forehead.

Sue motioned toward Mac and winked at Elenore before returning to her table.

She'd barely gotten seated and her napkin returned to her lap when Mac leaned forward, his hands clasped in front of him. "Sometimes you worry me, Secretary Sue."

"I do?"

"Yes, you do." He didn't elaborate since Marsha the waitress appeared at that moment with their orders.

Sue closed her eyes and thought a quick prayer of thanks only to open them and see Mac staring at her.

"If you want to say grace, that's okay."

She shook her head. "Already did, thank you."

He rolled his lips and nodded, waiting until she took a bite before cutting into his steak.

"How is it?" Sue pointed with her fork toward the meat.

"Really good. Not like I can do on my grill, but great for a restaurant."

She stabbed a piece of iceberg lettuce and touched it to the dressing on the side. "So we can add master barbecuer to your list of accomplishments?"

"Yeah, pretty much. I can grill about anything. That's one reason my mom wanted us to come for the Fourth. She can't grill for the life of her but figured if she mentioned to me she was going to I'd volunteer to take that job over. I fooled her and said I'd talk to you first. Eventually, I should tell her we're coming."

"You haven't told her yet?" That made Sue's nerves tingle. "Maybe she's moved on to plan B."

"My mom? Uh-uh. Her plan B is to discover another enticement to get me there to do the grilling. I'm waiting to see what she comes up with next."

"Now that's mean. I never thought of you that way." Sue studied his face again. Could she be wrong?

"It's not like that. She knows I'll be there. And I know she'll get me to grill. It's a game we play. Mom is the best, and this is how we tease." He paused with his fork partway to his mouth. "Maybe it's time I call her. Okay, you win."

"What did you say?"

He chewed with exaggerated patience, then finally swallowed. "I believe I said it's time I call her."

"No, the part after that."

"What part?" A smile toyed at his dimples.

"You're perfectly aware of what part. You said it. I heard you. I just want confirmation. Say it again."

He dabbed his napkin at the corners of his mouth. "Oh, you mean that bit about winning?"

The man was exasperating, but he was also more fun than anyone she'd talked with in a long time.

"Yes. That. Say it again."

"Okay. You. Win. Satisfied?"

Sue leaned back in her chair and grinned. "That wasn't so hard, was it?"

"Maybe not for me, but you sure seemed to be working at it." Mac winked, and she giggled. "Eat your rabbit food. I have an idea, but we need to get done here."

Sue wanted to grab him and shake the idea loose so she could approve or disapprove it, but he was now focused on his baked potato. Her mother's advice trickled in right then. *Don't come between a man and his food.* Mom was pretty sharp. She'd heed the advice. Returning to her salad, she cut the portion down the middle and stopped when she'd finished half. Then she set aside her fork, blotted her mouth with her napkin, and pushed the remnants of her meal away.

"You're done?" Mac still had a good portion of T-Bone and a third of a potato left.

"I don't like to overeat."

His eyes took on a worried stare. "Are you sure you won't be hungry later?"

"If I am, I'll eat then. I'm fine now."

"Finishing your salad isn't gonna put that weight back on you, you realize that, right?"

Sue averted her eyes. "I understand. This is all I need."

"Well, prepare to have my mom entice you with all sorts of foods. She might not be able to grill, but she sure can bake. She's sort of the neighborhood cookie pusher." He grinned.

She'd have to remember that and be on her guard. "You finish eating. Don't let me stop you."

"Oh, you won't." He cut another bite of steak and popped it in his mouth. "Mm-mm-mm."

"That's not going to get me to eat more either."

"Fine then, I'll keep my enjoyment to myself." He forked a bit of potato, making sure to have some sour cream on it.

Yet it was only a few minutes later that Mac shoved his plate away. "I can't believe my eyes were that much bigger than my stomach. There are little kids in China going hungry, and I'm wasting food."

"Don't worry. I sent them my cereal the other morning, and they returned it."

"What? Secretary Sue made a joke? Okay, I am aware that my leaving food on my plate will in no way harm those kids. Still, it does remind me to be grateful and to consider what I can do to help." Mac really was a good guy.

Sue needed to relax in his presence. Not be so uptight. This could be a new chance to succeed with... No, she wouldn't use the R word, even in her mind, for fear she'd jinx it.

Mac stood and came to her chair. "Ready?"

"Ready."

He paid for lunch and escorted her to the truck. The air had warmed more, and despite the windows being rolled down, it was sweltering.

Mac pulled into a parking spot on South Webster. She checked out the corner lot though she knew where they were at. Why had he brought her here? He came around to her side—Sue stayed put so he wouldn't rush—and helped her out.

"Have you ever been here?"

She scanned the manicured lawn, the turn-of-the-century mansion, and the wooden sign and plaque announcing *The Elwood Haynes Museum*. She'd stood outside this place many times but never had the courage to go inside. Once she'd hoped to be a docent for the place. Then with

Mom becoming ill and dying so soon after she returned home, plus all the care Danny had needed... Then, of course, with her reputation worthless, there was no way she'd be hired. Even if she were, someone who'd heard the rumors in Alto at some time would come through those doors and tell her employers about how she treated men. They'd never look at her the same again. Might even fire her on a morals clause.

"Your brother said you had studied to curate a museum, so I thought this would interest you. There are some funny stories. Do you know much about Elwood Haynes?"

She shook her head. Did taking a chance on Mac mean she had to take a chance on herself? What could it hurt to look through the place? Aside from her bruised ego that assured her she'd never get to work there.

"No, no I don't. I'd love to see inside." She accepted his outstretched hand and automatically their fingers wove together. This would be good. It would be safe. She was with Mac, and he would protect her. He didn't have to say it. She knew it was true.

Perhaps she'd let him kiss her. And maybe, just maybe, she'd kiss him back.

Mac couldn't get over how right Sue's hand felt in his. Like it had been made just to be held by him. He glanced her way, noting she still had color in her cheeks that might or might not be due to the day's heat. The woman moved him.

They got to the porch of the converted mansion, and he opened the door for her. Going inside, it was definitely cooler, and the darker woods of the early twentieth century brought the temperature down even more.

Mac was drawn to Sue's face as she took in the entry. Elegant and refined, she belonged in places that celebrated history and greatness. He imagined her as a curator of this place.

"Oh, Mac, this is amazing. I knew he was an inventor, but did you notice how many things we have today because of him? Look, he came up with stainless steel. And the thermostat. And, oh my, he took something that was considered waste and turned it into a product we use every day. Gasoline. I had no idea."

Yep, she seemed right at home discovering and learning. Why hadn't she been here before? It wasn't as if she were new to the area.

Sue tugged at his hand as she led him toward the dining room, all set with lots of dishes and period-dressed mannequins. "Oh, that china is exquisite."

He supposed it was pretty, maybe a little too busy for his style, but then it was for eating off of, so who was going to notice the pattern until the plates were empty? Besides, watching Sue enjoy the museum was enough entertainment for him.

They wandered into the kitchen. "You know this is a historic spot, right?"

Sue shook her head. "No, what happened?"

"Well, it seems that Mr. Haynes purchased a motor that had been designed for a boat, thinking he might adapt it to a land vehicle. This very kitchen became his workroom, and he got the engine attached to the chassis and ran his test." He smiled, waiting for her to react.

She smacked him on the arm. "So? Are you going to tell me?"

"Are you going to quit hitting me?" He cocked his eyebrow. Something his father used to do and as a kid Mac had practiced in front of his mirror until he could do it too. It came in useful at times, saying more than words.

"Only if you finish the story."

"Fine. The result was loud with great shaking that damaged his framework and his wife's kitchen floor. Mr. Haynes was banned from experimenting in the house after that."

"No. You're kidding me. What man would try running a gasoline engine inside? Especially in the kitchen. What was he thinking?"

"Probably that it wasn't going to be as destructive as it was. Now, ask me how I know." He realized he was smirking and that she'd rather smack him again. Still, it was worth it.

"Oh, great one, how do you come to know that story is true?"

It was time to impress her. "My grandpa was a childhood friend of March Haynes, Mr. Hayne's son. They were playing upstairs when the racket happened, and my grandpa heard the whole conversation. So there."

"You are a man of many mysteries, Mr. MacKenzie." She squeezed his hand, and he nearly forgot where they were.

"I'm not so mysterious. You are welcome to figure me out."

She didn't reply, but she did lean against his shoulder.

He could get used to this. "Where else should we look? Upstairs?"

"Why not? Lead on, McDuff."

He shook his head. "Not McDuff, just Mac." He tried to remain serious, but she caught him hiding his grin.

"Oh, you!" Then they laughed together, and the music of that sound bounced around in his heart.

They climbed the free-standing staircase to the second floor where bedrooms and what was then considered a modern bathroom were on display. It didn't take long to check it all out. Besides, Mac had seen it all before, and they hadn't gotten to his favorite part yet.

Back downstairs he paused as Sue studied the brochure. "Where are the cars?"

She'd started to figure him out. "This way." He led her to the carriage house where the 1923 Haynes Speedster that had once been owned by Governor McCray sat behind velvet ropes. A little further in, the 1923 Apperson Jackrabbit sedan was parked behind its own maroon barriers. "You are now at my favorite part of the museum."

"I understand why. These are gorgeous. The brochure says he first invented a car he named the Pioneer. Why isn't it here?"

"It's at the Smithsonian."

Sue nodded. "Oh, I see."

"Have you ever noticed the sign out on Pumpkin Vine Pike?"

"No, but I've heard of it. Where he did his test run of his first car with the Apperson brothers, right?"

"You remember your Hoosier history. Yep. My grandpa used to take my cousin and me there and tell us the stories. Seems the 1920s did a number on the family's fortune. March ended up selling the house in the 1950s, but his sister bought it back a few years ago and donated it to the city. That's how we got this museum."

"I'm impressed. If this was all about music, it wouldn't have surprised me. But—"

"I do have other interests. Cars? And I can appreciate great history."

"I didn't mean to imply anything. I'm enjoying this side of you." She smiled at him, and it took his breath. "What? No witty comeback?"

Mac mentally shook himself. Just staring would only get him into trouble. "Call me multi-faceted. You ain't seen nothin' yet."

That made her giggle.

"How about I treat you to an ice cream cone?"

Sue did that leaning into him thing again, and he had to force himself to focus. She paused before nodding. "I'd like that. A small one, please."

They headed for the truck where he got her situated in the passenger seat before climbing in and firing up the ignition. "Too bad ol' Elwood didn't live to see what all his kitchen experiment led to in today's culture. Passing away in 1925, he sure missed out."

"Yes, he did. The man was a genius."

Mac nodded. "Maybe. He lived his convictions, but he also wasn't always the best employer. No one is perfect, but I'll give him credit, he sure tried to be."

"Maybe it isn't in the effort. Perhaps it's in the acceptance of Jesus's perfection and gift." She did a quick glance his way that said more than her words had.

"I think you're right, Miss Mitchell." No need to point out that she didn't let herself fully feel His grace. Because if he did, he'd have to point to himself as well.

"Why thank you, Mr. MacKenzie."

The conversation slowed to silence. Not necessarily uncomfortable. In fact, it was more relaxing than anything he'd experienced all day. However, experience taught him that prolonged quietness of any kind could explode into chaos and destruction.

As if on cue, he glanced in the rearview mirror as the mom-and-pop grocery burst into flames. Did he race to help or get Sue out of danger? The road in front of them opened as a mine took out the center. Mac careened around it on two wheels.

Jungle filled in between the building that suddenly changed to huts. A claymore burst to the right. He knew what was coming. His temples pounded, he had to outrun this. Not his other foot. No!

"Stop light! Mac!"

He braked hard, using his arm to keep her from flying through the windshield. "Sorry." He felt the blood drain from his face and his pulse slowing but a long way from normal. The world returned to everyday Kokomo. Safe. Not Viet Nam. "Sue, I'm sorry."

Her eyes were round with fear. "Where were you?"

How could he answer that? He couldn't tell her that for one moment he was back in the hell of battle and about to lose another body part. "Just got lost in my head. I'm sorry."

"You keep saying that. Now I'm worried about you."

She was worried? He was freaking out about himself. And about telling her. Would she become afraid of him? "I'm fine. Really. I'm more concerned about you."

"Well, the light is green, and I think you should go, considering the guy in back of you." To punctuate her words, a horn blared.

Mac shifted into first, let out the clutch, and stepped on the gas. How stupid could he get? It had been going so well.

"Perhaps you should just take me home now."

"Are you sure? The frozen custard place is only a couple of blocks away." Maybe he should.

She didn't respond at first, only stared at him like she was making an assessment. Would he pass the test?

"Okay, since we're close. You'd said you needed nourishment at the restaurant, but I thought you were only kidding. Besides, you ate plenty."

Mac did his best to sound calm as he rounded the corner and pulled into Frozen Custard's lot. "It's not that. You're going to think I've gone nuts, but I was back in the Nam." He braked into a space.

"Does this happen often?"

"Um, just sometimes. Usually when things get too quiet."

Sue turned, giving her full attention. "Is that why you have music playing all the time?"

Guess this was the moment. "Yeah. Sort of chases the demons. I can't understand why it keeps happening. Trust me, this isn't a memory I want to keep remembering. It's just in the quiet, the battle starts. I've got orders to get somewhere, but people around me need help. Do I stop and give aid? Do I obey commands and possibly end the battle or give critical information to those who can? That's what was going on when..." He cleared his throat in an effort to keep the scene from replaying in his head. "My jeep was hit. The driver was killed, but I was thrown free. Except shrapnel from the vehicle severed my ankle. I remember seeing it gone. Then nothing until some guys were putting me on a stretcher. I screamed. For my foot."

He glanced her way.

She still studied him, no judgment on her face.

"I didn't want to tell you. It's humiliating that I fight this. Explaining means being back in the pain and fear, but I promised you. Mainly because I'm falling for you." He ran his fingers through his hair and grasped for control. "I need to know if you can trust me, even with all this garbage—"

"You're falling for me?"

"Yeah. Hard. I think you are the most amazing woman I've ever met. I love how you challenge me, how you get so excited about what others have accomplished. You are kind to the girls in your group, but you are honest and make them respond with truth. Then there are the kitchen ladies who you help so faithfully. Besides, even though Tracy makes you crazy, you still left work to take care of her." He longed to hold her as he spoke these words. "You, Sue Mitchell, are kindhearted and honorable, and I can't believe I have the good fortune to know you."

She ducked her head.

"Hey." He gently raised her chin to capture her gaze. "You haven't answered my question. Do you trust me?"

Sue rolled her lips between her teeth and blinked before finally speaking. "You can't tell?"

He needed her response, clear and concise. "Would you please answer my question without another question? Secretary Sue, do you trust me?"

She sprang from her seat and hugged him tight. "Yes, I trust you."

He embraced her, letting the reality of this instant take hold. Sue was in his arms. He was holding her, and she had initiated it.

She drew back and for a split second, he saw something in her eyes. Was it fear? Did he frighten her? Or was she concerned she'd gone too far? That maybe he would kiss her.

Or that he wouldn't.

He had to touch her face, craved to trace her lips, know if there was a chance.

She kissed his finger and shyly smiled permission.

That was all he needed as he lowered his mouth to hers.

Sweetness and warmth cascaded over him. Who cared about ice cream? This kiss was the best dessert on the planet.

Mac groaned as another wave of tenderness gave way to more emotion. He could get lost in this moment. Completely. This silence didn't terrify, it was healing.

She broke it off just when he wasn't sure he could.

Mac licked the corner of his mouth for a last taste of her. "That was better than any frozen custard they have here."

Sue's laugh was soft. "I agree. Could we split a cone?" Her fingers ruffled against her bottom lip that had gained color.

He caught a curl alongside her cheek and twirled it around his finger. "Alright, but you need to know I don't share my ice cream with just anyone."

"Then I promise not to eat more than my half. You can even pick the flavor."

That was fine, but his new favorite had everything to do with Sue Mitchell's lips and nothing about what was on the frozen custard shop's menu.

Chapter 12

Tuesday, July 4, 1972

"Here you go, Sue. Just like the last time." Aaron held out a stack of reel-to-reels to her. "Stormy said if you can show up in the next fifteen minutes, they have a clear spot on their calendar."

"Thanks, Aaron." Sue set them on her desk. Would she ever become comfortable calling the music director by his first name? "I'll get them there now."

"If you want to lock up as you leave, that's fine. You helped me knock things out and get caught up. Thanks for coming in on the holiday. You might as well enjoy some time away." Aaron gave her a quick salute and headed for his office.

The remainder of the day off? She'd planned to leave around noon, but it was only five past eleven. She didn't know whether to be excited or nervous. Getting a chance to rest before meeting Mac's mother might turn into one bizarre scenario after another in her fertile imagination. She still had to deliver the reels before she could be finished at work, though, so she straightened her desk, filing the last paper away.

After closing all the blinds, she gathered her purse and the container of tapes and headed out, locking the front door after herself.

Sue's VW ran like a champ ever since Mac fixed it. Today was no exception. She set the box behind her seat and then rolled down her windows to let the breeze blow through on the short drive.

It only took a few minutes to reach Ferguson House. She checked her watch to make sure she was within the time frame given. She was right smack dab in the center.

"Secretary Sue."

Only one person called her that, and she loved how his voice sounded when he did. Maybe she was falling for him more than she'd admitted. The whole idea still scared the bejeebers out of her, but Mac somehow had turned irresistible. She waved to him as he headed her way. "What brings you here?"

"You." He winked.

"Seriously, I know it's not me."

"Don't sell yourself short. But yes, I do have another reason. I called Professor Day, and he said his daughter who plays the piano could meet with me about now. He also mentioned that you would be coming, so I figured it was perfect timing." Mac brushed a kiss against her cheek.

She was still surprised by his endearing ways. They'd talked the preceding two nights on the phone—Sunday after he dropped her off and Monday after he'd stopped by to see her at work to bring her a box of candy. Sue gave him first choice and tried a chocolate truffle at the office in front of him to prove she appreciated his thoughtfulness. She allowed herself one piece as dessert last night.

Now today, when they were going on their official first date in a few hours, they were again like magnets, seeking each other out.

"Which of his daughters plays the piano?"

Mac held the door for her. "I think he said Windy. She might be able to sing my last song as well. I still have some work to do on that, but I should have all my compositions ready for the musicians."

"That's wonderful. I can't believe you did all that. It's so impressive."

"Are you saying I'm not impressive?"

She was about to punch his arm and point out that is not what she meant when Stormy entered.

"Great. Thanks, Sue, for bringing these over. Dad has the best collection, and using reel-to-reel frees me up from turntable duty." Stormy took the box and set it on the coffee table.

Mac spoke up. "You wouldn't by chance know where Windy is, would you?"

Sue slipped her hand in his and felt his nervousness.

"Sure. She's out back setting up for her next client. Let me show you." Stormy guided them down a hall that led past an ornate dining room, obviously set up for cake tasting, and into a kitchen that appeared newly remodeled with all the latest in appliances. From there, they crossed through the enclosed porch and down some steps where Sue spotted Windy fiddling with a camera on a tripod.

"Hey, Windy, there's someone here to see you." Stormy left them then to return to the house.

The pretty blonde glanced toward them and smiled before she walked their way and offered handshakes to them both. "How can I help you?"

Mac squeezed Sue's hand before beginning. "Your dad said you play the piano and suggested I stop by."

"I do. Are you one of his students? I think he mentioned you. Mac?"

"Yeah. I need a pianist for my presentation, and he recommended you."

"Tell you what, why don't you give me more information while you help me? I have to adjust something with my new camera and hoped to do it before the clients get here, but I'm having a hard time. Would you stand in for them while you explain what you want me to do and when?"

Mac glanced Sue's way, and she shrugged.

"Sure." Rather than unison, Sue warmed to the harmony of his baritone with her alto voice in their simultaneous answer.

They followed Windy to a large, spreading sycamore tree encircled with a white wrought-iron bench.

"How about sitting together on the seat?"

They did, and Mac filled Windy in on the details. "I have most of the five pieces composed. The music is ready, so I can drop it off any time. I'd like to rehearse in the evenings because of my job. I still need to locate a couple of acoustic guitar players, and I'm thinking that a flute would work well."

"That sounds interesting. How many rehearsals are we talking?" Windy stared into her viewfinder. "Oh, go ahead and stand now."

Mac helped Sue to her feet. "I'm guessing since it will depend on how things come together, but maybe two weeks of four nights per week? If I get the music to everyone so they can practice their parts at home, then that should work."

Windy straightened and motioned them to step a little to the left. "Sounds about right. I know a few musicians in the church. How about I give you their names?"

"Your dad did already. They are on my list to call when we leave—"

"Well, I'll be." Windy looked up at them again. "Are you two dating or anything?"

Sue glanced at Mac as her cheeks heated, and she nodded.

Mac grinned. "How did you know?"

"Let's just say a little red bird told me."

"Huh?"

Windy peeked toward the back door. "My clients will be here any second, but to make a long story short, there's a legend with this sycamore tree. If you kiss under it and a cardinal lands on the branch, you are meant to be together. Oh, here they are now." Windy walked away, heading for the couple standing inside the back porch door.

"A kiss beneath the tree, huh?" Mac drew her closer.

"What if she's wrong?" Sue didn't want to find that out.

"What if she's right? May I?" He leaned in as if he wasn't giving her time to respond, but just before their lips met, he paused and waited.

Sue's heart pounded in her ears. She remembered Sunday's kiss as the best she'd ever had. What if it had been a fluke? What if that were only a onetime thing? Suddenly, she had to know. Her fingers slipped up his neck into his hair and pulled him the rest of the way until Roman candles exploded in her brain. Sunday didn't even compare. This was her independence day. She was free of Brad's memories. This was the man she wanted to be with, to care for, to love.

She pulled back, scaring herself, rolling her lips between her teeth and not making eye contact.

Mac felt it too, she could tell. There was a tremble in his touch as he brushed her hair behind her ear. "Sue. You are amazing." He wrapped his arm across her shoulders and guided her out to the front through the side yard, walking her to her car. "I'll be by to get you at three."

She nodded shyly, peeking at him as his dimples popped into view. "I'll be ready."

He gave her a peck on the cheek and closed her door before heading to his motorcycle. Watching him mount and start the engine made her almost hope he drove it to pick her up. Holding on to him would be so pukka.

Yet he wasn't leaving, and she realized he waited for her to pull out first. Ever the gentleman. Sue put her Bug in gear and headed for home.

Tracy beat her to the apartment, having gotten off early for the holiday. Sue had hoped she'd have a little time to get ready without her roommate's input, but there was that promise to let Tracy play Barbie. No matter how much she hated feeling like one.

"You need to wear something capri length. I'm compromising because you really ought to put on short shorts with those long legs, but I know you. Besides, I have the perfect top." Tracy raced to her room and came back with a white peasant blouse with colorful embroidery on the neck and shoulders. "This will go great with your navy pedal pushers. Grab your shower and then dress. Then I'll fix your hair and makeup."

"I don't need makeup. Mac likes me just as I am."

"I get that, but we're out to make him lose his mind. So trust me."

Sue shook her head. "Who said he should lose his mind? Can't I just enjoy his company?"

Tracy gave her the Popeye stare and tapped her foot. "You seriously want me to believe that? After Sunday, you should be hoping he kisses you."

Unconsciously, Sue stroked her bottom lip, impressions of that last kiss setting off more rockets of red glare inside her.

"He did. He kissed you again. When? Where?"

"I saw him for a few minutes after work and, well..."

"You're blushing. It must have been fantastic."

"The best kiss in the whole history of kisses."

Tracy plopped backwards onto Sue's bed. "Now that is historic. Then we absolutely want you to look spectacular tonight so you can experience it again."

Would she get to? Did lightning strike in threes?

She had no time to figure more, though, especially once she was out of the shower. Tracy took her in hand, and the funny thing was, Sue wanted to look pretty for Mac. She longed to see that glimmer in his eyes that said she wowed him and that he was glad she was there only for him.

However, she did put her foot down on fake eyelashes. That was more than she was willing to do. She also called a halt after the third coat of mascara, but the person looking back at her from the bureau mirror was someone who could wow Mac. She hoped.

This time, Sue agreed to let Tracy trim her bangs. When her friend was done, Sue's hair was stylish and didn't need bobby pins to hold it back.

Just as Tracy dabbed some Wind Song behind Sue's ears, a knock sounded.

"He's here." Her heart pounded. Had she grabbed hold of a live wire? Jolts of electricity caused her to shake.

"Settle down. I'll answer it. Take a couple of deep breaths. You look divine, my friend." Tracy blew her a kiss and then closed the bedroom door on her way to let Mac into their apartment.

This was it. Would he like was he saw? What about his mother? Would she think Sue was too made up? Would she consider Sue a tramp and demand her son have nothing to do with her? She slipped her glasses on. They hid nothing.

She needed to wash her face and brush out her hair. That meant racing from her bedroom for the bathroom. Tracy would spot her and stop her. Then, of course, Mac would see her. Oh, what had she agreed to? Her bathrobe lay on her bed. She could throw it on and maybe she'd make it to the bathroom and lock the door before Tracy could catch her.

One arm through a sleeve—

"What are you doing?" Tracy stood in the doorway, knowing perfectly well what was happening.

"I… uh, I have to, …uh."

"Do what? Go greet your guest?" Tracy tipped her head with that stare of hers that said she'd given her the correct answer, now she needed to take it.

Sue let all the breath in her release in defeat and sat on her bed. It's what she had to do. Even if it meant she was ruining every chance at happiness she could have with Mac. "How does he look?"

"Handsome. Despite his bruised nose. Happy. He'll lose his ever-lovin' when he sees you. Now go." Tracy held up her hand. "Gimme." She wiggled her fingers until Sue finally handed over her security blanket—her black cat-eye frames. "Now, enjoy your time with him. This will work out."

"Okay." Sue stood, a prisoner headed for the gallows. She'd allowed this, she'd see it through. Tomorrow she'd mourn for what could have been.

When she reached the living room, Mac rose, his eyes wide, and a grin sinking his dimples deeper.

Will wonders ever cease? Maybe Tracy was right.

Not that Sue would ever tell her.

"Wow." The word slipped free before Mac finished thinking it. It definitely didn't express his thoughts to their fullest. Sue was stunning.

He'd known all along she was a beautiful woman. There was no hiding that. But this afternoon, she took his breath away.

As well as the ability to conjugate sentences apparently.

"Should we get going?"

He was supposed to say something, but words failed him. Somehow, he got his head to nod.

Sue crossed the room, took him by the hand, and led him to the door.

"Bye, you two. Have a good time." Tracy's laugh followed them outside.

"Where are you parked?" Sue gently squeezed his fingers and his brain clicked into gear. Finally.

"I brought the Harley. Thought it might be fun if you're up to it."

"Yes, I am. What were you going to do if I said no?"

He hadn't figured that far ahead but came up with an answer in that split second. "You would've had to drive." He shrugged. And she smiled.

At the bike, he handed her a helmet. "Sorry about your hair, but you can fix it at my mom's."

She didn't say anything but strapped it on and waited until he was seated and the engine purring.

"Hop on."

Without hesitation, she climbed aboard, as if the invitation were enough and she had complete trust.

He'd been worried she'd think about his prosthesis and change her mind, but she didn't. Even after he told her the whole story, she hadn't shied away from him.

At least not yet.

Sue wound her arms around him and held on. Not too tight, just the perfect amount. Her head rested against his back, and he'd never felt more suited to his Harley, like he could ride forever this way. Too bad his mom lived only ten minutes from Sue's.

He pulled into Mom's driveway and parked the bike on the side of the garage next to the path leading to the back yard. "I'll take you in through the front so you can stop at the bathroom if you want." She slipped the helmet off just then. "Though I don't think you need to. Your hair looks fine to me."

"I'd like to believe you, but I better check for myself."

He wove his fingers with hers and led her up the front porch steps and inside. "The downstairs powder room is over there." He pointed to a door in the middle of a short hall.

"Thanks." And that quick, his hand grew cold without her warmth as she headed in the direction he'd indicated.

"Hey, sweetheart, figured you'd just come in from the back." Mom entered from the kitchen, wiping her hands on her apron. The click of the powder room door caught her attention, and she quickly moved to his side. "You brought her? I'm so glad. Can't wait to meet her." Her words were only for him, and she finished with a kiss to his jaw.

"She's fixing her hair. We rode the Harley, and she wore my helmet." He paused, knowing Mom would understand.

Sue returned then, just as beautiful as when she'd come out of her room to see him. "Mom, this is Sue Mitchell. Sue, my mother, Alice."

The women exchanged pleasantries, and Mom guided them out to the back yard that already hosted a few guests. Neighbors and friends from his mom's church.

"Wasn't it supposed to be just family? What happened?" Mac realized she was up to something.

"Oh, honey, it's no big deal. I simply mentioned that we were going to barbecue and watch the fireworks, and I felt sorry for people who had nowhere to go, so I included them." Mom shrugged. Like she could convince him. There was more to it. Maybe she was excited to show that her son had a girlfriend. Finally. Of course she'd never say that, but somehow he sort of figured that was the idea behind it all.

Well, he did have a girlfriend. A lovely woman friend who he hoped would become more before too long. So let Mom celebrate all she wanted. He was pretty happy too.

"Can I get you something to drink, Sue?" Mom turned before heading back to the kitchen.

"A Tab is fine if you have that. Or a glass of water."

Mom grinned. "A girl after my own heart. I've got several cans of Tab. Mac, what can I bring you?"

"A Coke for me. When do you plan to eat? Should I start the grill?"

Mom shook her head as she mounted the porch steps and turned. "If we eat around five-ish, you don't have to light it for a while. Say a little after four? Show Sue around. I'll be back with your drinks."

"Well, you heard her. Let me give you the nickel tour." Mac winked and got their hands rejoined.

The yard was good sized and filled with lots of childhood memories. "You see that oak?"

Sue nodded.

"My cousin Smitty and I built a tree house in there. Not much left after all these years, what with storms and winters, but it was fun. Of course it couldn't have been all that sturdy if it's fallen into such disrepair by now. You see this scar?" He pointed to a faint white mark that lived above his right eyebrow. "Got that after a disagreement over where to put the entrance. I still say it should have been on the bottom like a trap door. Oh well."

Sue traced the scar with a feathery touch. "That only makes sense. Where did you end up putting it?"

"Right there." He pointed to where a small part of the platform remained. "We attached the ladder to that side and crawled on our bellies to get inside from there."

"Your talents were definitely underestimated."

He chuckled, glad to hear she had faith in him.

The tour continued, and with most spots he had a coordinating scar story. The more he told her, the more he realized his cousin had been a terrible bully his whole life. Why hadn't he seen it before?

Mac glanced at his watch, noting it was five after four. "Time to heat up the charcoal. Want to be my assistant?"

"Sure, but then I ought to offer to help your mother. I hate that she's doing everything all alone."

"Trust me, she's been planning this since we got off the phone from me telling her we were coming. I'll bet the fridge is stocked with salads and goodies."

"All the more reason for me to help her."

Though he didn't want to let her out of his sight, the fact that she was offering kindness to Mom only added to his feelings for her.

"I guess. Maybe you could tell her that I'm about ready and that you can bring the patties and wieners out in a bit."

She saluted him. "Aye, aye, Captain BBQ." And followed up with a wink.

"Captain BBQ? I like that. Or how about grill master extraordinaire? That oughta go on my resume."

"Absolutely. Next to international spy and world saver."

"Hmm. Does it sound a little pretentious? I mean, I probably should keep the spy bit under wraps, right?"

"Whatever you say, oh great one. No need to get the paparazzi involved."

"Now you're just making fun of me, so you might as well go help Mom. Let her tell you what a saint I am."

She took a couple steps backward while tapping her chin. "Maybe I should do that. Bet she's got some wonderful stories."

"On second thought..." Too late, she was racing for the house. At the porch door, Sue turned and waved before going inside.

Man, this felt so right. It'd been too long since life had fit this nice, like a well-worn pair of Levi's. Comfortable. He had no doubt that Sue and

Mom would hit it off. Sure, there'd be embarrassing photos and stories, that was Mom's way, but it would be good.

"Mac?"

He glanced up from the grill to see Rachel approaching. Mom wouldn't have invited her, would she? Not when he'd told her he was bringing Sue. But he and Rachel had agreed to be friends, had been most of their lives, and there was nothing Rachel could do to change his mind about Sue.

"Hey, Rache. How ya been?"

"Okay. You?"

"Never better."

"Got a minute?"

He did, but he didn't want to say he did. Still… "Sure, what's up?"

"I know you hate talking about Smitty and me, but I might need to break up with him. He won't set a date and I think he only gave me the ring to…" Her cheeks filled with pink.

"I'm not the best person to give you advice. You knew about Smitty and his ways back when we were in high school. He won't change, even if you are the only girl to get him to buy a ring. I don't know. Maybe it will work out, but I'm not going to tell you what to do."

"Okay, that's fair. I shouldn't have asked. Oh, Alice told me you were bringing a date today. Where is she?"

"In the house, helping Mom. Are you staying?"

She glanced toward the back door. "Yeah, for a bit. Smitty's supposed to pick me up here. Said he had some errands to run but he'd be by later."

Somehow, that news irritated Mac. He didn't want his cousin meeting Sue. That's how he lost Rachel. However, if Smitty and Rachel were together when he made introductions, there shouldn't be a problem.

Shouldn't being the operative word.

Besides, Sue'd never fall for someone like Smitty. She was too refined. Too special. Maybe it wouldn't be so bad, and that way Rachel would know for sure there was nothing left between her and Mac.

Chapter 13

Sue's desire to make a great first impression with Mac's mom added to the vociferous pother of nervous energy overtaking her stomach from just being with Mac. He excited her in ways she'd never known. Yet it felt so good, so right. She didn't deserve either. Though she was trying to get there. Could God be showing her acceptance by bringing her this relationship gift?

Sue took a moment. With a cleansing breath, she blew away those thoughts, focused on the now, and pulled open the back door. "Mrs. MacKenzie, is there anything I can do?"

"It's Alice, dear, and sure. I'd love your help though there isn't a ton left. How are you with cutting up veggies?"

Sue smiled. "That's right up my alley."

"Good. I need a couple of onions sliced for the burgers and another minced for the wieners. Oh, and would you slice those tomatoes over there?" Alice pointed to a bowlful of the bright red orbs with a soapy knife she'd been washing. "There's a platter in that cabinet." Again with her sharp pointer. "You can get the slices all set on that and put the chopped onion in a bowl, same cupboard."

"Got it." Sue washed her hands and chose a knife from the wooden block. "Mac gave me a tour of your back yard. It seemed to be filled with memories and matching scars."

Alice shook her head and stared out the window while she washed a pan. "That boy was always getting into a scrape. I know he's my brother's son, but Mac's cousin was not a good influence. I'd hoped since they've grown up things would change, but I haven't seen that, though I do appreciate that Smitty found Mac a job at the steel mill. It's been helpful for him since he got back."

"My brother was over there too. He doesn't like to talk about it, but he's healing from his wounds and has a better attitude than I would've had." The snick of the knife slicing through to the cutting board added her punctuation.

"Mac won't talk either, but I see more of the old him now that he's met you."

That made Sue pause mid-slice. "I really like him. I hope we can get to know each other better."

Alice dried her hands and turned to face Sue. "Me too. I think you are good for him."

Sue finished up one onion and reached for another when she stole a glimpse out the window and noticed someone, a woman, walking up to Mac. The breath in her lungs turned to cement, and the knife slipped from her hand, clattering on the table.

Alice peered a moment, then glanced toward the backyard where Sue continued to stare. "Oh, that's Rachel. She lives next door. She and Mac have been friends since they were toddlers." She caught Sue's attention. "Nothing to worry about."

Sue shook herself and picked up her knife. It wasn't so much jealousy, though to be honest, there was a little. It was something else. She recognized the girl talking with Mac. Had seen her before. That night when she'd driven to Brad's house to surprise him. And peeked in the window. She'd spotted him taking Rachel—that was her name, right? Taking Rachel in his arms and kissing her. That was the woman Brad was cheating on. With Sue.

The thought made her sick, but she'd never let Alice know that. Plus, there was no telling Mac. She had to suck it up, make them all believe that everything was fine. Nothing to see here. Focus on the smiles and fun and don't check behind the curtain to find the tears and guilt.

Ow!

Sue dropped the knife again, this time noting she'd sliced her finger along with the onion.

Alice was beside her in a jiffy, guiding Sue to the sink to rinse the wound. "It's not too bad. Let me get a Band-Aid."

She was gone only a split second, but it was long enough for Sue to gaze out the window again. Mac didn't appear happy. Perhaps he didn't want to see Rachel? Or he didn't like something she said? Or maybe he missed her? Did he prefer Rachel to Sue? Who wouldn't, with her long dark hair and classic beauty?

"Here, want me to put it on?" Alice held out the bandage.

"No, thank you, I can do it." She did, dropping the scraps into the trash along with the onion slice with the blood streak, and then after a quick rinse, she finished her task. "Should I take the meat out to Mac?"

Alice pulled out an aluminum foil-wrapped platter from the refrigerator and handed it over. "Sure. And it's okay. I promise, you've no need to worry."

Sue forced a smile. "Thank you." Steadying her nerves, she carried out the raw burgers and wieners. "Here you go."

Mac flashed that grin she loved, minutely calming her. "You've got pukka timing. How are you and Mom getting along?" Was he worried?

"She's wonderful." Smiling more for the fact he'd worked pukka into his sentence than that he was happy she enjoyed working with his mom.

He chuckled. "Tell me something I don't already know. Oh, Sue, this is Rachel Stafford, Smitty's fiancé. Rache, Sue Mitchell."

Rachel's smile was genuine. No hint of knowledge of the wrong Sue had done to her. She held out her hand. "I'm so glad to meet you. Mac was saying he'd met someone special."

Sue focused on the last part of her words, ignoring the view of the diamond on the woman's left ring finger, and shook Rachel's hand. "Thank you. Alice said you two grew up together."

"Yeah, I was always trying to tag along with him and Smitty." Rachel showed no guile, completely veridical.

Sue wanted to bathe for a year. Would she ever feel clean?

"I'd better get back to the kitchen. Still have more veggies to attack."

Mac spotted her Band-Aid and captured her hand. "What happened?"

Right. Like she was going to tell him that. Sue shook her head. "Just got a little careless. Alice keeps her knives much sharper than Tracy does." Once more, she summoned a smile.

Mac raised her finger to his lips, kissing the bandage before pulling her closer and dropping another peck on her cheek.

If only she could hibernate in his arms right now.

She blew him a kiss as she headed inside. At the door, she turned back in time to catch someone else entering the backyard from the side.

Sue's eyes took in the impossible, and her nervous stomach was out of control. Now she really had to vomit.

Brad, in the flesh, walked up to Mac and playfully punched his arm, before pulling Rachel into a side embrace and dropping a kiss on her crown.

Sue's stomach roiled, jumping as if on a trampoline. She needed the bathroom. Now. Where was it? Right, down that hall—

"Sue, are you okay?" Alice's voice traveled after her.

There was no time to answer.

It wasn't as if she'd eaten much. The chaotic dance her nerves performed all day at work and then at home removed nourishment from the equation. But that didn't stop the gag reflex from taking hold of her as she closed the bathroom door. Dry heaves hit. She knelt before the toilet and begged God to get her out of there. Anywhere away from Brad.

What was he doing here? Why?

Of course, he was Rachel's boyfriend. Fiancée.

Finally, with her stomach under control, she stood, checking herself in the mirror. The shaking in her hands would have to calm if she were to finish her kitchen task. Plus, the raccoon eyes from where her mascara smeared needed to be fixed.

It took another couple of minutes, but she pulled herself together enough to venture out of the bathroom.

As she opened the door, Brad, hand in hand with Rachel, walked past. "It was great meeting you, Sue. Oh, this is my fiancée, Smitty. Hon, this is Sue Mitchell. She's the one I mentioned was dating Mac."

"Nice to meet you, Sue." Brad's smirk revealed more than she wanted to know. "Guess we'll see you later. C'mon, baby." He guided Rachel past but peeked back over his shoulder to toss Sue a wink.

No, he did not just do that.

Sue needed to go home. However, if she made Mac leave his mom's party, there would be questions, and she absolutely didn't want any gossip about her and Mac. Or anyone else. Could she hold it together until after the fireworks?

There was no choice, she had to. Then Mac would take her home and she could hide in her room until Jesus came back.

With another deep breath, Sue headed for the kitchen only to find Alice had finished the chopping and slicing. "I'm sorry." Shame engulfed her, almost more than she could tolerate.

"You looked like you didn't feel well. In fact, I was on my way to check on you. Are you okay?"

Sue nodded. She was not going to tell Alice about this, not when she'd already made such an awful impression. "May I start carrying things out?"

"I'd appreciate the help. Here ya go." Alice's smile beamed as she handed Sue the platter of sliced onions and tomatoes that now featured squares of cheese fanned down the middle like splayed playing cards. Then she grabbed two big bowls covered in aluminum foil from the fridge and led the way out back, setting her load on a card table decked out with a red, white, and blue tablecloth.

Sue set the platter where Alice indicated.

A few trips later, they'd laden the table with all kinds of Jell-O salads and sides and goodies for the meat Mac had finished grilling.

The guests all gathered together, and Alice asked a blessing before they formed a line and filled their paper plates. Several picnic tables were spread out around the backyard, creating little groups of conversation and feasting.

Mac led Sue to a table farthest from the house. "Mom will want to stay closer so she can keep hopping up to grab things. It's just the way she is. So if we sit here, we'll be by ourselves. Are you okay with that?"

"Your mom won't mind?"

He chuckled. "No. She'll get the idea I want to be with you. She's pretty smart." Mac winked.

It caused a clench in her gut, but Mac's gesture was friendly whereas... No, she couldn't go there. Instead, she pulled every brain cell in her head to focus on the wonderful guy who was opening up to her, sharing his world, and treating her the way she'd always wanted to be treated. Oh, she knew she didn't deserve it, but until he learned that fact, Sue would savor being appreciated and cared for.

An hour after enjoying a couple of bites of Alice's amazing cherry cobbler, Mac dumped their plates in the trash and laced his fingers with hers, leading her over to his mom. He hadn't made a comment about how she picked at the food and took no offense that she merely nibbled his grill master cuisine, for which she was grateful since it was only due to her iron will and numerous silent prayers that she swallowed and kept down what she did.

"Hey, Mom, we're gonna split now." He leaned in and kissed Alice's cheek. "Made some new plans, but I'll be over tomorrow to help you get things put away."

"Oh, hon, there's no need. Uncle Frank helped me set up, and he's volunteered to manage the take down. You two have fun. It was lovely meeting you, Sue, and I hope you won't be a stranger."

All at once, Sue was pulled into a hug. She caught Mac's grin over his mom's shoulder. "Thank you, Alice. I'd love to come back sometime."

Alice patted Mac's arm. "Make sure that he brings you. Maybe I'll see him more often that way." She pinched his cheek for good measure.

"Mom." He feigned embarrassment, but Sue knew he loved it.

Then they climbed on his Harley and backed out of the drive.

A few moments later, Sue realized he wasn't headed toward her apartment and remembered he told his mother he had new plans. She should have asked right then, but at the first stop light, she did. "Where are we going?"

"I thought I'd surprise you. We're meeting up with some friends to go watch the fireworks. We know a great little spot that's sort of hidden away but gives a spectacular view of the show Stellite puts on."

"Okay." But she wasn't okay. Especially when he turned into the parking lot at Woody's. "What are we doing here?"

"Just meeting up." Mac held her hand as he led her inside. Could he feel how she trembled?

Then she spotted the friends. Brad and Rachel.

Everything slowed to a standstill while her brain raced a million miles per second. Sue's immediate reaction was to yell "no" and tear from the place. Then she'd have to explain to Mac. She couldn't, not when Brad was his cousin. His cousin. That thought pounded like a sledgehammer.

Then she realized something. Something that gave her a drop of courage. Brad didn't want Rachel to know, either. As long as she stayed with Mac and Rachel, Brad wouldn't dare try anything.

Grabbing tighter to that hope and Mac's hand, she followed him to the table.

Mac glanced over at Sue whose face had grown pale. Couple that with how she gripped his hand, she definitely was ill at ease. Maybe something more, though he couldn't imagine what it could be. She'd gotten along with Mom just fine. Of course, he'd already figured out that Sue wasn't an extrovert, so perhaps meeting so many people had overwhelmed her.

He should've told Smitty no, but from the moment that Rachel mentioned to him about Sue, Smitty had insisted they needed to double date.

You'd think his cousin would have some inkling of how uncomfortable being around him and Rachel together would make him. However, not as much as Mac would have guessed. That was the weird thing. No streaks of jealousy, no wanting to punch Smitty for stealing his girl while he was laid up in a hospital bed recovering from trauma or working his butt off to learn to walk wearing a fake foot. But then, that was Smitty. He acted like everything he did that wounded Mac was an oops. Then he moved on and figured so should Mac. Well, now that he'd found Sue, moving on was exactly what Mac wanted to do with this extraordinary woman.

Maybe he should tell Smitty some other time and take Sue where there weren't so many people.

Rachel waved and motioned them over.

Smitty merely grinned, like he'd beaten another rap.

Well, five minutes. Mac could give them that. He let Sue slip into the booth first before sliding in after.

"Yay, you made it." Rachel smiled as if world peace had been declared. Maybe she felt that way, less guilty because Mac was now happy.

Sue grabbed a menu and buried her nose in it.

"So, how did you kids meet?" What was with Smitty? His cousin was a year younger than Mac. "This has to be a great story. I don't remember anyone catching my cuz's attention before."

Smitty had selective memory, considering he was fully aware of how Mac felt about Rachel and still he'd taken advantage of Mac's foolish request to check in on her while he was overseas. Yeah, he'd taken real good care of Mac's girl. One thing was for sure, Smitty wouldn't get within a stone's throw of Sue.

"You know that music class I'm taking? The professor also works at a church, and I had to go meet with him there. Sue's the church secretary. When I came out, her car wasn't working."

"So you turned into Sir Galahad and fixed everything and stole her heart, is it?" Smitty's cynicism materialized in a smirk.

Sue lowered her menu. "Yes. He was a gentleman and took care of my Beetle."

"Oh, you have a VW? Mac used to have one too. No wonder. I think he worked on his more often than he drove it." Rachel grinned, and he could tell she was thinking of the times she tried to help him only to get grease on her face.

"Yes. That was a stroke of good luck. I haven't had any problems since Mac fixed it." Sue leaned closer to him and squeezed his hand.

Not that he minded. If she needed him to be her security blanket, that's what he'd be.

"Hon, give me a quarter. I want to play the jukebox."

Smitty huffed but dug out a coin and slapped it in Rachel's hand before standing to let her out of the booth.

Mac couldn't miss her wounded expression as she left to choose her music.

"So, your name is Smitty? Is it like Mac, part of your last name?" Sue had a strange, unreadable glimmer in her eye.

"Sorta, but no. My real name is Bradley Smith Heflin III. But my old man is Brad, and Gramps was Bradley, so I got labeled with Smitty. The whole family calls me that, but in class I had to go by a form of my legal first name. That was the rule."

The light flipped on. "Hey, that's right, you two went to the same high school. Did you know each other there?" Mac glanced from face to face.

"No." They both replied at the same time.

Then Smitty added. "Not then." His grin grew wicked.

Sue's face drained of color.

"What do you mean, not then?" Mac had a bad churning in his chest. Something wasn't right.

"I mean, I didn't know Sue back in high school."

"Oh, I see." Mac didn't really, but he recognized the signs. Smitty was up to no good.

"Then later, I got to know her." Smitty's eyebrows danced.

Sue's grip on Mac's hand verged on breakage. "Can we go?"

"So you've met before today. You already know each other." Mac's heart thudded a Morse Code message, *Danger*.

"Oh, yeah. I know sweet Sue."

"Mac, let's go." Sue pushed him to get up.

He should be doing as Sue wanted, but glutton for punishment that he was, Mac didn't budge. "What do you mean?"

"C'mon, man. What do you think I mean?" Smitty leaned forward to touch Sue, but she slapped his hand. "Aww, Susie Q, we were so good together."

Now Mac stood and pulled Sue behind him. "Knock it off."

Smitty rose too. "Or what, cuz? You gonna hit me?"

"What's going on?" Rachel returned and stared at each of them.

"Nothing. We were just leaving." Mac turned toward the exit, keeping Sue away from Smitty.

Once they reached outside, Mac felt the grab on his shoulder. He'd promised his father he'd never throw the first punch. The last one? Sure. But not the first. As far as he was concerned, that grip counted. Mac spun and landed a fist on Smitty's jaw.

Smitty shook it off and grinned. "This has been coming for a long time, cuz. Now you're gonna get it." All at once he barreled head first into Mac's chest, knocking him off his feet, into the gravel.

Scanning the gathering crowd, Mac finally landed on Sue, whose eyes were now saucers. Then he caught where her vision focused, freezing his breath in his lungs. His pant leg. Stupid bell bottoms. The flipped-back flare revealed his prosthesis. With so many standing around, everyone saw. *Everyone. Saw.*

"Leave him alone!"

Mac raised his gaze to find Sue whaling the crap out of Smitty with her bag, swinging it over and over, while he cowered, covering his head.

"Sue." She didn't need to fight his battles.

Sue ceased her attack, pulled her purse strap onto her shoulder, and turned, marching toward the highway.

Smitty popped up, heading after her.

"No!" Mac scrambled to his feet, racing for his cousin before he could touch her.

Smitty latched onto Sue's arm, yanking her around.

She slapped him, and Smitty raised his hand to her.

Mac wrenched that hand behind his back, forcing Smitty to face him. "Leave her alone."

"Fine. If you want to be one of a dozen, go ahead. Bet she's learned a trick or—"

Mac's fist connected with Smitty's big mouth.

Smitty hit the gravel.

Rachel ran up, standing over him. For a second, Mac thought she was going to kneel and help his cousin. Instead, she twisted off her ring, dropped it on him, and stormed back toward Woody's.

Sue, on the other hand, was no longer in the parking lot. He searched the area until he spotted her walking along the highway toward her place.

He hustled for his bike, started it, and spun gravel pulling out. A minute later, he drew up alongside her. "Get on."

Sue shook her head, focused straight forward, and kept stomping through the weeds along the highway's shoulder.

"Now. I'm not going away, and I don't want to walk this bike for ten miles. So get on."

Sue stopped, still, a statue in the twilight.

He was embarrassed enough to want to ride off and not see anyone for a very long time, but if something were to happen to her, he'd never forgive himself. He tried a gentler approach. "Let's go, Sue."

She turned and walked his way, never raising her gaze from the ground. After settling onto the seat behind him, she managed to hang on yet keep some distance.

The loss was palpable.

No more words were uttered the entire trip. When he pulled up in front of her apartment, she climbed off and headed for her door.

"Sue?"

She stopped, and it took a few seconds before she turned to face him. "What I told you was the truth. I just never told you everything about Brad, or Smitty, or whatever you call him. I thought he loved me. Then I found him with Rachel. I never knew her name until today. And I hate myself more because she didn't deserve— She's too nice for him."

"Maybe." Maybe they deserved each other.

"Anyway, you saw me home. Night, Mac." She trudged inside and the air grew cold.

Mac spun his bike around and rode to clear his head, though he'd run out of gas long before that happened.

Chapter 14

Friday, July 21, 1972

Sue tore the weekend pages from her desk calendar and dropped them into the trash, making sure everything was set for Monday before gathering her purse from the drawer. A quick look around confirmed she hadn't missed anything. Desk clean. Check. Blinds straightened. Check. The church office was in good shape.

Why wouldn't it be? There was nothing to distract her from her duties. No motorcycle-riding diversion sporting a handlebar mustache and dimples with the power to make women swoon showing up with candy or his guitar to take her mind off what she was being paid to do. There hadn't been one for seventeen days, not that Sue was counting.

Mac didn't even come on Wednesdays to help with the kids any more. When the girls asked where he was, she shrugged. What she wanted to do was to beg them to never make a mistake like hers because it could cost. Dearly.

Maybe she should have told Mac about her one slip with Brad. But then, she hadn't known they were cousins. It all would have ended the same.

She locked the office and headed for her Beetle. Even that reminded her of him, his kindness, his silly sense of humor. Since he'd owned one, it was another thing that had whispered they might belong together. Everywhere she turned, something made that connection and, voila, he was on her mind again.

Tracy had tried to help. She'd offered to beat Mac up. Right. But even if she were able, he didn't deserve it. He'd stood up for her and delivered her safely home before he walked out of her life. Now Sue was terrified to go anywhere she might bump into him. What would she say? What would he? Or would they walk past each other as if strangers?

So it was work and home. Church on Sunday, but she sat on the back pew, unsuited to be closer to the front. Shame was a hair shirt that never came off.

As she started her ignition, Sue noticed a familiar truck parked at the opposite end of the parking lot. Where was he? She drove around to the main building, in front of the entrance to the narthex. Music filtered out through the doors. Mac must be working on his project.

She shut down her car, drawn toward the door, staying out of the line of sight of anyone inside. The melody captivated her, not only because she knew he composed it, but for the beauty. Sue closed her eyes and let it pour over her. It lifted her above the pain of stupid choices and lifelong regrets, carrying her soul to a place of pulchritude and peace as she swayed in rhythm.

"Sue?"

Her eyes flew open. He stood inside the darkened narthex.

She raced for her Bug and started it, exiting the parking lot as quickly as possible.

But when she glanced back, before turning onto the street, what she saw shattered her heart even more. If that were possible.

Mac hadn't followed her.

The realization stung her eyes and made her nose drip. She blinked and prayed she'd make it home without causing an accident.

God answered that prayer.

"Sue? Is that you?" Tracy called from her bedroom.

"Yes." No need to elaborate. All Sue wanted to do was climb into her bed and live there. At least until Sunday morning when she forced herself to go to church. Because whether she liked it or not, she needed to be there.

"What sounds good for dinner?"

Sue opened Tracy's door wider or tried to. Everything her roomie owned was pulled from her closet and dresser drawers. "What are you doing?"

"Oh, I decided to get rid of what I'm not wearing, pare down. I have too much stuff, and I'm sure there are others who might use these things." What sorting method was she using? Throw at the wall and see what sticks?

"But it's your turn to fix dinner. How are you going to get out of here?" Sue scanned the piles that looked as if the J.C. Penney's junior department had exploded.

Tracy stood, stepping over heaps to come closer. "Well, that's just it. I was hoping you'd fix something." She put her hands together as if in prayer and flashed a wide grin. "Pretty please?"

That was the last thing Sue wanted to do. Or maybe one of the last things because she could think of several other objectionable tasks far worse. "Fine. However, I'm not cooking. You have a choice of a salad or a PB and J."

"Whatever you want to fix is fine. I'm just grateful you're willing to do it. Oh, your brother called."

Danny? "When? Did he say what he wanted?"

"About five minutes before you walked in. See, I was able to get out of the room to answer the phone. He didn't say, just asked for you to call him back."

"Thanks. I will." Sue stepped over piles to exit. After changing out of her work clothes into an old pair of jeans and a tank top, she returned to the kitchen and dialed the number, hugging the receiver between her ear and shoulder so she could make Tracy a sandwich.

Her brother answered on the third ring. "Hello?"

"Danny, Tracy said you called."

There was a pause. "Hey, figured you'd want to know. Pop got hurt on the job, and they've taken him to St Joe's. I'd be there, but I don't have a way."

"I'm coming. I'll pick you up." Sue hung up the phone, cut the sandwich, and took it to Tracy. "Dad's in the hospital. I've got to go."

"Oh, Sue, I'm so sorry. Is there anything I can do?"

A million wishes flashed through Sue's mind. "Just pray. I'm on my way to get Danny and then go to St. Joe's. Setting your sandwich here on your dresser."

Tracy leaped over her piles to give Sue a hug. "Don't worry about that. I'll be praying. Let me know, 'kay?"

Sue nodded, grabbed her purse, and began her trek to Alto.

Danny was ready. It wasn't the first time she'd transported him, but it wasn't easy getting the wheelchair behind their seats. It was too big for the trunk. Danny helped all he could, and she was surprised at the strength he'd acquired in his arms. But now they had to drive back almost to where she'd started out.

"You're awful quiet, sis. What's up?"

Sue shook her head. "Nothing. Only tired. Long week."

"Hmm." She could feel Danny's eyes staring at her.

"What?"

"Just thinking. I haven't heard you talk about your friend."

Sue stiffened. "My friend?"

"Yeah, Mac. I had a feeling there was more to your story, but you didn't say word one."

What was she supposed to tell her brother? Did he have a clue what had happened to her? Or at least the truth of what happened? No doubt her father had filled him in on how horrid she was.

"Sue? Did he hurt you?"

"No, nothing like that. He's kind and good, even when I messed up."

"How did you mess up?"

She chewed her lip. Would she lose Danny now?

"You can tell me anything, you know that. There's nothing that will make me stop loving you."

Great, now she was crying and trying to drive. Seriously, she seemed to be bursting into tears every two minutes. Sue pulled into the first parking lot she found, wiped her eyes, and turned to face her brother. She cleared her throat. "Dad thinks I'm pretty loose. But I only messed up once with a guy I thought was about to ask me to marry him. I even imagined I was in love with him, though I now realize that it was more fantasy than the real thing."

She peeked at Danny. His expression hadn't changed, so she swiped at her cheek and went on. "I thought he'd cheated on me but learned he was already engaged, and he was cheating on her with me. Great ego booster that. So when I moved to Kokomo, I worked hard for a fresh start. Then I met Mac. I told him most of this story." Sue paused, checking if he understood. "Turns out, Mac and this other guy are cousins. There was a huge fight. Mac stood up for me, even made sure I got home safe. Then he dropped off the face of the earth."

"Have you tried to call him?"

She shook her head. "He knows how to find me."

"Maybe he thinks you don't want him to try."

She hadn't thought of that. "I guess. He's got a lot of things he's working on anyway. I'd just be in the way."

"Not if he feels for you the same as you feel for him."

"You don't understand. He's amazing. I'm a mess. Mac's better off without me."

Danny took her hands, holding them tight between his own. "Have you looked in the mirror lately? I see an incredibly brilliant woman, capable of enormous love and goodness. It's time you forgave yourself and stepped out to try your hand at the skills you worked too hard to attain."

Sue sniffed. "You've always been my champion."

"I always will be. Let's go check on Pop, and then you and I can brainstorm some ideas on the way home." He patted her hands before releasing them.

She restarted her Bug and pulled back out, heading for Kokomo and St. Joe's.

It took extra effort, but between the two of them, Danny got situated in his wheelchair, and she pushed him up to the reception desk. "We're here to visit Charles Mitchell."

The receptionist looked up the room and gave them directions. Their father was on the third floor.

When they got close, Sue faltered. "Maybe you ought to go in by yourself first."

"Why? He'll be glad you're here."

"No, he's never glad to see me. It's best if I wait out here."

Danny snorted. "He's going to want to know how I got here. Like I could drive myself? C'mon. It'll be fine."

Before she could answer, a nurse stepped out of their father's room. "Are you here for Mr. Mitchell?"

She and her brother nodded.

"He's resting, so please don't stay long."

"What happened? All we heard was that he got hurt at work." Sue squeezed Danny's shoulder.

He reached up and gripped her hand. "I couldn't get any information from the caller."

The nurse seemed to search their faces. "You are his children?"

"Yes." They both replied.

"Mr. Mitchell had become agitated with an employee, who I understand was giving him a hard time. Somehow, while arguing with the other man, Mr. Mitchell suffered a heart attack. As I said, he is resting, but he's asked about both of you. I think he was concerned that you wouldn't know where he was. It will put his mind at ease to see you. Go on in, but don't stay too long." She left then as someone motioned from the nurses' station.

Sue chewed at her knuckle. "What if I make it worse going in there, Danny?"

"How about if I wheel in and ask if he wants to see you?"

It was a better idea than just popping in, but if he refused, she didn't know if her heart could take another rejection. "Okay, I'll stay by the door."

Danny wheeled himself into the room, up to their father's bed.

Sue watched him lean in close and knew he was speaking softly.

Suddenly, he turned and waved her forward.

As she got closer, she heard Dad whispering her name over and over.

"I'm here, Dad."

"Thank God, you came. I didn't think you'd ever want to see me again." Tears dripped down his pale face.

"Oh, Daddy, I'll always be here for you. I love you."

"I love you, my little Susie."

She kissed him on the forehead and let him capture her hand that he brought to his lips.

How could she have missed this? Was it fear of dying that made him want to forgive her? Whatever it was, it was an answer to prayer.

Two prayers answered tonight.

Maybe she should take a chance and pray about something else.

About someone else.

Mac rubbed at the nape of his neck and returned to the sanctuary. "I'm sorry about that. Thought I saw someone. Let's take it from section B."

No one objected or commented on his racing out a few moments ago. Instead, like professionals, they picked up where he'd told them, producing harmonies Mac had only enjoyed in his head until these kind folks had agreed to help him. He had no money to pay them, which he'd initially figured was a deal-breaker, but they were all still excited. It took a couple of weeks for everyone's schedule to mesh, but now that they were committed, the results blew Mac away.

Windy had suggested a violinist instead of a second guitar, and that was a stroke of genius. Just hearing George play his part made such a difference, adding another layer to the piece.

Mac had shied away from a dictator image. Rather he had encouraged the group to share ideas, which led to them all becoming friends and invested in the outcome.

"We can stop for tonight." Mac didn't know what else to have them do. They were amazingly gifted with what they had. But that was the problem. What they had. He still needed to put the finishing touches on the final piece, the one with the lyrics. That was what held him up, the words.

"Are we on for tomorrow? Saturday morning at 9:30?" Eve, the flautist, had her calendar out. She was a secretary for the savings and loan president and was the most organized person he'd ever met. Almost. His mind slipped off to Sue. Why had she run? He knew before he finished asking himself. He'd embarrassed her, and she didn't want anything to do with him.

"Yes, my dad will meet us to let us in and lock up after." Windy answered Eve's question. He would have if his mind hadn't decided to take a stroll.

At least that got him back to the present. "Thanks, everyone. I can't tell you how much this means."

The group offered encouraging words. "Enjoying myself." "Beautiful music." "This is a pleasure." Then they packed up and headed out until only Windy and Mac stood at the church's front doors.

"So, have you finished that last piece?" Windy waited for her father to pick her up. Apparently, Professor Day liked to work late in his office when his wife, Cheryl, had play practice with the Civic Theatre.

Mac shook his head. "The words aren't coming like I hoped. I'm better at writing music than poetry." He scuffed his prosthetic foot against the concrete slab.

"It doesn't have to rhyme."

True, but it was the heart of the message that he couldn't grasp.

"What do you hear in the songs we're playing?"

That he knew. "Second chances. How what we label as ugly can be turned into beauty, even harmony, when uniqueness is allowed to shine."

"Then that's what you say. Put words to your music. But I ought to say something else."

"What's that?" Mac wasn't sure he really wanted to know.

"You should be the one to play and sing it. This is your heart message. It needs to come from you. I'll still perform it, if necessary, but really consider it."

If he needed her to? Was she kidding? There was no way he'd get in front of an audience and pour out from his core. The last thing he wanted was to be that visible, really seen. He was too scarred, too scared. "I'll think about it, but I doubt I'll change my mind." And he would think about it. About how he'd convince Windy that there was no way he could perform it.

"Oh, I see Dad coming. Thanks for waiting with me." Windy flashed a smile and hustled over to meet her father.

Mac headed for his truck. Too much on his mind to allow him to head straight home to an empty, silent house. He turned on the radio, letting the noise of Neil Diamond's "Song Sung Blue" soothe his senses. "A Horse with No Name" followed, and Mac could picture himself riding the desert without other humans in sight. Just becoming one with the landscape. But then DJ Kris Eric Stevens had to go and put Climax's "Precious and Few" on, jolting Mac from some solitary ride to seeing Sue's face in the moonlight right before she turned away from him. For good.

He'd let her down.

Laying there on the ground while she stood up for him.

She'd never look at him the same way as she did when he kissed her under that sycamore at Ferguson House. Their time had been too short, the memories too few, but oh, so precious—minus the last ones when he tanked it all.

The only good to come out of the fiasco was that he didn't need to deal with Smitty at the mill every day. Apparently his cousin went back into Woody's, got drunk and caused a scene that led to his arrest. Continental Steel fired him for missed work. Granted, he was in jail and unable to get to his job. Smitty had been smart enough not to call him or his mother for bail money. His father had cut him off a couple years ago. So he had to wait behind bars until his case was heard and then he was found guilty. Smitty wouldn't be bothering Mac for the foreseeable future. Some Independence Day.

The Carpenters had just started "Hurting Each Other" as he turned into the driveway. Not his, but Elmer's. It had been a while since he'd seen his buddy, and by this time, the guy had to be home. Mac was glad to turn off that song along with his engine.

The front door opened, and Elmer stepped out, his hand holding a salute across his eyebrows as he peered into the semi-dark. "That you, Mac?"

"Yeah. Took a chance you'd be home. Are you busy?"

"Nah, just watching TV. *The Brady Bunch*. You know Misty. She loves that show." Elmer shook his head and motioned Mac toward the house. "C'mon up."

Mac didn't need to be told twice. Despite the higher temperatures during the day, the evening cooled enough to make sitting on Elmer's porch comfortable.

"Can I get you something to drink?"

"Nah, thanks though." Mac sat on the red and white webbed folding chair, giving him a great view of nature's lightning bug show.

Elmer took the other one and leaned back, waiting for Mac to begin.

"Things fell apart with Sue. I blew it. And that music class I'm taking requires me to write at least one song with lyrics. I'm struggling. Can't concentrate on composing and can't stop thinking about Sue."

Elmer still didn't speak. At least he leaned forward, giving Mac his full attention, but what Mac needed was some answers.

"I'm stuck. You always have great advice. Can't you figure out something?"

Elmer scratched his head. "Where'd you come up with the idea that I'm some sort of guru with wisdom for the ages? I just tell it like I see it."

"So, how do you see it?"

"First, I don't think I've got all the puzzle pieces to understand what happened with Sue, and I'll bet you don't either. As for your music, do you have to write about something in particular?"

Mac shook his head. "Not really. It's my recital."

"Good then. If you can't tell Sue in person all you want to say, put it to music. Maybe she'll go see your program and get your message. Just an idea."

Just a brilliant idea. Could he do that? Could Mac actually write out what he wanted to say to Sue? If she realized how much he cared, maybe she'd not be so embarrassed by his shortcomings. "Thanks, man. That might work. And don't worry about what your nephew says about you, you're all right."

Elmer stood. "My nephew? What did that little twerp say? I gave him a job, I'm training him for a career, and he's talking trash behind my back?"

Mac stood too. "Hey, man, just joshing you."

Now Elmer cracked up. "You are too easy. See ya on the flip side, man. Peace." He patted Mac's shoulder.

"Yeah, see ya." Mac hopped down the steps and into his truck. A plan was forming. It might take him all night, but at least he didn't have to work in the morning, and he could give the completed piece to Windy to practice. She was the one who needed to sing the song.

It was possible he pushed the speed limit a bit, or a lot, but he made it home with his guitar and started crafting what he wanted to tell Sue. Writing it for her was personal, private, but if he penned it just right, no one would know who the message was for. Only her.

But how could he make sure she would hear his words?

Another idea took hold. He'd have to be careful how he proceeded. It also meant getting the final date for the recital on the calendar.

Sue normally handled things like that. Would Professor Day do it for him? He needed to take a chance.

Now the pieces were moving into place. All he had to do was make the stuff in his head a reality. Time to get to work.

Four hours later, Mac fell into bed, making sure his alarm was set to wake him for rehearsal. He instantly dropped off to sleep with dreams of Sue. She was smiling, happy, even playful. They laughed, teased, but then he made the mistake of taking her in his arms. Just as he was about to kiss her, she turned away. She was crying, and he no longer saw her face. As he reached for her, she shook her head and ran. He tried to run, but he only had one foot. As that hit him, he toppled over and lay on the ground while Smitty sneered over him. "Can't even stand on your own two feet. You don't have two feet. You aren't man enough for her. She can't want you after me." Then Smitty chased Sue while Mac struggled to stand. On one foot.

The clanging alarm roused him, and he was never so glad to wake up.

What if she didn't want only part of a man? Maybe she wanted a whole man. That's what she deserved. A whole man. He was stupid to think this song would do any good.

Mac grabbed a shower and got ready, remembering to bring the new piece to the rehearsal. Professor Day waited with Windy as he pulled up, offering the perfect opportunity to request a date on the calendar. He'd picked it out. August 2nd. If that was too soon, then he'd take the ninth.

His professor liked the plan. "I think giving the Wednesday night teachers an evening off would be great. People would already be coming here. They could have dinner and a concert. Might have to keep the baby nursery through kindergarten classes available so there'll be fewer interruptions, but I like your idea and that you are getting this scheduled early. Let me talk with the pastor just to make sure, and I'll let you know which date is best. Should be able to tell you after rehearsal today."

Mac thanked him and led his musicians into the sanctuary. Once everyone was in place, he handed Windy his new composition. "Check it out when you get home."

"I will." She set it beneath her purse on top of the upright piano and opened the music for what they'd planned to practice. "All ready?"

The others echoed in answer. "Ready."

The only problem was that they might be, but Mac wasn't sure he was. Or if he ever could be.

Chapter 15

Wednesday, August 2, 1972

"Thank you for calling, Mrs. Hartman." Sue actually had a nice conversation with the matron. Only weeks ago, the woman had been criticizing Sue's performance in the office. Now she was solicitous, wanting Sue to know that she and her family were in her prayers. And that wasn't the first phone call. People cared that Dad had a heart attack. At least he was out of the hospital recovering and she was with him. Things had improved on the home front, finally.

Sue moved back into her old room in Alto to be available evenings and overnight—a temporary fix until Dad was better. Danny handled most things during the day, and Dad wasn't bedfast. He just rested a lot but daily worked toward more activity. His cardiologist was pleased with his progress, and though Dad would need to take early retirement, his pension would help him get along. She might be able to return to the apartment with Tracy in another month. Basically, as soon as the doctor cleared Dad to start driving again.

It was weird the first night or two in Alto, way too familiar yet strange. It didn't matter though. Sue was determined to hang tight to the cord of her life in Kokomo. She continued to work at the church and attended services here.

Last Sunday, Dad and Danny made it to church with her. That's how the congregation learned what had happened. Seriously, entering with Danny in a wheelchair and Dad with his walker, they made quite the show. Several people greeted them. Of course, some only wanted the scoop, but others were genuinely moved. Like Mrs. Hartman. God bless her.

The office door opened, and Tracy breezed in carrying a brown grocery bag. "I know you, and since I can't keep an eye on making sure you're eating at your house, I figured I should bring you lunch." She plopped her offering on Sue's desk.

"What makes you think I'm not eating?"

"Have you looked in your mirror? Your clothes are a tad roomier."

A tad roomier. She'd heard that phrase before. In fact, just this morning before she left for work. "You've been talking to Danny."

"So what if I have? He's a wealth of information about you."

Her brother was gossiping? Sharing her confidences?

"Oh, not personal stuff. You can trust him, though if there are things like that—and I bet there are—you could've told me too. However, I'm not plying you with this wonderful cornucopia of luncheon cuisine to gather dirt. I'm worried about you, and so is Danny."

Sue had to smile. Those two were her closest allies. "Actually, you got all my gory details when I came home on the Fourth. There's really nothing else you don't already know." Except for maybe how Danny's encouragement to try applying her hard-earned skills where she'd be able to work in her passion kept flashing through her brain. When she wasn't wondering what Mac was doing, that was.

"Okay. So, check out what I brought you." Tracy rested her hands at her hips, grinning.

Sue eyed her. Her roomie's enthusiasm made her more than curious as she unrolled the top of the bag. She lifted out a Tupperware bowl of salad with a small container of Italian dressing first. There was even a fork taped to the salad's lid. Sue checked the bag for the next item, a thermos.

"That's gazpacho. Just the way you like it, though I included a few croûtons in a baggie. You know you want to, and you've lost enough weight over the last few weeks that it won't hurt you in the least."

One more small square Tupperware container remained. Sue lifted it to find two no-bake cookies. She recognized them from the recipe she'd shared with Tracy, one that she'd learned in Girl Scouts way back in the day. Sue had confessed that they were her weakness and she couldn't be around them anymore.

"Oh, Tracy, I can't eat these. I especially can't eat two. This isn't fair. You've loaded this with all my favorite things and gave me huge portions."

"Who said it was all for you? Don't I get any for my good deed?"

Sue chuckled. "Of course you do. Pull up a chair, but I only saw a single fork and one cup on the thermos."

Tracy opened her shoulder bag and pulled out a mug and her own utensil. "Voila! Now let's eat."

After Sue divided the food, Tracy asked the blessing, and they both dug in.

"Make sure you put those croûtons in your gazpacho. I'm watching."

“Yes, ma’am.” Would her stomach be able to handle this after all the meals she’d skipped lately? “I appreciate this a lot, Trace, but please don’t expect me to clean my plate.”

“I don’t. However, you will eat something. You can save the rest for later if you want. More importantly, you need to start eating regular meals. Even if they are smaller at first. Putting a little weight back on won’t hurt you, and I know you are active enough with all your walking and exercising that you’ll not mess up.” Tracy leaned forward. “I believe in you.”

What? Tracy believed in her? When was the last time anyone had ever said that to her?

“Oh, you have company.” Gloria Mussing came in from the back.

“You’ve met my friend Tracy, right? She brought me lunch today.”

“I’m glad she did. I was just about to suggest we go out so I could make sure you eat.” Gloria pulled up a chair. “We need to talk, and I believe we should include Tracy in this conversation since she’s looking out for you too.”

The food Sue had just eaten turned to lead in her stomach. “Oh? Is there a problem? I thought you said I was doing a good job.”

“Oh, Sue, you are. That’s not it. Although your excellent abilities, I believe, are being wasted. You, my dear, are working way beneath your potential. Now don’t get me wrong. I love knowing that this office is run with efficiency. I can’t fault a single thing you do here, but you and I both know you are equipped for much bigger things.”

Sue’s heart clenched. If she were out of a job, what would she do? “Am I being fired?”

"No, oh, no. I'd never do that. But you should start hunting for a position that will challenge you and ignite your passion. God has broader plans for you. Don't hide from His gifts." Gloria took Sue's hand. "I've been praying about this ever since God put this notion in my brain. I believe there is something bigger out there for you."

Sue's eyes burned as she blinked away the unwanted tears. Gloria had used the word passion. Was God trying to get a message to her? "My brother said almost the same thing recently."

"Then this is your confirmation, Sue." Tracy's face glowed with animation. "You've always wanted to work in a museum. We can make a list—"

"I know where I want to work. It's just that... I'm not sure I'm the right fit."

Gloria gave a gentle squeeze to Sue's fingers. "What makes you say that?"

Sue stared at her desk. There was no way she'd tell her pastor's wife everything. Maybe she could be vague. "I've made some mistakes in my life. Some serious ones. You all have accepted me here, and I feel safe."

"Everyone blunders. I'll bet more seriously than you, but the beauty of God's love and Jesus's sacrifice is that it all has been atoned for and is no longer remembered. You are forgiven. Until you accept this for yourself, it's like having a wrapped present sitting on your shelf and never opening the most precious gift you could ever receive. Let's start there, Sue. Unwrap God's gift of forgiveness, let Him dress you in the white robe of His righteousness. It's not what others say or think, or even what you say or think. It is what He says and thinks, and He loves you."

There was no holding back the tears now.

Tracy came around the desk and wrapped her in a hug.

Gloria stood on Sue's other side and stroked her hair. "Pray with me, Sue?"

Sue sniffed and nodded.

"Repeat my words. I'll pray them for you first. Father, I love You and I am sorry for how I hurt You." She paused, allowing Sue to make the words her own. "I ask Your forgiveness and that You'd wash me clean by the blood of Jesus." Another pause before she continued. "I accept Your gift of forgiveness and choose to forgive myself, moving forward this day to listen to Your direction and, with Your help, to remain obedient to Your will. In Jesus's name I pray."

"Amen." Oh, yes, amen. Sue raised her head, wiped her palms over her eyes, and stood. "Thank you, Gloria."

The pastor's wife pulled her into an embrace. "Never forget who you are and Whose you are. A child of the King of the Universe. A princess by royal decree."

She didn't feel like a princess, but Sue did feel more loved than she had in her whole life. And she felt clean. Strong and clean. Was there anything she couldn't do?

"Well, I have a few more things to finish before we have dinner and the concert. I've heard through the grapevine that the music is amazing. Jim has listened in a few times with Aaron, and they are both very excited."

The thought of Mac squeezed at Sue's heart. God had worked so much out, especially in the last half hour, but getting her and Mac back together might not be in His plans. Could she move forward even if her future didn't include Mac? "If Aaron is raving about it, Mac must be about to get a good grade." Sue attempted a smile. She only wished the best for him.

"That's a given. I'll see you at dinner or the concert." Gloria waved as she left the room.

"Are you excited to hear Mac's presentation?" Hope lit Tracy's face, and Sue knew her friend was plotting.

"It's not a good idea."

"Didn't we just deal with all that?"

It was time for a change of subject. "By the way, aren't you due back at work?"

"Nope, I took the day off. Said I needed to get some things done here. Besides, I've clocked in enough overtime in the last month that they were happy for me to take some time. So I'm here for the duration."

Oh, lovely. "Well, then, I'll put you to work, unless you'd rather go spend your day doing activities you'd like?" Please?

"I'm at your command. Plus, I'm great at sorting, or I can stuff envelopes. Or..." Tracy shrugged.

Sue could just imagine how Tracy would sort out something—piles of folders and sheets of paper everywhere. True, somehow it all came back together in a much more organized manner, but her methods made Sue crazy, and she could not have her well-run office destroyed. "I've been putting this job off, so you're the perfect person to do it. The programs for tonight need to be folded and bound into stacks of fifty. Can you manage that?"

"Pshaw. Piece of cake."

Sue pointed to where the delivery box from the printer sat in the room's corner. "You may use the coffee table here, or there's a taller table in the workroom." Choose the workroom.

"Here is fine."

"It could wreck your back bending over doing that."

Tracy wouldn't take the bait, like she was determined to never leave Sue's side. "I'm used to it from the shop. I'll get at it."

To Tracy's credit, she did, getting all two hundred of the programs ready. As she finished the last one, she brought it to Sue's desk. "Want to check it out?" Ignoring the fact Sue was typing something, Tracy fanned the brochure in front of her face.

"Hey, I'm working here."

"It only takes a sec to look it over." Tracy shoved it at her again.

"Please, I don't—can't. Let it go, Trace."

"Fine. Where do you want me to put them?"

"In the narthex on the table to the right of the big doors. The greeters will find them there."

Tracy scooped up the bound sets and left through the rear door.

Sue inhaled and blew it out. Having her friend gone for a moment gave her breathing room. Tracy was up to something, she could tell. Then, when the girl wasn't back immediately, Sue began to wonder.

Twenty minutes later, Tracy returned. She probably ran into someone and got to talking. That's what usually happened. Her roomie had yet to meet a stranger.

Sue came up with odd jobs for Tracy until it was time to shut down the office and go help with dinner, just as she'd done every week since she started working for the church. Sue jumped in to ready the drinks. The ladies were so sweet to her, more so than usual. Probably because most of them had met her dad and brother on Sunday.

Tracy made her get a plate of dinner and eagle-eyed her until she'd eaten a few bites. But after having had lunch, she wasn't that hungry. Plus, with the way her friend was behaving, Sue couldn't help the nerves that began to tingle in her stomach, making food intake difficult.

Apparently Tracy understood and didn't push too hard, accepting a bite or two as enough. When Sue claimed done and dumped her plate, Tracy followed suit and then linked arms with her. "I need to see you in the restroom."

Instead of taking her to the one in the hall, Tracy led her to the little facility at the back of the kitchen. "Here, put on some makeup. You're looking too pale." She shoved her cosmetic bag at Sue.

"What?"

"Just do it." Again Tracy tried to force the bag into Sue's hands. What in the world?

"I don't want to." What was the point if she was going home to bed? Dad and Danny didn't care how she looked.

Elsie came to the door. "Is she ready yet?"

Tracy glanced over her shoulder. "Not yet. She doesn't want to wear makeup."

The older woman wormed her way into the small room. "Look, there's not a lot of time. You can put it on or one of us will do it for you."

"What are you talking about?" Sue glanced between the two women. What *were* they talking about? Tracy and Elsie concocted a plot? Uh-oh. Her heart pounded as she backed up into the corner. "No, no, no. I am not going."

Elsie called out the door. "Girls, she says she's not coming."

The others were in on it too?

Tracy put her hands on her hips, dropping her voice to a whisper. "You better do your own makeup, or you might end up looking like Clara Bow."

That shot an arrow of fear straight to Sue's heart. "Fine, I'll put on a little, but you need to give me room. No pushing." Maybe if she gave them this much, they'd let her escape Mac's recital.

The ladies backed up, and Sue accepted Tracy's cosmetic bag. There was more in it than Sue would ever use, but she added some blush and mascara and lip gloss. That would have to do. "Better?"

"Yes!" The chorus rang out.

They'd all thought she looked bad?

Tracy brushed at Sue's skirt and adjusted her blouse. "Okay, your work outfit's gonna have to do. It's time to get you over there."

"No. I can't go in these clothes. I need to go home first."

Elsie stepped forward. "No time for that. We can do it the easy way or the hard way. Which will it be?" The rest of the kitchen ladies behind her nodded in agreement as Elsie cracked her knuckles. "Ow. Arthritis."

Sue froze a moment. She couldn't imagine how they might force her, but she also didn't want to find out. Suppose she sat on the back pew. It was where she felt most comfortable in church, anyway. Then once it got dark and the concert started, she'd slip off for home. "Fine. I'll go. But for the record, I'll remember this."

"I'm sure you will, dear." Elsie patted her hand. "Head'em up, move'em out. You're going to make us late."

"What am I, a cow?"

Tracy gave a little shove. "Hush and go."

As it was, they got to the sanctuary just before the lights dimmed. Sue slipped into her favorite pew and was suddenly surrounded by Tracy, Elsie, and the rest of the women. There was no way to escape without them stopping her.

The musicians walked onto the stage and took their places. Windy gave a count of four, and they all played at once.

It was awful.

A shock went through Sue, and she realized she cared that this was a success more than she wanted to.

Then Windy waved her hand and made some signals before she began again at the piano. As she changed keys, she pointed to the guy with the guitar, and he joined in. Soon, there was another key change, and another instrument was incorporated. It continued until all four musicians played together. Then they added variations as harmony emerged.

Someone shoved a program into her hands, and she finally glanced at it. Now it made sense.

Mac listened from the corner as the group played what he'd written. They hadn't missed a note or a beat. He couldn't have imagined it any better. They moved from piece to piece, getting closer to the final number, which tied his gut into knots.

Right before they started, Windy had handed him the sheet music to the song he'd composed, saying she couldn't do it.

"What? This is my grade. I'll fail the class if I don't have this song included. You said you would."

"I know. I'm sorry, Mac. This is from your heart. I'm happy to accompany you on the piano, but you and your guitar need to be out there singing those words. You received the message, now you give it. Don't hold back. Think about the fact that someone out there needs to hear this. It's not about you. It's about that person." Then Windy climbed the steps to join the others and start the concert.

Mac knew who needed the words. He'd written it for her. However, to sing in front of everyone present?

Windy was right. It wasn't about him. It was time he quit worrying what people thought of him and looked beyond himself. No one in the audience was concerned if he was all there or if he left his foot in the Nam. They wouldn't be hoping for him to mess up either. These people applauded after each one of the compositions. Enthusiastically. He'd even overheard someone whisper, "That was beautiful."

Soon, the final note of the-next-to-the-last piece sounded. The audience clapped. That was his cue. Only he was frozen to the wall, unable to make his feet move.

Windy glanced his way and gave an encouraging gesture.

It was now or never. No matter what happened to him, this was for Sue. He sure hoped Tracy and the kitchen ladies had gotten her to come. There was a moment when he would've sworn he saw her slip into the back row, but being so far away, there was no way to tell.

He'd just have to believe God got her there and do this.

Mac stepped forward and all but Windy left the stage. His heartbeat had moved from *adagio* to *andante*, picking up speed the closer he came to the stool and the microphone stand.

Should he say something? Could he get his voice to cooperate if he did? *Think of the audience, think of Sue. It's not about you, it's about her.*

Mac opened his mouth, and no sound came out. *You can do this.*

He tried again. "Good evening, folks. I appreciate, er, all of us here appreciate you coming to listen. This little group practiced and gave so much of their time. Would you give them another hand, please?"

The audience did, and it allowed Mac the moment he needed. As the clapping faded, he continued. "Here is our last number. Thank you." He strummed, turned to Windy and nodded, then began.

I see you staring at the frozen mountain top.
You wonder can you make the climb alone?
But still you can't imagine how to take a step.
When all your support is gone
If I could only hold your hand
And make this climb with you.
We could bring springtime to the frozen mountain top.
Sharing what's good and right and true.
Here in the valley where the pain can stop your heart.
This is where you're growing.
Nothing is easy when you do it all alone.
There's no one cheers bestowing
But if you would just hold my hand
I'll make this climb with you.
And we'll bring springtime to the frozen mountain top.

Sharing what's good and right and true.
Come, climb with me up to the mountain top.
We'll make this trek together.
I am here for you, and you'll be here for me.
Through fair winds and cold weather,
So please come now and take my hand.
We'll climb this, me and you.
And He'll bring springtime to the frozen mountain top.
Sharing what's good and right and true.
And then we'll find it, me and you.

Mac completed the riff at the end with his eyes closed and sat still, almost afraid to move. Was she there? Did she understand what his heart tried to say?

Suddenly, there was a roar of clapping.

He opened his eyes just as Windy touched his shoulder. "You did it." She gave a little squeeze and slipped off the stage, leaving him alone in front of a standing ovation.

Professor Day came to the front, microphone in hand. "Thank you all for coming. Please be seated. I know Mac is thrilled to have such a wonderful response." Aaron glanced at him and then turned back to the crowd and chuckled. "In fact, he might be a little shell-shocked. I also want to say how grateful I am for you all allowing me to bring this talented young man from my class here to Wabash Congregational and for giving him such a warm reception. Enjoy the rest of your evening, and once again, from all the musicians, thank you."

There was another round of applause before most of the people began their walk to the rear of the sanctuary and out the big double doors.

A few made their way to the front, shaking Mac's hand, thumping his shoulder, and offering congratulations on a wonderful presentation.

His mom came, and she gave him a quick pinch on the cheek with a reminder to call.

Elmer and Misty also stopped long enough to shake hands and say congratulations.

So many people with well wishes. He tried to give each person his full attention but couldn't help searching the crowd for that one face, the one he longed to see. Where was she? Did she stay to the end? Had he said the wrong thing?

Then, all at once, he was caught up in a bear hug. "Miss Elsie, Miss Elsie, let me breathe."

She released him and grinned. "I'm going to adopt you. I need another grandson."

"How many do you have?"

"Counting you?"

He nodded, still trying to unobtrusively peek over her shoulder.

"One." Miss Elsie winked, then grew sober. "She left."

"What?" His heart thudded to the floor.

"Oh, hon, she stayed for the whole thing. She didn't want us to see, but she was crying. Trust me, she got your message. Don't give up. It's not over."

Mac rubbed his hand over his face. "I don't know. What else can I do?"

"You need to get her where she's not going anywhere. Talk to her one on one. This was wonderful, and now she knows. Just encourage her to take a chance."

"Miss Elsie, I don't want to coerce her into anything."

His new grandmother shook her white curls. "Oh, no, no forcing. Never you mind. Simply make sure you can talk to her and that she has the opportunity to open up to you."

"How? How do I do that?"

"You're a smart fella. Didn't you just write a whole lot of music? You have brains enough to figure it out." Miss Elsie pinched his cheek, like Mom did, and headed back up the aisle to the exit.

Okay, so she thought he could come up with a strategy, but this had been his plan. Now, what did he do?

Funny how asking brought about the answer. "Thanks, God."

There was nothing he could accomplish before tomorrow after work. But then he'd definitely make sure they had their moment.

Chapter 16

"Where are you going?"

Sue spun around at the voice. Tracy dogged her race to the parking lot.

"I need to get h—"

Tracy grabbed her arm. "That's not home anymore. You told me you were helping only until your dad was strong enough."

"I know. Just a slip of the tongue."

"More like a Freudian slip, if you ask me."

Sue shook free. "Who asked you?"

"Hey. I've been doing everything I can to help you. Why are you pushing me away? Again."

Tracy was right. Sue knew that. Still, her emotions were in such turmoil, how could she be expected to have a reasonable conversation this instant? "It's been too much today. Just too much..." The tears that had browbeaten her all day won another battle. She was such a crybaby.

Fortunately, her best friend was there to hold her while she sobbed. "He sang for me." She sniffed. "He wrote that and sang it for me."

"Yep. I was there." Tracy flashed her a little grin. "He was trying to tell you something."

"He was. But..."

"But what? What has you so worried?"

Sue shrugged. "Everything is changing so fast. This morning I accepted this was my life. I knew I'd be coming back to live with you, but that's not a real change, just returning to something I feel..."

"It feels safe. Right? You don't have to answer questions or mix with a lot of people. It's a secure place to decompress, but you were made for so much more, Sue."

"I have to make that call tomorrow. What with Danny and Gloria both nudging me with the same vernacular, that had to be a God thing."

Tracy nodded. "I agree. What's the problem with Mac?"

"What if he only sees me as Secretary Sue? What if he takes it as if I'm reaching for something beyond my station?"

The derisive snort gave full evidence of Tracy's opinion. "Don't you imagine he has an inkling of who you are? If he cares as much as I'm pretty sure he does, this won't surprise him. In fact, he'll be an even bigger cheerleader than me."

"You think so?" Sue dug in her purse for a tissue before she ended up a total mess.

"I do."

"Fine. I'll talk to him, but I want to find out about the museum first. I don't need anyone hovering and asking questions I can't answer. Once I know, I'll call him."

"Promise?"

Sue hugged Tracy before holding up the Girl Scout sign. "I promise."

However, the drive to Alto had her mind churning up all sorts of reasons to put off talking with Mac. What if he couldn't get past what happened with Brad? That speculation came back with a vengeance. Not to mention that her old bed had developed new lumps that kept her awake half the night so that she woke to her alarm mere minutes after she'd finally drifted off. At least, that's how it seemed.

She was on her second cup of coffee the next morning when Danny rolled into the kitchen. "Mornin', Glory. Must have had a rough night."

"Do I look that bad?"

He shook his head and offered a sympathy smile. "No, I heard you tossing."

"Great, so I kept you up?"

"Nah. Of course, I was forewarned before you got here." Danny reached to pour some coffee, but Sue intercepted, taking care of it for him.

"My best friend has a big mouth."

He accepted the mug, setting it at his place. "Thanks. It wasn't like that. No details, she just wanted to make sure you got home okay and warn me that you'd had a rough day. Want to tell me about it?"

"No, but I will inform you that someone else agrees with you about my looking for a more suitable career."

"Oh?" Danny tried sounding nonchalant while hiding his face behind his mug.

"You already knew."

"Tracy sort of let that part slip. She really is very careful with your confidences but figured I might like to know that the pastor's wife agreed with me. What are you going to do about it?"

Sue sighed. "I planned to phone and ask if there are any openings. Maybe." If her gumption stuck around long enough.

"Good. It's after eight. I'll bet someone is in their office. Call them."

"Here? Now?" Sue's heart rate shot up, making her hands shake.

"Do it. Do it. Do it." He probably would have kept on chanting if she hadn't swatted his shoulder.

"Fine. I will."

Nine hours later, Sue straightened her desk in the church office, put her folders in the file cabinet, and closed the blinds. Another work day completed. The last thing to do was to give the letter to Pastor Mussing. She ran her hand over the white business envelope, knowing this would be the end of her safety net. But there was no other way.

God had to be in it. Everything not only fell into place, but it happened quickly. Just thinking about it left her in awe.

Sue hesitated, then squared her shoulders and knocked on the pastor's office door that was cracked open enough to see inside.

He glanced up and motioned her in. "Hey there, Sue. How can I help you?"

"I need to give you this." She handed over the envelope.

He paused, staring at the rectangle before catching her gaze. "Is this what I think it is?"

Sue nodded. "I've been happy here, but it's time."

"I see."

"I'll still be here for two more weeks. I insisted on that."

Pastor Mussing tapped the envelope against his palm. "I'm grateful for that. Is there anything you need?"

"No, sir. The letter says it all. I best be going. But thank you for the opportunity. This will still be my home church."

He grinned. "Well, I should hope so. We're family now. Go on. We'll talk more later. Have a good evening, Sue."

"Thank you, Pastor." She slipped out, knowing there was no turning back.

After retrieving her purse from the bottom drawer, she exited and locked the door. The pastors all had keys and could either leave through the rear or just relock the front as they left. Soon she'd be returning her set. It had been a sign of trust to her, one she had honored. Though excited about the future, it required the end of her present in order to step into it. And that broke a piece of her heart.

Thursday, August 3, 1972

The afternoon heat sneaked up on Mac, but even before lowering himself to slide under the Bug, those prickles that led to deodorant-killing sweat had started. He swiped his hand across his forehead, leaving his damp hair standing like porcupine quills.

Better get to it. He fiddled with the starter he'd installed.

But as he shimmied back out, a shadow crossed over his legs.

"What do you think you're doing?"

Mac sat up and used her fender to stand. "You talking to me?" He glanced around as if there were multitudes in the parking lot she could choose to speak with.

"Of course I'm talking to you. Did you take something off my car?"

He grinned and held up the part. “Oh, this old thing? It’s called a starter. In fact, it’s the same one I put on a couple of months ago. You remember that, right?”

She winced.

He’d purposely never told her how much he’d paid. Now he watched those wheels spin like crazy in her brain. “I’m sorry. Tell me how much it is, and I’ll pay you.”

He tapped his chin. He could have some fun with this. “Hmm, let me see. What is my price?”

“C’mon, Mac. I just want to get home. It’s a long drive.”

“I heard.” He paused. “Yeah, I figured if you wouldn’t talk to me, I’d dig up my details another way.”

“What do you mean?” Then her face pinked as she knew what he meant. “You set that all up yesterday? You got Tracy and the kitchen ladies to make me go to your concert?”

Uh-oh. “Make you? They were only supposed to let you know you were invited and that I hoped you would come. What did they do?” He stepped toward her. Maybe Tracy and the ladies took their job a little too seriously.

She cleared her throat and glanced away. “Yes, they did that.”

“So you were there?” Another step closer.

Sue nodded, all sorts of emotions roaming over her face as she met his gaze. “You sang your own song.”

“Yeah, I did. Don’t ever want to have to do that again.”

“Why? You were wonderful.” She took a step. Finally.

“You thought so?” Time to be honest. “I was singing for you.”

She blinked repeatedly, but one tear escaped, dripping down her cheek. "I know."

Mac closed the gap and caught the tear with his finger before it dropped from her jaw. "Aw, Secretary Sue, don't cry. I never wanted to hurt you. I thought I'd embarrassed you."

"Oh, no. Never. I thought you weren't interested anymore because of—"

"Don't even say his name. He's an imbecile. You're the one I've dreamed of my whole life." His hand slid down her arm to link their fingers together. "You don't have to be alone." He pulled her close and held her, whispering the words of the song in her ear. "So please come now and take my hand. We'll climb this, me and you. And He'll bring springtime to the frozen mountain top, sharing what's good and right and true. And then we'll find it, me and you."

"Oh, Mac." Sue cupped his cheek as he lowered his lips to hers.

He'd been starved for her affection, taking in her closeness as Independence Day fireworks exploded through him. Her hands slipped around his neck, drawing him closer. She was everything he'd longed for and more when he dared to dream, and she accepted him. Saw him as a whole man. A man who would protect and cherish her. He'd do all that and more.

Someone pulled into the parking lot, and Mac broke off the kiss, drawing her to his side.

The car parked, and Windy got out. "Hey, glad I caught you, Sue. Hi, Mac. I'd been debating about giving you this, and my dad just told me on the phone that you're leaving. He figured you might want it, so I was going to put it on your desk." She handed Sue a manila folder.

Sue lifted the flap as he watched over her shoulder. "What is it?"

"I only have a minute before I pick up Heather, but remember that time you helped me with my new camera? Well, when I came out from the house, I spotted you two and snapped the photo supposing I could give it to you one day. But then I heard you'd stopped seeing each other and that it might not be a good thing—"

"It's us, Mac."

Mac's face heated as he stared at the photo of him kissing Sue. It appeared as passionate as it had felt.

"But look. See that there?" Windy pointed to a red flutter on the branch over their heads. "You got a cardinal. You two are meant to be."

"Isn't that just a superstition?" Sue glanced up at him.

Mac shrugged, clueless.

But Windy smiled. "Maybe. All I know is that the people who kiss under that sycamore and have a cardinal land on that branch when they do seem to find a way to keep their relationship strong. Rather than a superstition, perhaps it's a reminder, like a rainbow. I just thought you'd enjoy it."

Sue traced the bird in the photo with her finger. "Thank you. I do."

"Well, I'd better get back, but before I go, I also wanted to say that you'll be missed. Dad already told me he'll be lost without you."

Mac spun her to him as Windy slipped away. "Where are you going?"

"Oh, about that. You can't call me Secretary Sue anymore." She ran her finger over the logo on his shirt without making eye contact.

"What do you mean? Sue, I don't want to lose you. Not now."

Her finger rose to trace his bottom lip, making his knees want to buckle. "I don't want to lose you either. I just took another job."

"Where? Doing what?"

Sue winked at him. "You are nosy. Has anyone ever told you that?" She continued to run her finger over his lip, making him want to start the fireworks again with another kiss. "You are looking at the soon-to-be curator of the Elwood Haynes Museum." Her speech quickened and Mac felt the excitement running through her.

"Seriously, it was so fast, I thought it was a dream. I called them this morning to see if there were any openings. Turns out they've been interviewing for a few months, but no one had the qualifications they required. I went there on my lunch break, and we talked about my studies and degrees and my ideas for the place. They said they would let me know, but my office phone was ringing as I got back to the church. They offered me the job. I start in two weeks, which gives Pastor Mussing time to find a replacement and the museum a chance to check my references. Mac, I'm going to work in a museum." Sue bounced on her toes.

He picked her up and spun her in a circle. "I'm so proud of you. And you're right. Secretary Sue doesn't fit. Museum Sue doesn't have the same ring." He put her down and took her hand. "What about My Girl Sue?"

She paused and then shyly met his gaze. "Yes, I am your Girl Sue. For as long as you want me."

"For as long as I want you? Then hang on for a long ride with that title. Until maybe we're ready for another." Then he kissed her.

Epilogue

Monday, October 9, 1972

"This is so cool!"

Sue spun toward the young voice, smiling to herself. She shared the sentiments of the fourth grader who was awe-struck at the display their class examined. Sue had led the charge to get this new exhibit set up before the elementary school field trips started rolling in, and it looked to be a success, sparking the wonder she had imagined it would. *Thank You, Lord.*

Just glancing around reminded Sue of how amazing God's provisions were. Here she was in her dream position with a team of employees who shared her vision and drive.

She'd made a few friends, though Tracy and she were as close as ever, and with help from a counselor recommended by Gloria, Sue was maintaining an appropriate weight and exercise routine. Her body image no longer ruled over her.

Even her relationship with Mac had bloomed, making her bloom. It was the first time she'd felt like her true self in a very long time. Not what someone wanted her to be, but who God had created her to be. She didn't know where this thing with Mac might go, though there was no doubt about what she prayed would happen. Mac was good and kind, growing in faith like she was. He never pressured her inappropriately, but he made sure she knew she was desirable, and not just for her looks. Like he'd told her last night, "I love you for who you are inside. The outside is a bonus, a really great bonus, but God created the Sue Mitchell I've fallen for."

It wasn't the first time he'd said he loved her, which gave her hope of more. She had zero doubts she loved him.

Speaking of Mac, he and her brother had turned into good friends. They'd contacted a few other Viet Nam vets in the area and had regular times to get together. Mac said that he hadn't had a flashback since he'd started talking with the guys.

"Hey Sue, you've got company." Teri Crenshaw, her secretary, caught up to her. "I'll stay with the class while you go to the parlor."

Sue thanked her and headed to the front of the Elwood Haynes Museum. Mac stood near the door, watching out one of the lace covered side windows. Just the sight of him made her pulse race. What could have prompted him to not wait until after work? Was something wrong?

He must have heard her because he turned, a big grin making his dimples shine. "You'll never believe this!" Mac crossed the room and picked her up, twirling her around. "I had to come show you."

The suddenness wiped the air from her lungs, so when he put her down, she needed to draw in a breath.

"Are you okay?"

She nodded as a chuckle slipped free. "I was about to ask you that before you left me breathless. This must be big."

He guided her to a maroon velour-tufted settee but paced while she sat. "It is the biggest. I'm..." Mac shook his head. "I'll show you." He pulled out a business envelope and extracted what could only be a check and handed her a typed page.

Sue scanned the letter, then caught his gaze. "You sold the song?"

"Professor Day told me he'd submitted it to some people he knew in Los Angeles, with my permission of course, but I never expected anything to come of it. He'd suggested it might be good for James Taylor or David Loggins. I thought he was just trying to encourage me. But they want your song, plus the rest of what I presented, and offered me a contract for ten more songs. They even have a lyricist to work with me. The check is for what they bought and an advance on the future songs." Mac shook as he finished.

Sue embraced him, pulling his head to hers so their lips met. The fireworks that went off in her every time they kissed did so again. She didn't care where they were, only that he loved her and raced here to share this good news with her. A moment later, she pulled back enough for him to meet her gaze. "I'm so proud of you, and I'm glad others see the talent I know is in you. I can't wait to buy the album and say my boyfriend wrote this."

Mac cupped her cheek. "Boyfriend? Any way we can up that status?"

Sue's heart began an erratic rhythm as he steadied himself with the Demilune table to lower to one knee.

"My Girl Sue, I can't believe I've had the great joy of you in my life, but it isn't enough. Even calling you My Fiancée Sue falls short, but I'm happy to step up to that title for a little while if you'll agree to change it to My Wife Sue. What do you say?" Mac pulled out a box from his pocket and held it out to her, opened, revealing a princess-cut diamond. "I've been paying on this, but now, with the check, it'll be paid off. We can even buy a house. Is that a pukka idea with you?"

Sue couldn't tell whether she laughed or cried. Maybe both. All she knew was her dream was coming true. She nodded, her hand over her mouth.

"Say something. Please."

"Yes, I love your very pukka idea, and I love you. Yes, my fiancée, Mac, I will marry you."

The table steadied him again as he rose to his feet and claimed her left hand. "I'm hoping this fits." Mac slid the ring down her finger as pure joy danced around them.

The ring fit. Perfectly.

He held her face between his hands and kissed her again, erasing all other time and space elements until a soft cough shattered the moment.

Teri stood in the doorway. Backed by about sixty students and their teachers.

A fleeting thought darted through Sue's mind. Would this destroy her reputation here?

Then she noticed the smiles from the adult women and giggles from the kids. She held up her hand and wiggled her fingers so the light would catch the diamond. "Mr. MacKenzie asked me to marry him, and I said yes."

Mac pulled her close as the cheers from their audience made her cheeks warm.

Sue leaned her head against his chest, but he raised her chin with his finger.

"You said yes, My Fiancée Sue, and I'm holding you to it."

She smiled. "You never had a worry about my answer. Remember the cardinal?"

"True, but until we say I do, I'm going to keep pinching myself to make sure this is real."

Teri crossed the room to speak quietly to them. "Excuse me. Sue, there isn't much left to do here. The kids will board the bus in ten more minutes, and I can oversee that. Why don't you enjoy the rest of the day and celebrate?"

Sue met Mac's gaze, and they grinned together.

"Great idea, Teri. I think I'll take my new fiancée, Sue, to dinner." Mac tossed her a wink.

"Let me get my things." Sue ran to her office to grab her purse and keys before locking her door and rejoining Mac. "I'm ready."

"Let's go." He wove their fingers together and nearly pulled her from the building.

"In a hurry?"

"You bet. I want every second I can spend with you." He stopped before his Harley and handed her his helmet. "Strap it on and let's get going."

She obeyed. "Where are we off to?"

"We're heading into our future together. How does that sound?" Mac straddled the motorcycle and started it.

Sue swung on behind him. "Pukka. That is unequivocally pukka."

And to prove it, she held him tight as they drove away.

Acknowledgements:

Abba Father, once again I say thank You for your wonderful ideas and encouragement. Who knew that a second career at my age would be fun—You did!

To my wonderful P.I.T. crew who prays me through each story keeping me accountable—Annie, Deb, Lori D., Julie, Alyssa, and Dorothy—you ladies did it again! Thank you! You are the best!

Thank you to my cover artist, Stephanie at Alt 19 Creative. I love that you get me and I'm excited to see what you come up with next.

My Beta Readers and Street/Launch Team, you are such a huge support. Thank you!

Thank you to my writing buds—Jennifer Crosswhite, Diana Brandmeyer, Liz Tolsma, Angela Breidenbach, Kristin Billerbeck, Julie Carobini, and Katheryn Karrol. You are all such amazing authors but even better friends. Thank you and I love you!

Speaking of Liz Tolsma, my editor and friend. I'm so tickled to work with you again. Thank you and hugs!

My extraordinary family is so encouraging—Phil, Jaime, Jonathan, Alyssa, Juan, Natalia, Meg, Mat, Owen, Kami, Amy, Rick, Rusty, Sandi, and all my extended loved ones. I couldn't do this without you all.

Miss you, Mom.

And, as always, E.B. I still miss you.

Author's Note

This was a toughy, dear reader. There's been a lot of upheaval and I'm missing one of my biggest fans—my (step) mom, Mary England. She usually read advanced copies, and definitely did her best to get the first paperback released. With *Judy in Disguise*, hers was delivered more than a week before I got my author copies. In fact, I think it showed up at her house the day after the book went live. Trying to write while grieving is hard, but I believe she cheered me on from that cloud of witnesses.

You'll notice if you read the *Weather Girls* trilogy and *Cheryl's Going Home*, a few references. Not crucial to the plot, but fun Easter eggs for series fans. Something else you might want to know is that Tracy will be getting her own story probably sometime next year. In fact, I'm thinking that four books in this series per year should work (should being the operative word—you know, if the Lord is willing and the creek don't rise). If that plan comes to fruition, I think the titles might be *Ronnie*, *Carrianne*, *Tracy*, and *Shiloh*. Not necessarily in that order. It's not set in stone, but I'm leaning in this direction.

I have to tell you about the Elwood Haynes museum. This is a real place. When I was a child, my best friend's last name was Haynes. Turned out she was a relative of the man. And of course, since he was an amazing pioneer in automotive innovation and steel alloys, he was well respected in Kokomo. It was a blast to read up on him as an adult. Those of us from Kokomo consider him to be the father of the automotive industry. If only we'd had better water ways from the Great Lakes like Detroit, Kokomo might have ended up with that nickname—the Motor City.

But the shipping costs proved prohibitive.

And though technically there was one American motor vehicle invented for driving the streets before Haynes and the Apperson brothers came up with their Pioneer, it was actually a horse-drawn wagon that had been converted to use an engine. For that reason, many consider Elwood Haynes's design the actual first American car.

I don't sound too boastful of my hometown, do I?

I still say it was a wonderful place to grow up, and I'm happy to keep the stories about Kokomo coming.

Which brings me to our next installment of the *Weather Girls Wedding Shoppe and Venue* series—*Cracklin' Rosie*.

I'm a few chapters in so far and I think it's going to be funny—makes *me* giggle anyway. If you want to see what I mean, keep reading. I've included Chapter One, though it is early in the process, so things will most likely be edited before I launch *Cracklin' Rosie* sometime around August or September 2023. But you can get an idea of what's coming.

Last but not least, thank you for reading my stories. You make this fun. I hope you get a smile, a giggle, and a warm hug from what you read.

So, until next time...

Abundant blessings!

Jenny

Sneak Peek: Chapter One, Cracklin' Rosie

Monday, August 21, 1972, Kokomo, Indiana

Rose Cackinbush knew better. However, the phone call came, just before she tore out of the office, saying the sign would be left on her front porch.

Yes, she ought to go straight to the meeting—Doc said this was important and would be exactly what she needed. That attending this meeting would give her another boost toward her goal.

Not that the meeting wasn't important to her, but this sign was the first tangible piece of the puzzle to go into place saying that her dream might really come true.

So whether Doc approved or not, she made the detour. Good grief, it was basically a matter of crossing the street since the VFW could be seen from her front window.

Rose had left Doc Carlsen alone at the office while she was supposed to attend a Veterans of Foreign Wars meeting—one that Doc insisted would move her dream closer to reality. That was the plan. It's what she'd intended to do until that last minute phone call came through.

But now she *had* to stop by her new residence/soon-to-be-office to see the sign in person, if only for a minute. Just to touch it.

Okay, maybe that wasn't quite the truth, but that's how it felt. Besides, it would only take a couple minutes and she'd be on her way, no one the wiser. It wasn't as if she was driving across town first. Her house was within walking distance of the VFW.

On top of that, Doc had worked solo out of his office for years before Rose came on the scene. And she'd moved patients around so that it should be fairly slow while she was gone. Therefore another a few minutes added on wouldn't hurt him. She repeated that thought to herself to stifle any feelings of guilt.

She couldn't wait until this evening to come home and check out the sign. She just couldn't. No matter what her watch said. Oh, she was cutting it close.

Rose parked in front of her aging Victorian and raced from her car up the old concrete steps to her open wrap-around porch. There, leaning against the house behind her swing, sat the package.

It was heavier than she anticipated, so she balanced it on a white railing as she removed a portion of the covering, then gasped.

Dr. Rose Anna Crackinbush, D.C.

This was real.

Of course, she had been treating patients with Doc for a few months now, and even had returnees who requested her. This is what she and Doc were aiming for—to get her set up so she could finally open her own practice here, in her very own house.

Seeing the sign that would hopefully soon grace the front of her home caused tunnel vision while she stared. Everything else blurred away, time screeched to a halt.

This instance was the best. Ever.

She'd read about people falling in love and could imagine that it must be sort of like this. There was no way it could be better. In fact, she couldn't conceive of anything surpassing this magic moment.

"Miss? Yoo-hoo, Miss!"

The world rushed back along with the realization that she needed to be on her way. A glance at her watch told her she still might make it. Maybe.

"Hey, there. Are you all right?"

Rose turned to the voice to find an elderly lady waving a hankie and calling from the porch next door. "Oh, I'm fine. Is there something you need?" *Please don't need me.*

"I was wondering if you've seen my cat. Her name is Miss Kitty. She's an indoor cat but she's not inside the house and I'm desperate to find her before something awful happens."

Rose glanced around her porch and then over the railings, finally spotting something orange and fluffy-looking. "I think I see her." She returned the sign to where the messenger had left it and tiptoed down her front steps to the azalea bush. "Here, Miss Kitty. That's a nice girl. Come to me now."

Pfft! The cat shot out her paw.

Rose narrowly got her hand out of the way in time. Little monster. Another peek had her amending her thought. Fat monster.

Rose straightened. "She's here but she doesn't seem to like me."

"Oh, she's only playing. Nothing to worry about. Miss Kitty is as sweet as her namesake." The elderly woman didn't move toward them. Why couldn't she come get her own cat?

Neighbors should get along with each other, and Rose wanted amicable relations with hers. But she also needed to be at that meeting. With her hands on her hips, she took another gander behind the bush. Where was Mat Dillon when she needed him?

Miss Kitty was comfortably grooming her tail.

Okay, one more time. Rose stooped and this time she reached in quick. She'd probably get nailed and end up walking into the meeting with deep scratches, but she had to put a stop to this now—

OW!

"Bad Miss Kitty." Rose held on tight. So did the cat.

The neighbor met her at the top of her porch steps. "Oh, thank you so much. You can bring her inside for me."

"I'm sorry, but I'm in a hurry. Can't you just take her?" She didn't want to be lured into the house, tricked into being company for a lonely old woman. Rose had places to go, things to do, a meeting she shouldn't be late for.

"She slips out of my arms these days. Guess I just don't have the strength I used to."

Sounded like someone who could use Rose's services. However, not this minute. She carried the cat to the door and the neighbor held it open.

"Will you be able to keep her inside if I set her down?"

"Follow me. You can put her in her carrier until you leave." Rose's neighbor led her to the back of the house where the carrier sat on the kitchen table.

After unloading and locking the naughty Miss Kitty in her jail, Rose turned to leave.

"Oh, my, I didn't think she'd get you so bad. Let me find some Merthiolate for you."

"No, no thank you." Just the thought burned worse than the scratches. Besides, now she was going to miss the first part of the meeting. "Since Miss Kitty is where she belongs, I really ought to scoot. I'm running late."

"Oh, and I've kept you. I'm sorry." The neighbor walked Rose to her front door. "Please feel free to stop by any time and thank you for rescuing Miss Kitty."

"That's okay. It was nice meeting you." Rose got as far as the sidewalk.

"But I didn't tell you my name and I don't know yours."

She turned and forced a smile. "I'm Dr. Crackinbush."

"Oh, a doctor, and I've held you up. Probably from an emergency! Just tell them Amelia Whitehead is to blame."

Rose shook her head, wiggled her fingers in a quick wave, and grabbed her purse from her car.

The VFW building sat across the street and down about three houses on the corner—not far, but since she was already late, she didn't want to add to it.

While closing her car door, she got a good look at her arms and hands. They appeared to have been raked with deep red furrows, and though blood didn't pour out, it did ooze somewhat. Now she'd have to stop at a restroom to rinse off and hope that would be enough—she better remember to keep a first aid kit in her car, or at least Band-Aids in her purse. She was a medical professional, for goodness sakes. Rose took off as quickly as her shoes would allow.

After walking halfway around the old building, she found the entrance. By now her feet were screaming at her. From her wedges.

This was so not her plan for the day as she got ready this morning.

Still these were the shoes she needed. Any device to help add height to her petite frame kept men from looking down on her.

As long as she didn't break her ankle sprinting like an Olympian.

The restroom was just inside the door, and she made a beeline there to try to remedy Miss Kitty's damage. Once she'd run water over them, her arms and hands didn't look quite so bad. She patted them down with a paper towel, thankful this place was more hygienic and not sporting one of those fabric loops for drying hands. They must not get a lot of women in here because the restroom looked almost new. She'd done the best she was able to with her wounds. Now to get in there.

Signs pointed toward a conference room on the other side of the foyer. Rose made her way, opening the door as quietly as she could, and slipped into the first vacant seat.

The man beside her flashed a smile.

Of course he did.

Well, maybe he was merely being friendly, though she'd been through enough to not trust a male, no matter how affable his grin.

He handed her a bulletin. She'd missed seeing any on her way in and nodded her thanks.

As she scanned the plan for today's meeting, she noted the presentation. The reason why Doc encouraged her to come. Very interesting.

A new speaker rose to the podium. "I too want to welcome you. Could we take a moment and have a show of hands for those who are here for the first time?"

About four others raised their hands, along with Rose and the man next to her.

He leaned closer, his voice dropped to a whisper. "I had a feeling." Now he held out his hand. "I'm Brett Shoffner. You?"

Rose glanced to the front. Was anyone looking their way? No. She shook the man's hand, her firm I-mean-business grip. "I'm Dr. Crackinbush. Nice to meet you."

"Doctor? I am too. What's your specialty?"

"Let's talk after." Rose nodded toward the speaker up front.

"Okay." He turned back but not before Rose caught the smirk.

Well, yeah, he'd been smiling before, but she could tell the difference and hear his thoughts. *A woman doctor. Right.*

The speaker continued. "...and with this bequeath, we are to interview several of you in the medical field. You do not have to be a veteran to be eligible, but having a heart for our vets would go a long way. The plan is to put together a medical team of various specialties to form a group to monitor and treat our members. We would be building an expansion where you would have offices. Now we realize that you all have your own practices, but depending on how many we divide this between, you'd be able to set up a schedule and donate time so that our guys here have someone who'll monitor things. There is also a chunk of money for each one chosen to be part of this new co-op that can be used to provide materials and supplies. If this sounds like something you'd like to learn more about, please come see me afterward. Thank you."

The speaker stepped away and the first man returned.

Rose half listened to him as she mulled the idea of claiming that award's check. Doc had been right. This could help and she should be part of this thing. She had a growing practice—slow growing, but still.

And helping the vets wasn't such a bad idea. It would help her meet others who might become patients.

"So we are looking for volunteers to aid in this fact-finding project."

This was her chance, an opportunity to show she cared. Rose shot her hand up.

So did the guy next to her. Brett.

The speaker looked their way. "Great! You two were first, so come see me after the meeting and I'll get you the particulars. Thank you. And now, feel free to grab a cup of coffee and one of the cookies donated by Puckett's."

He stepped away and the low rumble of voices in conversation filled the void.

"We'd better go find him. By the way, what happened to your hands and arms? Looks like Elsa the lioness attacked you." Brett began singing "Born Free" until Rose put up her hand. Andy Williams he wasn't.

"My neighbor's cat got out, but I'm fine."

"Happy to examine your wounds if you want. I'm also a doctor. By the way, you never told me your specialty."

Here we go. Rose opened her mouth but before she could utter a sound, the speaker spotted them. "Thank you for volunteering, and right out of the gate so to speak. I'm Frank Brown, my law group is overseeing this whole venture. It's such a large bequest and the stipulations are stringent." He stuck out his hand.

Rose grabbed it first. "Dr. Rose Crackinbush."

That touch of smirk teased Brett's lips again as he shook Frank's hand. "I'm Dr. Brett Shoffner. Glad to be here. You said this is a fact-finding project?"

"Yes. Not every veteran in town is a member of the VFW though they may qualify. We'd like to see if there are more vets who could benefit from having medical help here on site."

Rose would love to see who all she could help. "How do you see us doing that?"

"Here's the idea we came up with. We have a list of various citizens who've served in the military. If you check in with those on the list, request they do a quick verbal survey with you—the questions are on the back of the list, then record their answers to our questions and bring it back to me, that's it. Maybe start by phoning for an appointment but assure them that the questions are brief. We would just like to know if this would be of interest to them and what has kept them from joining."

"Oh, I see. How do you suggest we divvy up the work?" Rose was all for splitting the list, divide and conquer. At least she wouldn't have to spend as much time with this nosy Joe Gannon wannabe. Kokomo was not L.A. and though the hospitals here were good ones, they didn't compare to TV's *Medical Center*.

"Actually, we really liked that you two chose to work together. We figure that a team approach would be better and having it be a man and woman, which will feel more like family—which is how we hope the vets feel here. Like family."

Being chosen for her gender was almost as bad as being blocked because of it. Rose's blood pressure kicked up another ten points. "So you really want us to work together. With each one."

Brett shrugged. "That won't be so hard. We can do it. When do you want the data?"

Frank looked past them and raised a finger. “I need to speak with someone, but I have the list here. Just get it back to me in two weeks? I know you both have your own practices, but I’m hopeful this will go quick.”

Rose knew that look. The guy assumed Brett would be in charge.

“It’s been nice meeting you. Good luck.” He threw the last two words over his shoulder as he shoved the list into Brett’s hand.

So Mr. Frank Brown wasn’t as enlightened as he pretended. It figured.

“Well, Dr. Crackinbush, would you like to go with me to make a plan? Or do you trust me to manage things?” The corner of Brett’s mouth twitched as if the whole thing were a giant joke.

“I think we need to plan this together, or I’m happy to be in charge.” She smiled sweetly.

“Well then, maybe we could grab a cup of coffee and come up with a strategy?” Brett’s smile finally appeared more genuine, friendly.

Rose supposed she’d have to since he didn’t like her idea of taking the lead. Might as well get it over with. As long as this counted toward her winning a part of that bequest. “Kresge’s isn’t far.”

“Kresge’s it is.” He opened the door for her and waited until she walked through.

Two could play this game. Rose made it to the exit doors first, holding it out for him.

And waited to see if he’d walk through.

Boy, oh, boy could he pick'm.

Brett shook his head before motioning Dr. Crackinbush through the door. If he'd heard it once, he'd heard it a million times. Ladies first. And this women's libber wasn't about to change all the work his mother had poured into making him a gentleman.

"I've got it. You can go on." Her determined green eyes flashed a dare.

Brett needed to work with the lady. So he swallowed his pride, hoped no one he knew saw him, and exited the building making sure that he was on the outside of the sidewalk while they walked to the lunch counter at the small department store.

Was everything going to be a challenge? Oh, man, he hoped not. He needed to find some kind of neutral ground. "You mentioned your first name is Rose. May I call you that?"

She pressed her lips tighter but then nodded. "I guess. You probably want me to call you Brett then?"

"That or Omar Sharif. That would work just as well." He dazzled her with a smile or attempted to.

Her persimmon expression let him know he hadn't succeeded.

He cleared his throat. "Sure, Brett is fine. So have you always lived in Kokomo?"

"No. My family is from Lafayette." No elaborating, no pleasant reciprocal questions.

"I'm from near here. Ever hear of Russiaville? For those who think it is pronounced like it's written, Russia Ville, I'm here to set the record straight. *Roosh*-a-ville."

"Lafayette isn't that far away. I've heard of Russiaville. Especially about eight years ago when that tornado hit." She never looked at him, just straight ahead, her pace keeping him moving.

Rose couldn't realize what her words had done to his gut, twisting it into knots. She'd mentioned tornado as if it were just another storm. Only he remembered. Far too well.

Now she glanced at him. Guess he'd been too quiet.

They'd arrived at their destination, and he wasn't about to let her hold another door for him. Brett reached around her to grab the handle.

Rose shot him a glare, or maybe he read more into it because she also said, "Thank you," before heading into the store and making a hard right toward the lunch counter.

Brett followed and took a seat next to her. "Two coffees, please." He held up two fingers before turning to Rose. "How do you like yours?"

"Paid for with my own money."

Geez Louise. He'd never met a woman so prickly. "I apologize. It was my idea, I invited you, and wouldn't have done so if I didn't intend to pay. I'm not trying to buy your good will, just being polite."

Rose sighed and her expression softened. "You're right. Now I apologize. I've had too many people, men, try to take over for me as if I haven't a brain. I am capable of paying twenty cents for a cup of coffee, but I appreciate your kindness."

"Let's start over. I don't know how we ended up like a couple of porcupines but I'm sure we can get along just fine, working together on this project." He stuck out his right hand. "Hello, I'm Brett Shoffner, a local general practitioner fun guy—not fungi as in mushroom." He winked and hoped that would help.

She shook his hand, just as strong as the first time, and sort of smiled—she'd be very pretty if she really smiled. "I'm Rose Crackinbush, a local doctor of chiropractic medi—"

"Chiropractor? I thought you said you were a doctor." Oh, boy. That slipped from his brain and out his mouth way too fast to stop it.

From the storm clouds filling her eyes, he should have tried harder.

"Chiropractic is a long accepted practice and has been regulated for over fifty years. Before I could receive my license to practice, I had to meet rigorous educational and competency standards set forth by the National Board of Chiropractic Examiners *and* the state of Indiana. My training after finishing my undergraduate degree was as long as your medical school training. I *earned* my title of doctor, at the top of my class, mind you, and no one, especially a GP, will treat me as if I am a quack. I don't even possess sugar pills."

The lightning sure flashed in those gorgeous green eyes of hers. It was almost worth her ire to see the storm surge. "Again, I apologize. My aim was not to attack your intelligence. But I'm sure you understand how cracking someone's back... Cracking." He stared and knew he was about to get into more trouble, but he couldn't help himself. "You really are Cracklin' Rosie."

Rose dug in her purse and slapped two dimes on the counter before spinning off the stool and marching for the exit.

Brett's mother's voice whispered in his head that he should run after and apologize for the third time. Three's the charm, right? But Rose was too hot to handle at this point.

He'd call her this evening and try groveling again.

But a chiropractor? Come on. What did she think he would say? And with that profession and a name like Rose Crackinbush, what was he *supposed* to say?

You were supposed to keep that big mouth of yours shut and those silly thoughts locked up in your head.

Thanks, Alma. Like he couldn't figure that out already. It was bad enough hearing his mom correct him. Why did he need his big sister in his head too?

It wasn't the first time his mouth had gotten the rest of him in trouble. You'd think he'd have learned by now. But seriously. Rose Crackinbush, Chiropractor. Didn't that just scream Cracklin' Rosie to everyone?

He drank the rest of his coffee and left a good tip along with payment before beating a path out of there.

Even though his stalwart receptionist/secretary/everything-that-the-office-needed-besides-a-nurse (or doctor) Belinda had cleared his afternoon so he could take the VFW meeting, he knew he had scads of work waiting for him. He might as well head there and use the quiet of the afternoon to finish up paperwork.

Brett retrieved his car from where he'd parked, and after a quick stop at the bank headed toward his office off South LaFountain. It still sounded weird to call it his office. It had been Dr. Eilert's for as long as he could recall, even back when he was a little kid getting his shots and vaccinations for elementary school. Emil, that is what the man wanted to be called. Brett needed to remember they were colleagues now, peers. Sort of. Dr. Eilert would always be his mentor and the man who saved his life. Nothing about taking over the established practice changed that.

He pulled into the office lot and parked in his designated spot. Belinda's car was still there. She was a workhorse and Brett learned more each day why he was blessed she stayed on. He'd given Pam, his nurse, the afternoon off since he wasn't sure how long the meeting might last. Now he wished he hadn't. There could be an emergency. But he'd made arrangements with Dr. Forrester to handle anything urgent that came up this afternoon, so it should be quiet. As long as no one noticed his car in the lot.

"Hey Boss, how was the meeting?" Belinda's smile, the original surrounded by photos of her kids and grandkids sporting the same toothy grin, welcomed him back.

"The meeting itself wasn't bad but..."

"But what? Something bad happen?" Now she was all concern with two furrows sprouting between her eyebrows.

Should he tell her? Why not. Get an unbiased opinion. "What comes to mind when you hear the name Rose Crackinbush D.C.?"

"Oh, she's a chiropractor?"

"Yeah, but doesn't that remind you of something?" He leaned in a little, his hand moving as if to pull the correct answer from his audience.

Belinda shrugged. "Should it?"

"Neil Diamond's 'Cracklin' Rosie.' Don't you get it?"

Her face lost color. "Please tell me you didn't say that out loud." She stared at his face, and he knew she could read the answer without him saying a word. "You did." Belinda groaned while covering her face with her hand.

"What is so horrible about that?"

"Boss, I need to tell you something and please don't fire me for it." She took his hand and patted it, just like his mother would. "You are not as funny as you think you are. Now those of us who love you can find some things humorous but I'm betting this is the first time you've had a conversation with this Rose person. Right? You've gotta know your audience or one of these days I'm going to be visiting you in the ER because you said the wrong thing at the wrong time."

"You're fired."

Belinda gasped, then smirked and smacked his arm. "You couldn't function without me."

"Oh, if only that weren't true. Fine. But don't speak to me unless it's an emergency. I need to suffer in my office. Not funny? That was harsh, Belinda." He shook his head but couldn't help the tiny smile. She only confirmed what he knew all along. Rose was not the type of person to tease like that. But not funny? He'd show her funny. Just wait and see.

He started through his stack of to-do work—some he'd left for himself, and some Belinda had added because it needed his signature or attention. Usually there wasn't a lot of time during the day to get at this. He really needed to hire an office manager who could deal with the medical things Belinda couldn't.

Pam had the qualifications, just not the time. Nor inclination for that matter. She was a working mom with school aged kids. Staying to deal with paperwork deprived her family of their only parent. Belinda was in a similar situation—working because she had to—though her kids were now grown.

That got Brett to thinking. Why did Rose feel like she had to work? Wouldn't she want to stay home with her children when she and her husband started their family? True, he hadn't noticed a ring on her finger, but didn't most women want that? A husband, a house, and a family?

Okay, maybe that was presumptive of him. But it didn't lessen a woman's intelligence to care for the next generation. Didn't today's kids deserve moms at home to be there for them when they needed a parent?

Brett knew before he voiced any of this not to do it in front of a female. Today's women were sure they could do it all, and without a man. Yeah, right. There were a few things they still required the male of the species for so he didn't think his gender would become extinct like the Dodo, but he could envision a poster touting scarcity of the antiquated gentleman.

The train of his thinking made him depressed. Somewhere out there, there had to exist an old-fashioned girl who would love to marry a funny—

You're not funny. Belinda's voice invaded his musings. What were the women in his life doing? Having a coffee klatch in his brain?

He tried again. Somewhere out there existed an old-fashioned woman who would succumb to his charms and want to build a life together. It had worked for his parents. Even when his dad had been stationed overseas. It wasn't a matter of a woman being weak or brainless. His mother was neither. But she was satisfied, happy even to raise her family and create a loving home.

Was that too much to ask?

About the Author

Historical Christian Romance author, Jennifer Lynn Cary, likes to say you can take the girl out of Indiana, but you can't take the Hoosier out of the girl. Now transplanted to the Arizona desert, this direct descendant of Davy Crockett and her husband of forty plus years enjoy time with family where she shares tales of her small-town heritage and family legacies with their grandchildren.

You can contact Jennifer via her website www.jenniferlynncary.comOr use this QR code.

Also By Jennifer Lynn Cary

The Crockett Chronicles Series:

The Patriarch: : Book 1

The Sojourners: Book 2

The Prodigal: Book 3

Tales of the Hob Nob Annex Café

The Relentless Series:

Relentless Heart: Book 1

Wedding Bell Blues: Book 2

Relentless Joy: Book 3

Silver Bell Christmas: Book 4

The Traveling Prayer Shawl

The Weather Girls Trilogy:

Sunny

Stormy

Windy

The Forgotten Gratitude Journal

Cheryl's Going Home (A Weather Girls Novel)

The Weather Girls Wedding Shoppe and Venue Series:

Judy in Disguise (Book One)

Sylvia's Mother (Book Two)

Nonfiction:

When God Holds Your Hand

Or use this:

QR code for Amazon Author page

Made in United States
Orlando, FL
19 May 2023

33262092R00178